WHITEWASH

ANN GRECH

Ann Grech may be contacted via the following email address:

ann@anngrech.com

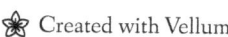 Created with Vellum

Reef and Ford are back, and they're playing for keeps. For their forever. It's hard; harder than they ever imagined. But they're strong. And even though falling for each other was unexpected, they'll do whatever it takes to be together, including overcoming any obstacles in their path.

Pro snowboarder, Reef Reed, is on the precipice. His chance of winning the world championship is within reach. But he's navigating a treacherous path, one which is full of incredible highs and soul-crushing lows. Crippling stress, insurmountable distances between him and his boyfriend, jealousy, and illness threaten everything he's worked for. His relationship with Ford is tested in ways Reef couldn't have fathomed.

Ford Wallace will do anything within his power to help his man soar high and achieve his dreams. But the season has been hard on both of them; watching all Reef's hard work unravel from afar is unbearable for the healer at heart. So he fights—they both do—for their happiness and love, and they emerge on the other side stronger than ever before.

Whitewash is book 3 in Ann Grech's international hit male/male romance trilogy, Unexpected. It can be read as a standalone, but it's recommended that you've read Whiteout and White Noise first. You'll fall for these two men who are absolutely made for each other.

To everyone who has been in my corner since the beginning, you mean the world to me. You've stuck with me through thick and thin, supported me and kept me sane. I couldn't have survived this last year without you.

ACKNOWLEDGMENTS

In White Noise I said that I was truly lucky to have an amazing team of people around me who I could call on for support. That team hasn't changed. My family – thank you for everything you do for me. You continually push me to be a better person. Your support during those endless months of uncertainty (okay, it was four, but it felt endless) meant everything to me. Your patience while I expressed every ounce of my frustration into this story was exactly what I needed. Despite feeling like I had no control over my destiny, like my entire future was being determined by three people, you kept me grounded and you did (and still do) make me laugh every day. I love you always.

My friends who have helped me to bring Reef and Ford's finale (although not goodbye) to you, you're amazing. Kariss Stone, Sassie Lewis, Susan Child, Willsin Rowe and Maci Dillon, I adore you guys. I'm privileged to work with you.

And for all of you who have fallen in love with my boys, here's to you *raises my glass to you*. The bloggers, readers and fans, I'm so incredibly grateful for you all. Your support, your selfless help in pimping, promoting and reviewing was so much more than I could ever have dreamed of. I shouldn't be surprised (because each and every one of you are amazing), but I'm continually blown away for the love the romance book community shows me. I hope that the finale to Reef and Ford's story gives you all the gooey, sweet feels.

Ann xx

CHAPTER ONE

PRO-SNOWBOARDER, Reef Reid, was next up on the complex freestyle mountain course. It was already a couple of months into the season, and this event in The Netherlands, and every other heat was critical. He was behind on points. Not by much, but enough that he had to work harder, smarter, better than the current world champion, Caden Lambert, to beat him. He'd be damned if the *snowboarding king* was keeping his crown at the end of the season. Caden was going to be dethroned. Reef was done being a bridesmaid, but never the bride. It was *his* year. *His* championship.

Closing his eyes he tried to tune out everything—the crowd, the announcers, the groan of the chairlift and the annoying clank as each chair turned and began its descent down the slope—and breathed deep. The arctic wind lashed the only uncovered part of his body, the lower half of his face. The cold could have passed for fire, burning his lungs as he filled them. He was instantly transported, the memories of the fateful storm colliding into him, the same one which brought him the love of his life, Ford Wallace.

. . .

REEF WATCHED his guide as Ford made a bee-line toward the mountain pass ahead of them, using the man as a guide-point to focus on in the failing visibility. Ford's red jacket stood out like a neon light against the white background, though through the orange lenses of Reef's goggles, every-thing was monochromatic. The clouds pitched and rolled overhead like stormy seas, darkening the rich cerulean sky. The blizzard was descending, fast. Snow fall was getting heavier by the second, the temperature dropping even quicker. The cold stung his lungs with each inhale.

Keeping up with Ford wasn't easy; the man was a pro on a set of skis, and shot along the ridge like a bat out of hell. When Reef closed the distance between them, he called out, "Ford, how long will it take us to get to the ranger's hut? We won't make it before the weather really sets in, will we?"

"No. I've never seen a front move this fast." The worry in Ford's tone was obvious.

They'd skied until they had to unbuckle and trudge up the steep icy slope between two towering monoliths. To get to the ranger's hut, they were following what Reef imagined was an age-old track, used by the New Zealand Maori for centuries. The protection the hut afforded was within reach. But it was a hard going, exhausting trek as they scrambled for purchase on the icy slope in boots never intended for hiking. One slip and they'd tumble down the mountain face without any chance of slowing the fall. Reef's fingers ached from trying to grip non-existent hand-holds on the perilous surface, and the cold having long seeped into his bones. For what could have been hours, they clambered up toward the peak together. It seemed never-ending as they struggled through the patches of thigh-deep snow and ice.

Resting a moment, Ford clamped his arm around Reef's shoulder and squeezed. Reef leaned into the touch, bringing their foreheads together. The contact—the reassurance—was exactly what he needed. Reef was shitting himself, absolutely petrified of dying in that frozen wonderland.

Reef's heart was pounding out a rumbling bass line— deep, hard beats that sent the blood pumping through his veins almost violently. The thought that he could have lost Ford before he even had him, spiked Reef's blood pressure. As futile an attempt as it was, Reef tried to push aside all thoughts of Ford and focus. Adrenaline coursed through his system, but instead of helping his laser focus like it normally did, this time the adrenaline high made him antsy. He couldn't rid the background noise from his mind. Building and building, it coalesced into a ruckus that was so loud it rattled his brain, and completely destroyed his concentration.

Growling in frustration, Reef knew he needed to meditate, to get back his Zen. Concentration was everything, but strapped onto the new snowboard his sponsor had presented him with for the competition didn't exactly help him use his yoga training. He did what he could. Stretching his arms out wide, he inhaled slowly and brought his hands together above his head, joining them palm-to-palm like he was praying. Breathing out slowly, he pressed them down until his hands were in front of his chest and repeated the process a second time. Standing in the weak sunlight on top of a Dutch mountain, his hands joined before him, Reef slowly found his focus. Quiet descended upon him as he breathed again. A hand on his shoulder should have startled him, but Mason Canning, his trainer, knew his warm up ritual. No words were spoken as Reef opened his eyes and Mace stepped back.

Surveying the slope before him, Reef mentally mapped out his lines. Just like one of those TV cop dramas where the protagonist gets flashbacks and puts the pieces of the puzzle together to solve the crime, Reef did the same. Piecing together his memories of the many test runs he'd done in the preceding days, the patches of ice, thicker powder, slow and fast spots, humps and dips in the skiing surface were all highlighted on his mental map. He knew the jump—a backward five-forty spin with a tail grab. He knew the course. Now he had his focus back, all he needed to do was execute.

Reef raised his gaze to the sky. Grey clouds hung low, blotting out the view of the surrounding mountains, but that didn't matter to Reef, nor did the crowd of people below chanting and cheering. Panning down again, Reef zoned in on the path he would follow. Barriers framed the steep slope keeping the spectators out of the competitors' way, but close enough that he could high-five a few toward the bottom where he would land. He had to give it to these crazy fans—standing outside in this freezing weather for hours, watching snowboarding's elite do their freestyle maneuvers must have been hellishly cold. But whatever, he needed to focus. Tilting his head to the sky once more, he breathed deep, shook his arms, and blew out the breath. Pointing the nose of his board down, he looked to Mace and nodded. When Mason tilted his head in response, Reef started his slide down the fast slope. Not wasting time or losing speed to cut and turn along the run like many of the other riders did, Reef headed straight for the naturally formed jump part way down the mountain. He was aiming to hit it at a different angle to the other boarders, adding a complexity to the landing which the others hadn't mastered in their jumps. Every point in this competition counted, and Reef had a few to make up.

He could do it.

He had to.

Powder swirled around his calves as he flew down the slope in a barely controlled charge. Knees bent and arms out wide holding his balance, Reef shifted his weight, turning the nose of the board into the precise position to hit the jump. Particles of ice slammed against his face, each like the prick of a needle. Wind buffeted him, blowing across the slope sending mini-tornados of snow into the air. Reef's fingers were numb, his thermal lined gloves not holding up in the miserable cold. It was just one more distraction that he didn't need when he was busy calculating the complex launch and landing zones. He saw them like physics equations scrolling through his brain, the unknown 'x's' quickly being resolved and matching up with points on the ground or in the air. But his concentration was off, the distractions creating a cacophony of noise vying for his attention. Reef stopped fighting his mind and relaxed into the moment, letting muscle memory take over and guide his jump. The small ledge was coming up fast, and with every passing second his fate rested in his body's ability to repeat the jumps he'd mastered during pre-season training. From there on in, Reef just had to stay upright.

He hit the ledge and pushed up, launching his board in a high arc above the falling slope. The rush of the air below him, all around him, gave Reef the sensation of flying. In reality, he was falling really, really fast and with any luck, a little style. Reaching back, Reef grabbed the lip of the board, adjusting his hold until it was secure. He twisted his body to execute the first one-eighty degree spin, until he was looking up the mountain. The second had him facing forward again and the third, spun him to, once again, see his launch point. The ground was approaching fast. Letting go of the board, Reef adjusted his stance minutely. Leaning toward the slope, he counteracted the pull of gravity, which would see him land on his ass and tumble backward if given half a chance.

As the snow rushed toward him, Reef held his breath, hoping he'd nail the backward landing. Bracing for the impact meant tensing—something he tried not to do. A hard landing was hell on points and his joints. More than one of the boarders in the competition that day had fallen after executing a perfect jump because of the icy surface in the landing zone. The wind howling along the ridge-line had shifted most of the powder against the barriers and buildings, or blew it right off the edge of the mountain.

Rather than a smooth glide, his landing was more of a thud, a three-story drop onto pavement. Reef knew instantly what he'd done wrong—his knees were too close together and his hips had twisted as he hit the snow with an 'oomph'. Reef's snowboard slipped, his weight shifted too far back and his arms wind-milled as he fought to right himself instead of falling on his ass and tumbling the rest of the way down. Crouching lower, he tightened the muscles in his abs and forced himself to lean into the slope to right his balance, before spinning to face forward.

"Fuck," Reef growled. "Shit, shit, shit."

He plastered on a smile and skied over to the waiting crowds cheering for him to high-five a few of the kids as he slowed to a crawl. He pulled off to the side and took off his beanie, running his gloved hand through his hair as he waited for the scores to be broadcasted over the loudspeaker.

"That was Reef Reid's last run for the competition. An

unanimous panel has awarded the competitor ninety points. That places Reid in second position for the competition and second overall in the world championship placings, still behind current champion, Caden Lambert."

Disappointment surged through Reef. Three points. Three fucking points and he would have beat Lambert. Three goddamn fucking points and he could have had him, closing some of the gap between them. Grinding his teeth together, Reef shook his head and spun toward base, heading in the direction of the change rooms.

———

FORD RACED over to the radio which had crackled to life. "Mountain Rescue this is Farrujia, come in please."

"Reading you, Carlo. Go ahead." Ford readied his incident report sheet and pulling a pen from his pocket, noted the time and date of the radio call.

"Ford, I need you to come up to the big lift. I've got a girl who's hurt herself coming off the chairlift."

Scribbling notes, Ford answered automatically, "Coming off the chairlift? What happened?"

"She tripped over her feet when she was skiing off, fell and the chairlift bumped her head. She's got a bit of a scratch there, but it's her knee she's saying is hurting more." Ford raised his eyebrows and shook his head, blowing out a breath. Carlo was a great guy, but he had no idea how serious head injuries could be, especially ones that were caused by a metal frame moved by a few tons of pulling power.

"Okay, Carlo. Hiro and I are coming to you. Over and out."

"Received. Over."

"Hiro, we're up. Grab the bag and I'll get the sled."

"Where are we going?" the other paramedic asked as he threw on his red ski jacket and zipped it up.

Ford spoke as he donned his gloves and beanie. "Top lift. Knee and possible head injury."

"Okay, I'm set," he called out, slipping the straps of the large medical pack over his shoulders and clipping them together. Ford dragged the rescue sled behind him as Hiro held the door open.

The slope, in the Italian ski village of Santa Caterina di Valfurva, was too steep to take the snowmobile up, so the two men skied over to the chairlift and, much to the annoyance of the people waiting, cut in, heading straight to the front of the line. The operator stopped the moving cars so Ford could load on the sled and Hiro could get seated with the heavy pack on his back. As Ford lowered the bar and gave the nod to the attendant, the chairs started moving again. Clearing the housing, the seat lurched, swinging back and forth as it began the quick climb to the top of the mountain. It was a perfect day, the sun bright over the Italian Alps, but the air was cold. Ford zipped up his jacket and tugged on the goggles he'd had stuffed in his pocket, shielding his eyes from the harsh glare. Rugged black cliffs at the very top of the mountain contrasted against the stark white beauty of the ski slopes, only slightly dimmed by the grey lenses he was now looking through. Ford enjoyed the relative silence, broken only by the odd whoop from passing skiers and the breeze whispering over the stunning vista before him.

This place was his second home, the other staff his friends, but this year it was empty, lonely. Ford's heart was elsewhere—currently in the Netherlands with Reef—and the sense of detachment he was experiencing was hard. As the top of the chairlift came within sight, Ford could see the small crowd of people gathered around, getting ready to launch down the intermediate and advanced slopes, and further away, the easier beginner's trail.

Carlos stopped the chair as their seat levelled out and they could safely step off. After lifting the bar, Carlos helped Hiro stand and adjust his balance to account for the pack, while Ford slid the sled out from its mounting.

Ford immediately saw their patient off to the side of the lift, clutching her knee as someone held a snowball to the bleeding lump on her temple. "Small scratch, my ass," he muttered, turning to Hiro and shaking his head.

Hiro smirked at Ford's annoyance and skied over to the lady. He went to work quickly, introducing them and asking her a barrage of questions while shining a pen-light into her eyes, assessing her vision and searching for signs of a concussion. Ford concentrated on her knee, feeling for signs of a dislocation or break. Finding nothing but swelling, Ford wrapped an ice pack around it just as his cell rang. Ignoring it, he laid out the splint, preparing to immobilize her leg.

He couldn't help his smile, the memory of Reef doing this very thing to him was the beginning of their whirlwind relationship. Reef rescuing him, their first soak in the tub together, their first date, first kiss—in that order—all stemmed from Ford's banged up knee. They were some of the best moments of his life. Of course, there were a few shitty things that'd happened since he'd met Reef too—only just surviving the snowstorm they were trapped in was far too close for comfort, then there was the avalanche which followed that put Ford in need of rescue in the first place. Neither was exactly wonderful, but both were pleasant compared to coming out to his fucked-in-the-head parents.

Ford's hands worked on auto-pilot fastening the clips on

the splint as the memory of Reef's interrogation at the hands of his mother and father hit him like a freight train.

"*So, what is it that you do, Reef? Is that your birth name? Reef?*"

"*You play for a living?*"

"*How many world championships have you won?*"

"*And your education? What do you have to fall back on when your sporting career is over?*"

"*So, what about children, Reef? How do you plan on giving my son offspring to carry on the family name?*"

The questions and the judgement behind them hurt, but his mother's diatribe after he'd defended Reef stung the most.

"*Stratford, you're throwing your life away with this man. He's uneducated, clearly not from a respectable family— listen to his accent—and it's an embarrassment to your heritage to be with a man. If you have to be gay, fine. Just don't bring it here. Find a nice lady who you can marry and keep a man on the side. What you do in private is nobody's business, but you must maintain appearances.*"

They'd left soon after only to have to deal with Ford's father offering Reef fifty grand to walk away. Hearing Reef say the words, what minute respect he had left for his parents had irretrievably shattered. He didn't want to have anything to do with them from that point on, but Reef insisted Ford give them another chance. He'd managed to ignore five of his mother's calls in the last two days, but she was getting more persistent.

As if right on cue, his cell rang again. Ugly Kid Joe's '*Everything About You*' blared through the speaker. "Ford, will you please answer the call?" Hiro demanded.

"No, I'm working," he replied tightly. The last thing Ford wanted to do was speak with his mother. A dentist's visit, walking barefoot over shards of glass, hell, getting circumcised without any anesthetic would be a whole lot more pleasant. He resolutely ignored it as the call went to his message service, only for it to start ringing again. This time, he took it out of his pocket and hung up on his mother. She usually got the message that he couldn't answer when he did that, but not so much this time. His cell rang again only a moment later.

"It's okay, you can answer it. I'm fine, I just don't think I can get down the slope by myself and they won't let me ride the chairlift back down if I'm hurt," the young lady said. She couldn't have been more than eighteen or nineteen, with flushed cheeks and a red nose from the cold. With her head bandaged up and Hiro nodding his agreement, Ford yanked off his glove, swiped the screen and stood, stepping away from Hiro and their patient as he answered.

"Hello?"

"Hello, Stratford," his mother answered happily.

"Mother, I can't talk. I'm in the middle of a rescue."

"Why did you answer, Stratford? You know your father would be disappointed if you disregarded your responsibilities to your patients."

"Did you forget that you just called me three times, even after I hung up on you? And just so you know, I don't give a flying fuck what Father thinks about how I do my job."

"Stratford, that's no way to talk to me! Show me the respect I deserve."

"Mother, when you decided to disrespect Reef and me by trying to pay him off and have me cry on your shoulder, you lost any and all respect I had for the two of you. So, unless you're ready to apologize and go to some serious lengths to make amends to Reef, I don't want to hear anything you have to say. Now as I said, I need to go. I have a patient waiting." Ford hung up his cell and dropped it in his pocket before slipping his glove back on and trudging over to the injured girl and her group of friends.

"Right," he said more brightly than he felt. "We'll get you on the sled and I'll ski down with you."

"You okay, man?" Hiro asked.

"Yeah, just fine, mate." He hadn't opened up to Hiro, or any of his other friends about his recent experiences with his parents. Except for Gabriela, he'd told her everything, but that's the sort of relationship the two of them had. They'd spent enough winters together now that she was one of his closest friends. He'd seen her at her worst, and she'd been there for him when he was especially missing Reef. He adored her. He'd be disrespecting their bond if he hadn't shared everything with her, and he loved her far too much for that.

CHAPTER TWO

"So, whatcha think, Reef?" Caden asked as they sat on high stools at the bar of the mountain pub.

Resting his elbows on the well-loved countertop as he spun a cardboard Heineken branded coaster in one hand, Reef considered the world champion's question. The dimly lit room could have been anywhere in the world, but this old pub in Norway was pretty cool. Dark wood paneling lined the walls, and stacked behind the opposite end of the bar were barrels of Akvavit, the Scandinavian spirit, and other liqueurs distilled locally. They were seated at the end lined with shelves containing every liquor bottle you could imagine. Behind the bottles was a mirror reflecting the tables gathered around the wrought iron pot-bellied stove heater. High stained glass windows let in the muted early evening light from outside, despite it being two in the afternoon. During the long winters so far north of the Equator, daylight was in short supply; competitions only ran for a few hours each day unless the bowls were flood lit. Reef's last run was twenty minutes ago. Mace, his trainer, had hotfooted it down the windblown slope pretty quickly after his run so the two of them could get some warm food and a few drinks into them. Even Caden, who'd stayed behind to sign some autographs, had soon joined them.

"I dunno man. You're right, we have to be able to do something to help get more funding. Shit, we're pro-athletes, you're the World Champion." Reef dropped the coaster on the countertop, fighting back his frustration at that comment. Pursing his lips together, he paused in thought. "If nothing else, at least we've got some media contacts. That's gotta help us raise some money."

"Yeah. Yeah, you're right. Surely we can use that to do some good."

"Whatcha talkin' about?" Mace interrupted, stealing a handful of peanuts from between them.

"Fundraising for breast cancer research," Caden replied. "After Mom... Well, I feel like I need to do some-thing." Locking his gaze with Mace, Caden's expression was intense. They stared at each other, the tension radiating between the two of them, making the air crackle with testosterone.

Suddenly uncomfortable with intruding on what seemed like an intensely private moment passing between the two men, Reef cleared his throat and added, "I'm all for it, man. Whatever I can do to help, I'm in. My only problem is that I've got no ideas. Absolutely no clue how to do it."

"Try speaking with someone from promotions," Mace offered before squeezing Caden's shoulder and striding away.

"Momma Bear's helped with a few of Dad's donation drives. I'll ask her for some suggestions." Reef turned to Caden again. He looked as exhausted as Reef was. They were already a couple of months into the hectic season, the Euro-leg of the tour almost over. Reef never got used to the low when the adrenaline left his system after a day's heats ended. It was even worse after the two-day competition finished. He was shattered.

"It's gotta be big, go viral like that Ice Bucket Challenge."

"Yeah, the more money, the more research." Reef nodded. "Hey, um, I know I've said it before but I'm sorry you lost your mom. It sucks."

"It does. Now my baby sister's a high risk for cancer too." They fell silent after that, Caden clearly lost in his thoughts as he took a swig of beer and Reef fought to keep his eyes from closing.

"So, you're keen to get involved? I mean, I know we're competitors but—"

"Shut up, Caden. Of course I will. Ford too if we're together."

Caden stopped lifting the bottle to his mouth again and looked at Reef alarmed. "Whatcha mean 'if you're together'? I thought you two were solid."

"We are." Reef couldn't help the smile that split his lips as he nodded, followed closely by the pang in his heart. He hadn't seen his man since the beginning of the season and the distance was killing both of them. But those gooey sweet feels when he thought about Ford—the same ones that left him wearing a goofy grin—were even stronger. Butterflies fluttered in his stomach and warmth spread through his veins when he pictured Ford doing...well, anything. "I meant he'd get involved if we're in the same country. I think he lost his aunt to breast cancer."

"Well, see, that's just it," Caden replied excitedly. "You don't have to be in the same country. It's the perfect way to kick start it internationally."

"Yeah, okay. Think up something and put me down to

do it." Reef held up his beer bottle to Caden and they clinked the necks, toasting their deal.

"How you goin' being separated from each other? It can't be easy," Caden asked, concern etching his brow.

"It sucks donkey dick. But we knew going into it that we'd be apart for most of the winter. Doesn't make it easier though."

Caden choked, getting Reef's attention. Peering across at him over the lip of his bottle, Reef watched as he coughed again and sprayed more beer from his mouth. Reef couldn't help his smirk as Caden shook his head and wiped spilled beer from his chin.

"You right?" Reef asked, amused.

"Yeah." Caden coughed again and Reef thumped him on the back, chuckling. "I wasn't expecting you to compare missing your boyfriend to sucking donkey dick."

"Shit, dude, that's gross." Reef cringed and shook his head. "So wrong."

"Hey, you're the one that sucks dick," Caden replied playfully. Reef didn't respond other than to grin wickedly at Caden. Well, his dick responded, thickening at the thought of kissing a trail down Ford's chest and abs, tasting and teasing all that beautiful skin.

"So, can I ask a question that's kinda private?" Caden asked tentatively.

"I might tell you to fuck off, but you can ask."

"So...um...isn't it weird being with a guy? Don't get me wrong, Ford's great, but don't you miss the curves, the softness, the smooth skin? I mean, I'm assuming he doesn't like shave his legs or pubes. He's got a dick. Whaddya do with it?"

It was Reef's turn to choke on his beer as he tried not to spray it out his nose at Caden's naiveté. Between coughs

Reef sucked in a breath and couldn't help but laugh. "Dude, whatcha think I do with it?" Still smiling, Reef shook his head. "No, I don't miss being with girls. The ladies I've been with weren't the right ones for me—Ford is. It's as simple as that, and that's what makes it so good between us. Yes, Ford has a dick and...." Reef nodded and pursed his lips to stop the moan suddenly begging to break free.

"Ford's different from a woman in every way and that's a hell of a turn on. Having his strength, those muscles, between my legs or wrapped around me is fuckin' hot. And the hair..." Reef again had to stop talking, biting back a moan as he thought about his man.

Caden cleared his throat and Reef turned to look at him. He didn't expect to see the heat in the other man's gaze directed at the mirror he was staring at. Reef searched the reflection following Caden's line of sight, but he was clueless. *Who is he focused on?* He couldn't see any ladies who stood out.

"Yeah, I get it; I saw the spark between you. Seeing you two together was pretty unexpected, though. Have to admit I was surprised given you were with Addilyn before."

"Sometimes the unexpected is the best gift you could ever receive."

Caden huffed out a sigh that sounded almost like longing and downed the rest of his beer. "I'm beat. I need a hot tub and a smoke."

"How the fuck can you compete at this level when you smoke, man? I'll never get why you put that shit into your body." At Reef's comment Caden shrugged.

"Helps me unwind and it's only one cigarette after a comp. Don't worry, my body's still a temple and all that shit you're into."

"Whatever, dude." He waved as Caden slapped a few

Euros on the countertop before walking away from the bar. Reef downed the last of his beer and followed suit, dropping some cash next to Caden's before leaving through the double doors.

Zipping up his jacket against the cold, Reef stepped onto the street, crossing the road to his hotel as he pulled his cell from the pocket of his ski pants. Ford was due to finish his first shift soon but with only an hour's break before his second one started, they didn't have long to speak. Reef had just enough time to get to his room before Ford would call.

THE DOOR HAD BARELY CLICKED CLOSED when Reef's cell rang. He smiled at the photo that appeared. It was a close up of Ford's ass in all its glory, encased in the sexiest pair of low slung, tight black, Calvin Klein boxer shorts he'd ever seen. They were in the little Canadian ski-resort Reef called home during pre-season training. Ford was splayed out on the bed fast asleep and Reef couldn't resist snapping the shot of him.

Answering the call and holding the cell to his ear, he said, "Hey, hon. I've missed you."

"Reef, God, it's good to hear your voice," Ford sighed. "I miss you, too. How'd you go today? I haven't seen any footage yet." Reef closed his eyes and leaned against the nearest wall, letting his lover's deep voice soothe his soul.

"Ninety points overall," he said. His disappointment couldn't have been any clearer.

"That's brilliant, sweet cheeks," Ford replied. "I'm so proud of you. How'd Caden go? You kickin' his ass?"

Reef managed a small smile, encouraged by Ford's ever-lasting faith in him but supremely disappointed that he was going to let Ford down.

"Ninety-three," Reef replied quietly. A crushing sense of defeat filled him, weighing him down with the pressure of the monumental importance of the season.

"You've got this, Reef. Keep gettin' mad air like you were doing with Mace during training and you'll have the championship in the bag. Complete whitewash, you'll see."

Mason, Reef's trainer going on five years, had given a hell of a lot of constructive criticism but it took something really impressive to get the man's praise. And Mace's pep talk before the first event of the season showed Reef just how much faith his trainer had in him.

Mace stepped in front of him, grasping his biceps through the thick jacket. Locking eyes with him, the fierceness in the other man's gaze held Reef captivated. "Seize that championship, Reef. Strap in, focus, and breathe." Reef closed his eyes and took the deep breath Mace instructed him to. "Feel the slope. Feed off the energy. Harness the rush, channel it. Fly. This is your *season,* your *time. You're not ready to be the best, you already are. Show the rest of the world what we know. It's* your *world championship. Reach out with both hands and grab that bastard. Bring it home."*

Now he just had to do it, he just had to win. Minor details. *Yeah, right.*

Reef knew Mason had never been as confident in him as he was this season. He'd always been a good motivator —it was kind of a necessity for every decent coach and trainer—but this season was different. It was now or never and they both knew it. The winter he'd taken off to recharge had done him the world of good, both professionally and personally. It gave Reef time to find himself again, to remember why he loved competing. It revived him. After the break, he took his skills to the next level, rocking his pre-season training by landing more of the complex jumps and bowl tricks than ever before. The time off and knowing he had the support of the four people who mattered most, Momma Bear and Coach—despite the hiccup when he and Ford came out to them—his trainer and now his man, gave Reef the confidence to try and nail many of the riskiest tricks he'd ever attempted. And it had been paying off, drawing with Caden once and even winning a couple of competitions. Then he lost a few and was now behind the eight-ball. Yeah, the point gap between Reef in second place and Caden in first place, was the smallest it'd ever been at this point in the season, but he was still second. Still the bridesmaid.

Reef sucked in a breath. Confidence. That's what he needed. He needed to suck it up and get over this impending doom he was constantly plagued with. With more self-assurance than he actually believed he had, Reef responded to Ford, "This is the year, hon. I'm gonna bring it home for us." Reef was ready. He had the skills, he'd honed his talent to be the best in the world.

"You'll win it, sweet. Without a doubt."

Reef loved his man's optimism and he would do it, be number one, but the pressure to win was like a crushing weight. For now he needed to switch off, to reconnect with Ford and just be. "Thanks, hon. So, how's your day been?"

Ford sighed. "Urgh, I spoke with Mother for a minute. She called a few times right in the middle of a rescue. I told her that unless she was ringing to grovel, she could leave me alone. But good news is that my first shift is finished and I'm on an hour break. Then I'll only have another six-hour stint to go."

"How long are you guys gonna have to do back-to-back shifts? Surely the resort can't expect it to happen for long?"

"It's a bitch but at least I've managed to get a bit of paperwork done today between call-outs."

"That's not the point. You're tired."

Reef heard Ford huff out a breath. He could just picture him shrugging his shoulders. "I am, but what am I gonna do? At least I should finish the supply stock take tonight if there aren't many injuries." Ford yawned before mumbling his apology. "You never know with night skiing though. Accidents are bound to happen."

"You have no idea how long you're stuck with those hours?"

"Management said they're interviewing another rescuer tomorrow to fill in for Roberto until he's out of his cast. Hopefully they'll hire whoever they're looking at. They have to get someone. If we keep going at this rate, we'll be too damn tired to function in a few weeks and the season won't even be halfway through. I've already picked up a mistake that Gabriella made yesterday which could have been fatal and during one of our rescues this morning I fucked up. Wouldn't have even known if Hiro didn't spot it."

As much as it killed Reef to end their conversation, Ford needed rest. "You need some food and sleep so I'm gonna hang up, hon. Close your eyes for a bit and recharge. Call me again when you get back to your apartment tonight, yeah?"

Ford gave what sounded like a frustrated groan. "I want to have more than five minutes to talk to you, sweet. It wasn't supposed to happen like this. I should have been there yesterday and today to cheer you on. You're only a few bloody hours away from me. If Roberto didn't break his leg on his first fucking day, I probably could have met you in Austria too. It sucks."

"I know, but it's okay. We can get through this," Reef said with more confidence than he felt, something he'd been doing a lot of lately. "They'll hire the fill-in and you'll be back to normal shifts in no time, you'll see. I'll be in Austria in a couple of weeks. Maybe there'll still be time to book a flight once this new hire starts."

"Yeah, hopefully. I'll try to get a couple of days off. This shit of not seeing you for over two fucking months is a ball buster."

Reef snorted out a laugh as he listened to Ford's frustrated muttering and a door slam, quietening the background noise at Ford's end. "Do I still have you, hon?"

"Yeah, Reef. I was going into one of the offices to get a bit of privacy. Wanted to be able to talk to you without anyone hearing. Whatcha doin' now?" The sultry tone in Ford's voice had Reef sighing, wishing he was close enough to touch and to taste every inch of his man.

"Right now, I'm walking across the room getting' outta my snow gear. I'm gonna go and soak in the hot tub for a while. I need to relax a little."

Ford paused before he asked, "Yeah? You gonna be naked?" his voice went from sultry to gravelly with desire.

Hearing how affected Ford was by his innocent response had Reef's cock thickening. And his own husky voice gave away his arousal. "I'm gettin' naked now. I'm down to my thermals; you know the ones I wear—the tight ones you like so much. You peeled me out of them so many times after I got done training for the day."

"Take your shirt off, Reef. Cup your cock through your pants and stroke it just like I would. Pretend it's me." With his free hand, Reef tugged the neckline of his thermal tee from behind his head, pulling it off and tossing it to the floor as he passed by the bed. He stepped out onto the balcony where the hot tub stood in the freezing darkness and lifted the heavy cover off it. Reef watched, mesmerized by the steam floating off the hot surface. With the light behind his back illuminating his movements to anyone on the street below, Reef quickly slipped out of his thermal leggings and stepped into the water. He put Ford on speakerphone and rested his cell on the edge of the tub. Sinking down into the welcoming heat, he wrapped his fingers around his rigid shaft and tugged slowly, sending a shudder through him.

He moaned. "This is heaven, hon. Wish you were here with me."

"Close your eyes, Reef. Can you feel me? I'm right in front of you." In his mind's eye, he pictured Ford leaning in close, lips almost touching as he caged Reef with strong arms. "You're hard for me, aren't you?" Ford's words may have been framed as a question, but his tone left no doubt what he expected Reef to say. Didn't matter anyway, Reef was hard enough to hammer nails just from the deep rasp of Ford's voice. "You're so damn sexy lying there like that— legs spread open with me kneeling in front of you, my hand wrapped around your cock."

Reef stroked his cock harder, his hips rocking of their own volition. He moaned, practically feeling Ford's touch.

"Yeah, sweet. Just like that. Seeing you spread open, your hole on display for me makes me want to sink into you. You're so tight around my fingers." Eyes still closed, Reef's other hand went to his tight pucker and teased the ring of muscle, rimming himself with barely-there touches. His muscles clenched in sweet anticipation of being stretched, the yearning to be filled by his man overwhelming.

"I need you, Ford," Reef panted. "Want you inside me so bad. Get naked too. Wanna hear you wrap your hand around your cock and fuck your fist." A moan, followed by rustling on the other end of the line, let Reef know his man was stripping off his snow gear.

"I'm here, sweet. Feel my fingers stretching you." Reef pushed two fingers in, breaching himself and sliding his digits as deep as he could with the water his only lubricant. Reef's gasp was loud as sensation ricocheted through his body. "That's it, Reef. You're hugging my fingers so damn tight. Can't wait for my dick to be buried in you."

"Do it, Ford," Reef moaned, stroking his cock harder and seeking out that spot deep within him which made him see stars. His fingers brushed the sensitive bundle of nerves just as Ford hissed.

"Oh, God, yeah." Reef worked his cock faster, his fingers pumping in time with the strokes of his hand. Ford's moans sounded through Reef's cell, mirroring the noises he was making, spurring him on.

"Ford, I'm so close. Fuck, you're so deep in me." The tingle at the base of his spine started and spread fast from Reef working the fuck out of his prostate. He sucked in a breath as a wave of heat flowed through him and his ass clamped down on the digits lodged deep within. "Nghunhn," Reef grunted as the first stream of his spunk shot from his cock into the water. Never slowing his hand, Reef exhaled in a rush, whispering Ford's name like an entreaty while more cum pulsed from his dick.

Reef was dimly aware of Ford's moans and harsh breaths on the other side of the call as he slowly came back into his body after his epic orgasm. His satiated limbs still uncoordinated, Reef fumbled, nearly dropping his cell when he took it off speaker.

"Phone sex with you is hot, Reef, but next time it's gonna be skin-on-skin. I need to kiss you or I'm gonna go fucking insane," Ford whispered.

"I love you, Ford. I miss you," Reef replied breathlessly.

"Love you too, sweet. Austria, okay? I need to hold you."

"Austria." Reef nodded. There had to be a way they could get a couple of days together. Hell, even a few hours would be enough.

———

FORD STEPPED out of the office and closed the door behind him. Rubbing his forehead he closed his eyes. The headache he'd been battling all day reared its vicious self again. Stolen moments with Reef weren't enough but he was right, they were doing the best they could with the limited time he had. Ford cursed Roberto's stupidity. How could the dumb ass have broken his leg skiing – seriously, the dude was supposed to be alpine rescue.

Ford had to eat and get some sleep but that wasn't gonna happen with only a half-hour left on his break. A hot drink, that's what he'd start with. At least he had a stockpile of his favorite tea stashed in the staff kitchen.

Gabriella startled Ford when she linked arms with him as she caught him in the corridor. "*Ciao*, sexy," she purred in her Italian accent. "*Stai bene?*"

"Yeah, I'm okay. Just tired and frustrated. Reef came second in a comp today and I haven't even seen it. I should have been there watching him. He's in the Netherlands for fuck sake. He's only a few hours away but I'll be lucky to see him before Christmas at this rate. Austria's our last chance." Ford knew he was complaining, but the frustration was overwhelming.

"I'm sorry, Ford. Why don't we watch his competition online when we're doing the stock take tonight?"

Ford looked down at her and smiled affectionately. "I'd

like that. Thanks, Gab. Sorry I've been miserable, but this is so much harder than we expected."

"You love him." Her smile was almost wistful as she turned her gaze down. "Come." She directed him to the open staff room and pushed Ford onto one of the sofas as she made her way into the small kitchen. Ford sunk down on the soft cushions letting his tired muscles recover from his morning shift. The freezing conditions outside, the multiple rescues he'd performed that morning and the fact he hadn't eaten for a few hours were catching up to him. Usually he'd do a six-hour stint and then the evening crew would take over in the afternoon ready for the night skiing to begin, rarely backing up for a double. Now he was rotating 12-hour shifts with Gabriella and Hiro, the other full-time paramedics and Jose, the part-timer, so that they could cover a five-person job.

Ford closed his eyes and sighed, trying to figure out how he could manage a few days off to see Reef. His man's schedule was pretty tightly packed until the Christmas break and it picked right up again after the holiday for the rest of the season. There was no way Ford was waiting near on two months to see him.

"*Bere questo*, Ford." He cracked his eyes open at Gab's order to drink, seeing her holding a cup of tea.

"Thanks, love," he murmured, gratefully taking it from her and sipping the steaming liquid. She dropped into the seat next to him and rested her head on his arm. They had an easy familiarity together and he loved being with her.

"Is Reef's next competition in Austria?"

"No, the UK. He leaves tonight. Austria's a week away."

"His erm..." Gabriella stumbled over the word, pausing as she often did to think of the right one to say in English.

Giving up, she substituted the word in Italian. "His *programma* is tight."

"Yep," Ford sighed. "We're spending Christmas together, but he's all over the place between now and then—the UK, Austria, three different states in the US, Korea, Japan, then Istanbul. I was hoping I could see him more during the Euro-leg of the tour. But now it probably won't happen for most of November and December."

Gabriella had their roster open on her cell. "If you change this shift with Hiro," she said, pointing to one of the days, "You'd be able to get the afternoon and evening off." She continued on, planning out a series of swaps they could do between the four of them to give Ford two nights with Reef.

"You think they'd go for it?"

"*Assolutamente.*" Gabriella's smile was brilliant, reassuring him she'd work her magic on their co-workers and get them to agree. "You're unbearable. They'll be happy to have a break from you."

Ford winced. He'd been pretty down in the dumps, but he thought he was hiding it better. "It's okay, Ford. We understand. We've all been separated from lovers when we work," Gabriella reassured him, patting his arm affectionately as he finished the last of the hot drink.

"At least you're here to brighten me up, love." Ford kissed her hair before resting his head back on the cushion and stretching the kinks out of his neck.

"Eh." she shrugged, nudging her shoulder against his arm as she moved. "It's what I do, but for now you need to eat."

"Yeah, you're right. I'll get something now." Smiling at her and reinvigorated from Gabriella's assurances, Ford hefted his tired body from the sofa and bent down to kiss her once more. "*Grazie bella mia.*"

Gabriella smiled back at Ford and patted his cheek before he grinned and sauntered to the diner, an extra spring in his step. Making his way through the crowded tables to the counter, he picked out a calzone and, after paying, exited the main building of the ski resort. He stood in the snow to the side of the outdoor dining area and took a bite. Mushroom, olive and cheese burst onto his tongue. Ford savored the taste and pulled out his cell, thumbed the message app and typed out a note to Reef.

Working on it, sweet. I'm trying to get us together. Love you.

He didn't have to wait long for Reef's response.

Love you too, Ford. We'll be okay no matter what happens. Remember, you held my spot.

With a goofy love-struck grin plastered on his face, Ford took the final bite out of his calzone and crushed the paper plate in his fist, tossing the rubbish in the trash. He awkwardly trudged up the steep slope in his rigid ski boots to the First Aid building, not bothering to wait for Gabriella to join him for the day's second shift. For the first time in a while, things were looking up. He had a plan. Knowing exactly what he had to do to see Reef again gave him hope and had his lips tilting in a grin.

CHAPTER THREE

REEF SCROLLED through his social media app while he shoveled a forkful of scrambled eggs into his mouth. Pictures of what looked like a great night out were plastered all over his feed. Ford's friends had tagged Reef in every post, labelling themselves as his personal cheer squad. They were in a bar somewhere and by the looks of it, watching Reef's competition via YouTube on the big screen. The posts and various comments had Reef smirking. Well, the ones in English anyway. Ford's friends had clearly gone from tipsy to wasted, cataloguing every moment of their night. Ford standing on a chair screaming at the screen in obvious frustration made him laugh. There were also a few pics of the group of friends grinning happily at the camera and another of Ford celebrating, his arms up in the air and drink held high. Reef's heart flip flopped in his chest. God, he missed his man. He kept scrolling, pausing on the last picture. It made him lose his appetite. Ford was hugging a stunner of a girl, and she was draped all over him, snuggled into his side. They looked comfortable together, familiar. *In love.* Based on Ford's description of Gabriella it could have been her, but he'd promised Reef they were only friends. *Are they still 'just friends'?*

The lead weight in his gut grew heavier the more he scanned the photos. While he'd been sitting at the airport waiting to catch his flight to his next competition in the UK, Ford was out partying with friends. Dammit, Reef wanted that. He didn't want to be flying around, miserable and lonely when the love of his life was waiting for him. Well, not exactly waiting for him, but still.

Reef was supposed to be the one having a great time with Ford, not this girl. He was the one who should have been hugging him, touching him. Not her. In every photo, there she was, hands all over him. *Always* touching him. Touching *his* man. He sounded like one of those insecure psycho clingy bastards, but Reef couldn't bring himself to care whether his reaction was reasonable or not. He missed Ford with every fiber of his being. A soul deep void scarred him while they were apart, making the want and the need to hold him multiply until it overwhelmed Reef.

Anger and frustration pulsed through him. He may be acting like a three-year-old throwing a temper tantrum, but it wasn't fair. Reef balled his fists and took a deep breath resisting every instinct within him to slam the table, cementing his spot as a childish prat.

Stuck on repeat in his head, doubt circled him like vultures waiting for the death knell to sound. *Why the fuck is she touching him? Why is Ford letting her? He's supposed to love me. Does he still? What if I lose him? What if I already have?* The questions swept away any semblance of reasonableness Reef might have had and in its wake, left him shaking and ready to puke.

"Dude, you okay? You look like you're gonna be sick," Mace said as he sat opposite Reef. Reaching out to press the backs of his fingers against Reef's forehead, he continued, "You're not feverish. Is it the food? Is the taste off? It's probably the eggs. Stop eating." Mace pulled the plate away from Reef and dropped it on one of the nearby empty tables.

Reef shook his head, unable to answer. The burning behind his eyes wasn't from tears. He was missing Ford like crazy, but he would *not* be that much of a sad sap and cry. Fuck that, he had to get in the zone for his practice-run that morning. He was there to do a job—familiarize himself with the terrain so he knew exactly where to hit the jumps. Every mountain, every bowl was different. He needed to memorize the variances before he was doing it for competition points.

"Reef, talk to me. What's goin' on, man?" Mace asked.

Reef spun his cell around and slid it across the table to Mason, showing him the photo of Ford with his arm wrapped around the girl, both of them smiling at the camera. "Dude, what's the problem? They're friends."

Reef shook his head again which only earned him a disgusted snort from Mace. "Dude, even I can tell they're only friends. Look at their bodies. They aren't pressed tight like the two of you are when you hug." Mace pointed to the picture. "See, there's a space between them. And look, Ford's arm is slung across her shoulders. He's not holding her. Trust me, Reef, he's not cheating on you."

"Logically I know that, but this distance is fuckin' killing me. I'm this close," Reef said, motioning with his thumb and forefinger a hair's breadth apart, "to chucking it in just to be able to see him."

"Don't be fuckin' ridiculous," Mace replied angrily, glaring at him. "Suck it up, sunshine. You're here to do a job. Ford has one too. Remember? You can't live in a bubble.

Reality will eventually intrude. Make your relationship work in the real world, not the fantasyland you two have been livin' in since Queenstown."

"What?" Reef snapped back.

"You were on holidays and Ford wasn't working so you got to spend every minute together. Then you flew out to Fernie and Ford put his life on hold, doing some cruisy job he was way overqualified for so you two could play house together again. Face it, Reef, you've been livin' in each other's pockets since you met. Just chill."

"You know what? Fuck you." Reef growled, pointing at Mace. "You don't know shit about what's goin' on." The urge to punch something was overwhelming. Mace didn't get it. He'd never had what he and Ford did. Reef glared at him, Mason meeting his stare head on and looking entirely unimpressed with him. His frustration welled up fueling his rage until, with a quirk of Mason's eyebrow and an unspoken *you finished acting like a child?*, Reef's shoulders sagged. All the fight left his body as he acknowledged the truth of Mason's advice.

Mace's features softened and he reached out for Reef's hand, covering it and squeezing. The warmth seeped through Reef. "I know you love him. I've never seen two people more committed to each other than you guys are. And I know it's hard but you've worked so long for this, Reef. Don't throw it away when you're so close. You'll regret it for the rest of your life and it *will* affect your relationship with Ford. Maybe not now, but in ten or twenty years? Who knows? You don't want to risk dooming your future before it even starts.

"Please, focus on the here and now—you're nearly halfway through the season. You'll get a break before you know it. Then come back, win the championship and you can enjoy your off season. You'll have months together after competition ends, especially if you spend pre-season training with each other again. Do this for the both of you, for your relationship, for your future. He loves you, Reef. Make him proud. Make yourself proud."

Reef closed his eyes focusing on Mason's words. He wasn't going to lose Ford. He had more faith in his man than that. He knew Ford, knew he would never cheat on Reef. Acknowledging that it was the pressure talking, the ever-present stress of competition screwing up his brain helped in a perverse way.

Mason's pep talk worked too. Sort of. Reef knew that the lingering doubt which remained—all point zero zero one percent of it—wasn't him worrying about whether Ford could remain faithful. No, it was all on Reef. He needed to figure out a way to cope with the stress from this championship because if he didn't, there was no way he'd win.

Mace was right; he needed to suck it up. He had to focus, had to want the championship more than anything else going on in his life. Absolute focus, that's what he needed. He didn't have the headspace to doubt his relationship with Ford because the worry, the uncertainty, would bleed into his competition. He had to trust, put faith in the snow gods that he'd get through this rough patch in whatever way fate intended. Reef tipped his head up to the tiled ceiling and imagined the perfect sapphire blue stretching out to the horizon, a stark contrast against the flawless white untouched blanket of snow below his feet. Breathing in deep to center himself only filled his lungs with the smells of coffee, greasy bacon and burnt toast, not the blast of pure fresh air of the mountaintop. Trying to recapture his Zen would have to wait.

"That's my man." Mace smiled when he opened his eyes again.

Reef nodded, managing a small smile back. "Thanks, Mace. I needed that."

"Call your man. Get a pep talk from him too."

"Do we have any flexibility in the schedule? Can I get a couple of days between competitions so I can fly over and see him?"

Mace stood and squeezed Reef's arm. "Let's speak with Momma Bear. I'm sure we'll work out something." He walked away after patting his shoulder gently.

Reef brought up Ford's contact information, his thumb hovering over the call button. He smiled thinking back to their time in New Zealand. The wind had rushed through their hair, their delighted whoops echoing around them as they flew over the toboggan track high above Queenstown. Seated on the same luge with Ford's arms wrapped around him, they took the turns as tight as they could, leaning into each other as they laughed and smack-talked the other riders.

Before he had the chance to ring Ford, Reef's cell lit up, his man's gorgeous ass appearing on the screen. "Hey hon," Reef whispered, smiling.

"Hi, sweet. I needed to hear your voice. You okay this morning?" Ford's voice was warm, filled with love.

The burning behind Reef's eyes started again and he closed them as he rested his forehead on the heel of his palm, turning into the booth and away from the other tables. "It's been a rough morning," he murmured, unable to keep the wobble from his voice.

Ford's sharp intake of breath was audible. "Talk to me, Reef. What's goin' on? What can I do to fix it?"

"Seeing your pics online from last night was hard. I...."

Reef blew out a breath. "I kinda flipped out. I'm feelin' the stress here."

Ford paused. "Gabriella suggested we watch your comp during our shift, but we were too busy. We went to the pub instead. She's a hugger, Reef; she does it to everyone. There's nothing between us. Sweet, I'd never cheat on you."

"Yeah, I know. But this distance between us is killin' me. I need you, Ford. I miss you so damn much. This competition...I'm losin' it over here."

"I'm doing my best to get there, sweet. I'm trying to get Hiro and Jose to swap a few shifts with me. If I can sort it out, I'll be able to meet you in Austria regardless of whether we get the new hire. Just hold out for me for another week and I'll come to you."

Needing to hear the words, to have the reassurance he could wield as a shield against his self-doubt, Reef asked, "Do you love me, Ford?"

This time there was no hesitation in Ford's response. "More than anything on this earth, Reef. I'd do anything to keep you happy, to show you how much I love you."

"Me too, hon. I love you too."

"Listen to me, okay? Close your eyes." Reef did what Ford asked and listened to Ford's voice as he continued speaking. The deep rumble took Reef back to their pillow-talk, those whispered sweet nothings as they lay curled into each other late at night. "Tune out everything but my voice. Now think back to our first date in Queenstown. Remember what I said to you? That I wanted your hands in my hair and how I wanted to hold you and touch you, how I couldn't get enough of you? Remember our kiss? Our first kiss?" The moment was ingrained in Reef's memory—the moment he gave into temptation and claimed the one person he'd wanted above all others. Fire, passion and need all combined to create the single most explosive kiss Reef had ever had. There wasn't a doubt in his mind after their first kiss that he and Ford were meant to be together.

Ford continued on, "Right out there in the cold, leaning up against your rental in the middle of the night. We connected, Reef. From that moment— maybe even before then—our lives became totally intertwined. You're the other half of my heart, sweet. You complete me."

It took a second to register what Ford had said, but when it did, Reef snorted out a laugh, the grin firmly plastered on his face once more. "You didn't just say that. You didn't just go *Jerry McGuire* on me, did you?"

"Hey, made you laugh didn't it?"

"And you think I'm a nutter." Reef shook his head, still smiling.

"Reef, think of that moment when everything gets too much. This competition is one moment in your life. Important, yes, but don't let *it* define *you*. You control it."

Reef saw Mace tapping his wrist where his imaginary watch would be and motioning to the door of the hotel's restaurant. "Hon, Mace is telling me I have to go."

"Okay. I love you, Reef. I may not physically be there, but I'm with you every step of the way. Got it?"

"Yeah, I've got it."

"Good. Now go practice."

"I love you too, Ford. Thanks for...fixing me."

———

FORD PALMED his cell after Reef had hung up and pursed his lips together, furrowing his brows. Reef was normally so Zen. He did this thing where he'd take a deep breath and you could literally see the stress falling away.

For him to admit that the stress getting to be too much, he was on the edge. *But how do I bring him back from it? How do I tell him it doesn't matter, I'd love him anyway world champion or not?* It was easy to say the words, easy for Ford to think, but being the champion was a big deal to Reef. He'd been training for it since he was a kid. There's no way Ford would render meaningless those years of training, those years of being separated from his family and friends and the sacrifices he made by telling him the competition wasn't important. Reef had won silver at the Winter Olympics—the peak of elite sports— yet the world championship was what mattered to him. It was a childhood dream and he was so close, but was he going to snatch defeat from the hands of victory because he couldn't handle the pressure? Would he buckle under the strain? Ford debated for only a moment before swiping the screen to bring up Mace's number and sent him a message.

Mace, call me when you've got five mins apart from him. We need to talk.

Ford walked the halls of the staff quarters at the resort on his way to breakfast. It was a 1970s style building which hadn't been updated since it was built. Inevitably it smelled like old socks and sweat. The brown linoleum lining the floors was worn through in sections, the windows rattled and the draft from the ice-cold wind sent bone deep shivers through anyone who didn't stuff the oversized gap below their door with one of the old blankets every room was stocked with. After his few nights at the resort, Ford learned his lesson and went shopping for much warmer bedding.

It was only a short wait until he got Mason's call. He swiped his thumb across the screen and answered with a, "Hey, Mace. How are you, buddy?"

"Good to hear from ya, dude, but I didn't like gettin' a 'we need to talk' message. What's goin' on?"

"I'm worried about Reef. This isn't like him. He's the most bloody relaxed person I know and he's crumbling to pieces."

"He misses you."

"Yeah, I miss him too; it's damn hard being apart. But it's more than that. He said the pressure is getting to him."

"I read him the Riot Act this morning. He said he wanted to chuck in the competition to come to you."

"He can't do that, not when he's so close." Ford paused, Reef's comment *'This competition...I'm losin' it over here'* replaying in his head. "I'm doing my best to get there. But we need to do something in the meantime; he's at the end of his tether. He needs to unwind. He's putting himself under so much pressure." Ford took a deep breath to stop the words tumbling from his mouth. "I don't think he can take much more, especially if he doesn't start seeing some results."

"He can do it though." Mason's frustration was obvious. "He's making stupid mistakes and it's costing him points."

"Is he psyching himself out? Between everyone telling him he can do it and him wanting it so bad. God, he looks at those scores like a man possessed when he's on the snow...." Ford trailed off.

"He could be psyching himself out," Mason said thoughtfully. "After our little chat this morning, I was gonna try a different tactic with him today anyway. Maybe if I can get him to focus on the mountain rather than the competition, he'll relax. If I can get him outta his head, his muscle memory will kick in."

"Look after my man, Mace. I need him."

"Wouldn't dream of doing anything else. Take care on the slopes, Ford."

"You too, big guy." Ford hung up as he joined the line for breakfast.

"Urgh, I have a hangover from ginger beer," Gabriella mumbled from behind Ford as she leaned on him, prompting his smile.

"Is that even possible? God you're a lightweight." At Gabriella's scowl, Ford laughed.

Burying her face in his jacket once more, she grumbled again. "I hate you. Mornings are not happy."

"You'll be fine after your third espresso. Sit down and I'll bring you one." Ford motioned to the table they always sat at.

Slipping her arms around him, she squeezed Ford tight. "*Grazie, Ford. Ti amo.*"

"I love you too, Gab."

Shaking his head at her retreating back, he smiled and placed his order with the waiting server.

Lost in thought, Ford sat and toyed with the packets of sugar, tipping them to let the contents slide from one end to another. "It's called gravity. Been around since apples fell out of trees," Gabriella said playfully.

"Huh?" he replied, looking across to her. He'd forgotten she was sitting with him.

"What's going on? You're distracted."

"I spoke to Reef this morning. I'm worried about him and," he blew out a breath, "and I'm upset."

"Why?" Gabriella's brow furrowed, her head tilted to the side as she waited expectantly.

"He's having a hard time. The pressure of the comp is getting to him. Jesus, the bloody pic of us together last night made him freak out."

"I don't understand. What was wrong with the picture?"

Ford sighed. He knew exactly how Gabriella would react, but he needed to talk, to get it off his chest. "He didn't say the words but it made him doubt us and that, combined with all the other stress he's under, pushed him to the edge."

"Did you set him straight?"

"Of course. He's feeling insecure, questioning himself. It's making him wonder whether I still love him." Ford scrubbed his hands through his hair, frustrated. "He doubted me, Gab, questioned whether I was cheating on him."

"Why? How could he think that? You're miserable here without him. You lit up when he was on the television."

Needing her comfort, Ford reached across and curled his fingers over to grasp her small hand. "He saw us hugging and thought I cheated, Gab," he said simply, his heart breaking over the stress he'd added onto Reef's already large stash. She looked at him blankly for a moment then turned her gaze to their joined hands, before pulling her smaller one from Ford's.

"È stupido," Gabriella muttered.

"He's not stupid. He's insecure and stressed and missing his family and I upset him."

"He's jealous. That's a slippery slope, Ford."

"He's nothing like your ex. He just needed some reassurance."

Gabriella sighed and shook her head, picking up her empty coffee cup as she stood. "I hope for your sake that's all this is, Ford. I don't want to see you hurt like I was."

"Gab," Ford pleaded as she walked away. She waved him off when he called out again. Crossing his arms on the table, Ford rested his head on his forearms. The memories of the first time he met Gabriella slammed into him. She had every reason to be worried about a jealous, abusive lover. She'd experienced it first-hand. It was how they'd met, Ford rescuing her from her torture chamber.

"Gabriella, my name is Ford. I'm friends with Ricky and Angelo. Your brothers sent me. I'm here to help you," he called out as he knocked loudly on the door of the modest townhouse on the quiet laneway. Looking at it from the street, you would never know the horrors that went on inside. And his friends' little sister was trapped in there, imprisoned behind the steel bars and bolted door. The blinds in the window to the right shifted and his heart stopped. Before him was a timid woman, battered and bruised, her face swollen, one eye closed completely, the other bloodshot. *"I'm here to help you. I'm a paramedic. Are you alone?"*

Ford slumped back in his seat and scrubbed his hand through his hair, groaning out loud at the walk down memory lane.

"Hi, buddy," Hiro said as he slipped into the seat opposite him. "Headache?"

"Shitty morning. Hey, can we talk about swapping a few shifts in a week or so? I need to get a few days off so I can see Reef before he goes on the next leg of his world tour. It'll be the last chance I get before Christmas."

Hiro frowned. "Ford, you know I don't swap shifts."

"I know. I'm asking for a favor. I'm desperate. Take the extra shifts if you want them, you don't have to give up any of yours. Or you can take yours in a block so you've got a couple of days off too. I don't care, I just...Please, Hiro." *I'll do anything.*

Hiro shook his head, apparently being a pig-headed bastard. "I'm sorry, Ford. We're busy enough. I don't need to work anymore shifts than I already am. I don't want more."

Ford's desperation increased. Clenching his fists was working as well as a blocked release valve on a pressure cooker. *He has to help me.* "I'm begging, Hiro."

But like an impenetrable wall, Hiro didn't budge. Ford slammed his fist down on the table, his frustration getting the better of him. "Dammit, Hiro."

"Ford, it's not going to happen."

"Shit," Ford hissed. Then, a lot louder than he should have, growled, "Fuck." Standing abruptly, he turned on his heel and strode out of the restaurant, slamming the door behind him.

CHAPTER FOUR

"I'm sorry, sweet cheeks, I'm so sorry. I couldn't pull it off." The misery in Ford's voice tore at Reef, his heart breaking for the two of them. It was the last chance they had to see each other before Christmas, still two months away. The long lonely nights without having his man pressed against him, holding him, loving on him was like an endless desert stretching before him.

Desolate.

"I spoke to him, begged him, but Hiro wouldn't budge. When I'd calmed down enough to stop myself from hitting him, I went back and offered him a damn holiday. He still turned me down for fuck sake."

Reef sighed, unable to keep the disappointment from his tone. "That sucks. The saying no part." Stretching out on the sofa, Reef pulled the fluffy throw blanket over him as he laid in front of the roaring fire and stared into the dancing flames. He'd gone straight to the fireplace, lighting it as soon as they'd arrived back from the end of the day's competition anticipating Ford's call. He'd smiled the whole time as he remembered doing the same thing at Ford's house after their disastrous first date took a turn for the better. With the call, the smile had slipped, the day losing its shine. Beating Caden by two points and closing some of the gap between them suddenly wasn't so great anymore.

Warm and comfortable, Reef closed his eyes wishing his man was in front of him even for just one night. He fingered the white stitching which edged the teal-blue blanket as the silence stretched between them. Reef heard Ford's breath catch on the other end of the line, a small hitch that eviscerated him. Knowing he was on the verge of crying brought Reef to his knees. Ford's number one fear was failing, letting down those close to him. He'd no doubt be beating himself up, taking full blame for disappointing Reef. "It's okay, Ford. We can do this. We can get through it."

"That's not the point." Ford blew out a breath. "I'm supposed to be supporting you." The sound muffled like he was rubbing his face and Ford said, "Dammit, I'm supposed to be there for you and I can't even get my ass into the same fuckin' country as you. The one thing...the one fuckin' thing—"

"Ford stop," Reef interrupted, his tone firm. "You told me a few days ago that it didn't matter if you and I weren't physically together, you'd still be there every step of the way. That hasn't changed, has it? When we spoke this morning everything seemed okay, so don't do this. Please, hon."

Another exhale from Ford. "I'm worried about you, Reef. I don't think either one of us is handling the stress of being apart but you're under so much more pressure. I need to be there for you," Ford whispered to him.

Not handling the pressure—ain't that the truth. Taking a breath and slowly letting it out, Reef was thankful his voice was strong, steady. "I'll be okay, hon. I just miss you."

"Me too." Ford paused before continuing, pleading. "I need you to talk to me, Reef. I need you to call me whenever it's getting to be too much. I need you to talk to Mace and Momma Bear and Coach too. I can't risk losing you, sweet."

The gooey sweet feels wrapped around Reef's heart, washing over him like the warm rays of sunshine on a spring day. "I love you, Ford. You're right; I am stressed. It's hard to breathe—kinda like everything's sitting on my chest, weighing me down. The comp, constantly watching the points, the travelling; I just wanna curl up with you in bed and sleep. I'm tired, Ford. I want this season to be over. But Mace was right, I need to hit the heats hard and nail 'em. I need to do it for me, for us. And I'm gonna kick ass doin' it."

"I haven't even asked how you went today. So much for supporting you."

"Ford, stop. You're doing great." Ford's snort of disbelief had Reef shaking his head. "I followed your advice, focused on the mountain and pushed aside everything except us skiing together that first time. Well, before the storm set in anyway."

"And?"

"Two points." Reef's grin sounded through his voice.

"You're fuckin' killin' me," Ford growled.

"It was a good two points. I won." Ford's shout of joy had Reef's ears ringing. Doors slamming in the background and the fast footfalls of someone running filled the airwaves between them as he shouted out happily, "He won!" Laughing, Reef kicked off the blanket onto the floor, propping his feet up on the armrest at the opposite end of the sofa. Arching his back to stretch out the kinks in his sore muscles, Reef closed his eyes and smiled.

"Ford," he called. When he got no answer over Ford's enthusiastic rambling to whoever he was yelling out to, Reef called out again, louder this time. "Ford. Get your ass back into your room."

Reef made his way over to his bed, flopping down on the mattress as he heard Ford kick the door shut behind him. "I need to get some sleep, Ford. I'm wrecked."

"I can't wait to fall asleep next to you again, sweet."

"I miss my pillow. Who knew muscle could be so damn comfortable?"

Ford's chuckle had Reef smiling again. "Get on Skype, sweet. I wanna go to sleep with you. If I can't see you tomorrow, I'm sure as hell gonna spend some quality time with you now."

————

ANOTHER DAY, another flight. Or at least it seemed like that with the never-ending cycle of the competition circuit. The constant travel and everything that went with competing on the international circuit was like Groundhog Day. Reef could just picture the title of his memoir—cue the Hollywood style jazz hands——My Life on Endless Repeat. There was no way he'd get lucky and be compared to someone like Michael Jordan—hey, he got mad air too—nope, he'd well and truly be the middle-aged dude with bad 1990s hair. Reef sighed. Being a sad sack didn't suit him. He had hoped that the lonely competition trail would be filled with a few days of Ford's loving, but there wasn't any chance of that now thanks to that stubborn fucker, Hiro.

After landing, they'd been escorted to busses. The one he was on had collected a few of those traveling the world circuit, he and Mace included, for the trip up the mountain. Despite only being half full of people, the extra seats were filled with the ton of luggage the ten or so travelers were lugging around—boards, boots, ski gear, clothes, cameras, computers, you name it. And what were the odds? The one person who he'd tried to avoid driving with was there. Of course, no one else except Mace gave a shit that reporter-extraordinaire, Hailey Watts, was sitting across the aisle from them. She'd had a hard-on for Caden forever, following him and making everyone else's lives hell in the process. She'd reported Reef's ex, Addilyn's cheating; it was apparently her way of distracting Reef so he'd crumble under the pressure, falling apart and protecting Caden's season in the process. *Bitch.*

The fallout from the media coverage wasn't all bad though. His ex-girlfriend's cheating was exposed to the world and it gave him the out he hadn't realized he needed. Even if it was him who ended up looking like a bastard for driving her into the arms of another man. If it weren't for Hailey, he never would've taken time off, he and Ford would never have met, would never have ended up together. Did that make him want to spend any time with her? Fuck, no. But he could still smile at the crazy turn his life had taken.

Engine whining and straining, the bus slowly made its way up the winding mountain road which was rutted into rough corrugations that jarred Reef's temple as he leaned his head against the cold glass window. The little resort playing host to the next leg of the world circuit came into view. Every time he'd been there in the past, he'd liked it. The rooms were homey—big beds in apartment-style cabins with open fireplaces and sheep-skin rugs before them, room service and the view of the mountain towering over them visible through the picture windows. Perfect for a romantic weekend away.

And now Reef wanted to be anywhere but there.

He wallowed in self-pity, his mood dropping like one of those anvils Wile E Coyote always tossed on the Roadrunner. Mason hadn't said anything, instead, squeezing his shoulder as Reef slumped in the seat.

THE BUS LURCHED to a stop at the front entry to the resort. Reef took a deep breath and plastered on a fake smile, locking the façade in place as he disembarked the bus and stepped onto the stony surface of the drive. The great timber and stone structure of the four-story building that stretched out along the street towered over him, blocking the view of the ski slope behind it. Grey skies loomed above, the freezing wind cutting through them. Shoulders hunched, he stuffed his hands in his pockets and looked to the luggage being offloaded, wishing he didn't have to deal with the heavy load. His snowboards, boots and ski gear took up the most room, his other stuff crammed into two smaller packs.

"Why don't you leave these, Reef?" Mace squeezed his shoulder again. "I can look after them for you."

"Nah, it's okay." Reef shook his head, dropping his gaze to the gravel underfoot kicking at the small rocks. "It'll give me something to do."

"I'm sorry, man. Totally sucks that he couldn't get the time off."

Reef huffed out a breath and nodded. "Yeah, it does."

"Come on, let's get our shit organized so we can eat. I'm starving." Reef followed Mason's lead, picking up a couple of their bags and joining the line to check-in. As the bus pulled away, the view opened up before him. A heavy covering of snow blanketed the high-pitched roofs of the hotels opposite them, the competition flags blowing in the breeze. Tall pines swayed in the distance, the towering mountain range the resort was nestled in covered in a mist of white as the clouds swirled around their peaks. It would snow that evening. Even since arriving, Reef could sense the shift in the temperature. Leaving Mace in line, he wandered over to the arched windows, leaning against the frame as he watched skiers come down off the slopes and dodge the buses and SUVs as they crossed over to their own resorts and the myriad eateries.

Reef toyed with his cell, shooting off a quick message to Ford while he waited.

Skype in 20 mins or tonight, bunnykins? I wanna see you.

People swarmed everywhere around him, bundled up in heavy coats and scarves, like bees buzzing around a flower garden. Reef watched them from the sidelines, happy not to be in the fray. He wouldn't be able to stand on the outskirts and watch for much longer though. The event sponsors had set up a signing this time around, rather than the usual meet and greet required with every leg of the tour. Reef could already see the tables being organized in the open ballroom off to the side of the lobby. A bolt of excitement shot through him. Meeting his fans was a hell of a lot of fun. It was exactly what he needed to lift his mood. The little kids were always awesome, always made him grin nonstop. And the fact he even had fans who were loyal enough to stand in line to get something signed, or in the freezing cold to watch him still blew him away. Until then, he needed food.

Reef jumped when Mason joined him, leaning against the other window. "You tried calling him yet?"

"Nah, I just messaged him. I think he's got a double shift today."

"Come on, we're checked in. We're sharing a suite again, so let's do lunch then you've got the promo sesh."

Reef's tired muscles ached. Lifting his arms above his head, he stretched, leaning from side to side. "Do I have time for a quick workout? I'm so damn sore."

"Nope. We arrived late. You're gonna have to suck it up, buttercup. Smile and be your charming self for a while, then you can go for a run."

Reef groaned, but cracked a smile when Mace pointed to a guest carrying a hot drink. "Don't worry, I'll keep you caffeinated."

They stepped to the lifts and Reef's cell chimed with an incoming message from Ford.

NSFW.

The picture attachment was exactly that—not safe for work. Ford's hard cock—and it was definitely Ford's cock—took center stage. Rabbit ears, eyes and a grin were drawn on his crown with a bow tie just below it. 'Bunnykins misses you too, sweet cheeks,' was added as a speech bubble. Reef's snort of laughter cut through the quiet of the lift as it slowed to a stop on their floor.

"Whatcha lookin' at?" Mace asked as the lift doors opened and he looked over Reef's shoulder.

"Oh, you don't wanna see." He laughed, darkening the screen. "Trust me." Smirking at Mace, he added, "You really don't wanna see."

HIS BELLY uncomfortably full from lunch, Reef slumped in the armchair that was placed in the corner of his room, exhausted. It'd been a grueling few weeks and the non-stop travelling was catching up with him. Closing his eyes, he leaned his head on the backrest and groaned. He needed a workout; not more sitting around.

After a moment, he rummaged around in his bag and pulled out a few shirts. The tee Ford had surprised him with was on top of the pile. Smiling, Reef thought about the morning he'd received the gift.

He cracked open his eyes as the weight between Reef's legs shifted and a warm wet tongue lapped at the crown of his cock. God, had he ever been this hard? Reef moaned, bucking his hips and trying to increase the friction and suction on his throbbing shaft.

"Morning, sleepyhead."

"Suck me, Ford. Please," he gasped as Ford wrapped his hand around the base of Reef's dick and pumped him languidly. Ford knew every hot button to press and Reef erupted in record time to Ford fingering his ass and his tongue sneaking out to lap at his balls each time Ford deep-throated him. How he did that while using enough suction to rival a Hoover, Reef would never know.

When the world stopped spinning and Reef had caught his breath, he rolled Ford off him, caging him below his body. Grinding against his man's erection, Reef's spent dick perked up at the possibility of a second orgasm. "Gonna keep you in bed all day, Ford. You're gonna fuck me over and over until I can't walk straight. Wanna feel you for days."

"Oh God, yes," Ford moaned, gripping Reef's hips to press him down, sliding his cock against him. "Shit, wait," Ford grumbled. "Need to...." he trailed off, shifting on the sheets.

Reef pinched Ford's nipple and rocked his hips, murmuring against his throat. "Only thing we need is lube, hon. Gotta have you inside me."

Ford shifted again and Reef sat up giving him some

room. Arching his back, Ford pulled a wrapped package from beneath him, squashed when Reef rolled them over. Tossing it aside, Ford reached up to pull Reef's face down to his again, but Reef was intrigued. "What is it, hon?"

"No big deal. I'll show you later."

"Nah, I wanna see what you got me." Reef said playfully, reaching across the bed for the package now haphazardly balancing on the edge of the mattress. Tearing open the bright blue tissue paper, two bundles of material fell out. White T-shirts with black sleeves. On one was written He sucks *and on the other* I swallow. *Surprised, Reef turned to Ford who met his gaze with a sheepish smile and a shrug.*

"Aww, how romantic, bunnykins. You got me a shirt to wear next time we meet your Mom and Dad," Reef teased.

Ford laughed. "God, I'd pay to see that."

"You know, you might even get lucky later giving me gifts like this." Reef wiggled his eyebrows.

Laughing again, Ford replied, "That was the idea, sweet cheeks."

Reef's cell, beeping a message alarm, startled him back to reality. The words on the screen had him digging through his bags to find his tablet and loading up Skype so he could video-chat with his man. Ford would be on in ten minutes. Ten minutes and he'd be able to see him again. Grinning, Reef brought up the app. Ford was already online. He gave a sigh of relief and dialed. The familiar ringtone barely sounded before his call was answered. But the sight greeting him surprised Reef. A woman—Gabriella—stood before him smiling at the screen. Long dark brown hair and matching brown eyes, flawless olive skin and a face too pretty for anything other than a magazine cover had Reef swallowing. She was beautiful. No stunning. Stunningly beautiful.

"*Ciao*," she said happily in a strong Italian accent. "I'm Gabriella, Ford's friend."

Reef smiled. "Hi, I'm Reef."

"I know. Ford speaks of you all the time. *Un momento*, he's here. *Arrivederci!*" The vision onscreen blurred, as if the camera was being moved far too fast to focus and Ford's smiling face appeared.

"God, it's good to see you, Reef. I've missed you."

"I'm lucky, I got to see a whole lot more of you this morning." Reef grinned wickedly at Ford's blush.

"Too much?"

Reef laughed. "Mace almost copped an eyeful, but I'm always glad to see any part of you. If we're naming our junk though, I want something manly, like Chuck Norris."

"Yeah, okay. I'll go MacGyver then. Or Indiana Jones."

Reef clicked his fingers and pointed. "I've got it. Donkey dick."

Ford laughed. "Stallion could work. I could buck you all night long." Reef coughed out another laugh.

Putting on a fake drawl and tipping an imaginary hat, Reef responded, "I'll ride you like a Texan cowboy."

Ford's fingertips brushed the screen, giving Reef a warm smile. "I love hearing you laugh," Ford murmured and Reef's smile turned shy. They didn't have long—Reef had to be at the signing in a few, but there was no way he wasn't making use of every short-lived moment together. His heart fluttered every time Ford smiled at him. With every word of encouragement Ford uttered, Reef fell harder. It was so damn hard being apart from him. His heart ached from the distance between them, but these stolen moments meant everything. They were literally what kept Reef going. Knowing Ford was missing him just as much gave Reef some sort of perverse comfort—he didn't want Ford in pain, but knowing he wasn't the only one of them who was lonely was reassuring. And times like these, where they had a chance just to tease each other and get back to that levity they always had, lifted Reef's spirits. So, while he would do almost anything to have those strong arms wrapped around him tight—including playing hooky with the competition—Reef tried to use the desire as motivation. You know, for good instead of evil. But hell, it'd be good times to get Ford alone for a few hours again.

Reef's cock twitched thinking of all the despicable things they could do to each other. By the heated expression Ford gave him— all intense eyes and a slow wetting of his bottom lip with the tongue that could take Reef to heaven and back— he had clued into Reef's inner monologue. Reef stole a look at his watch. *Fuck it.* He didn't want to be a Debbie Downer, but he was way too short on time to do anything. And there was no way Reef could do a signing with a raging boner. He groaned and scrubbed his forehead in frustration. Thankfully, Ford took the hint and steered their conversation back into safer territory, telling Reef how Gabriella and Alfonso, the bar tender at their local, looked like they might finally make the move from friends to lovers.

"Shit, hon, I've got to go or I'm gonna be late. I'm sorry, I've got to get downstairs for this signing."

"Don't be, sweet. I'll take five minutes over nothing any day. I love you."

"Love you too, Ford. I miss you."

"Me too." Ford touched his fingertips to the screen and Reef followed suit, joining them in the only connection they could have in that moment. Hundreds, hell possibly even thousands of miles of road separated them, but for that instant, Reef was back in his arms in Queenstown dancing, or hugging him from behind as Ford stirred up a mean casserole on the stove in their townhouse in Fernie.

REEF DID up the buckle on his belt, wishing he hadn't had to say goodbye to Ford and stared at himself standing only in a pair of faded jeans before the mirror. The hickey Ford had given him on his collarbone had long since disappeared. He loved the mark, wore it proudly like a brand announcing to the world he was Ford's. Of course, the only person who saw it beside Ford was Mace. Living together for part of the tour meant they were bound to see each other in the buff, just like any other roommates did. He brushed his fingers along the spot, grinning as he remembered another of Ford's attempts at being a romantic—which he'd debauched—on their last evening together in Canada.

"You're all about the romance tonight, hon," Reef murmured as he plucked a strawberry from the bowl and dipped it in the chocolate sauce, before letting it drip onto Ford's pale skin while he lay prone on the dinner table. He danced the berry up the ridges and valleys of Ford's abs to the flat disc of his nipple, smearing chocolate on him. Ford arched into the touch, pre-cum dripping from his shaft as Reef tightened the grip of his other hand on Ford's hip. He'd leave marks when they were done, the finger-tip sized bruises a reminder of Reef for days to come.

Reef was buried deep, moving slowly in Ford as he touched and teased, licking the melted chocolate from Ford's salty skin. Hands curled over the edge of the table, his man held on with a white-knuckled grip as Reef bent his knees and surged in, changing the angle of his penetration. Ford had his legs wound tightly around Reef, holding him close.

His breathing ragged, his moans ramping up Reef's desire, Ford was the very definition of sin and sex.

Sex incarnate.

Taking the strawberry between his teeth, Reef leaned down to feed Ford, joining their lips together as he bit down and swallowed half of the delicate fruit. Dipping his fingers in the chocolate again, Reef wrapped his hand around Ford's cock and stroked, keeping up the same torturously slow rhythm of his hips. He swallowed Ford's moan as he kissed him until Ford pulled his mouth away, desperately gasping for breath. Reef's head spun, every nerve ending electrified as they made love. Ford clenched around him, shivering as Reef thrust again. His man was riding the knife-edge of rapture. And Reef was right there with him.

Licking a path down his throat, Reef danced his tongue against Ford's pulse-point feeling it beat at a frenetic pace. Strong arms held him close and Ford lunged, latching onto the spot at the base of Reef's throat. Biting and sucking as Reef slammed into him, they lost it together, Reef shouting as he pumped his seed deep into Ford, joining them for the last time before Reef's flight a few hours later.

CHAPTER FIVE

Ford was startled awake by his name being shouted at the volume of a foghorn, rattling what few brain cells he had left after his drunken binge the night before. The banging on his door going with the screaming could have woken the dead. And his brain didn't appreciate it. At all. Groaning he pulled the second pillow from his bed and pressed it against his ear, trying desperately to stop his head imploding from the noise.

"Go away."

"Ford, get up. You need to get packed. *Ora, ora, ora.*" Ford's head thumped out a rhythm in time with the bashing on the door and her shout of *now, now, now* the throb almost worse than the taste in his mouth.

Thank god he was doing the late shift that afternoon—he had time to die—and if he was still drunk when his start time rolled around, it was no skin off his nose. That fucker, Hiro, would just have to cover for him. Ford was sure he'd fail the breath test he insisted on giving every paramedic before their shift. He'd learned the lesson the hard way in New Zealand with Trent, the other mountain rescuer, showing up drunk to work more than once. And if he had to pull rank and kick his own ass out of the first aid building, he would. It'd serve Hiro right anyway, he shouldn't have been such a bastard. If his stubborn assed former-friend had just agreed to rearrange a few shifts with him, Ford would... well he definitely wouldn't be there for his next shift.

He blew out a frustrated breath at the continued beating on the door and the accompanying shouting. Louder this time, Ford responded, gripping his head tighter as the throbbing turned into the head spin from hell when he yelled out, "Gab, go away. I'm not in the mood."

"*Se non sei,*" she shouted back. His hungover brain took a minute to register that she was telling him she didn't care. "*Apri la porta.*"

Open the door? Why? Ford threw the pillow off the bed at the wall, the dull thud completely unrewarding, and kicked off the covers. Stomping to the door, Ford wrenched it open and stood in the opening, towering over Gabriella.

"What?" he growled as the cold air from the draughty corridor sucked the oxygen out of his lungs.

Her eyes trailed down his naked body and looking completely unimpressed, she pushed Ford back so she could step into his room and close the door. "You're a sorry sight, Ford and you stink like a bar. Get in the shower and make it quick. You have exactly twenty minutes to get ready, pack and leave. You're booked on the next flight to Austria."

Ford stilled and furrowed his brows. "Huh?"

"You heard me. You have three days off." As Gabriella clapped a few times, she spoke far louder than his hungover brain could handle. "*Via, via, via.*" *Go, go, go.*

"Gab, are you serious? How?"

"Shower Ford."

"Yeah. Yeah, okay." He spun around and dashed to the

closet to snatch up the towel he'd haphazardly tossed over the door together with the shower caddy he stashed on the top shelf. His hangover was clouding the tingling excitement now crawling over every inch of his body, but the blinding throb of the headache was clearing fast. He had his hand on the doorknob when Gabriella spoke again.

"Ford, you're naked. For goodness sake, cover up. It's like looking at my brothers' junk." Ford looked down, remembering he was naked. Unable to wipe the grin off his face at the possibility of seeing Reef, he wrapped the towel around his waist and yanked open the door once again, getting blasted by the cold draught howling through the corridor.

"Follow me, Gab. Explain how in the hell you've pulled off a miracle." Ford rushed to the shared shower rooms, looking behind him only as he pushed through the door. Gabriella was hot on his heels, a self-satisfied smirk tilting her lips upward.

Looking around the room to make sure they were alone, Ford moved to the side to let her in. As she strutted past him, she threw over her shoulder, "It actually wasn't that hard. I did Hiro a favor and he did one for you."

That stopped him in his tracks. "Gab, what was the favor?"

"Jesus, I didn't sleep with him."

Ford's embarrassment had him rubbing the back of his neck. "Uh—"

Waving her hand dismissively, she clarified, "It wasn't so much a favor as a swap."

After dumping the shower caddy on the seat in the closest of the curtained shower stalls, Ford turned to Gabriella, his hand holding the towel in place on his hip. "What did he want, Gab?" Ford didn't mean to sound suspicious, but he couldn't help it. He'd offered Hiro an overseas holiday and he still couldn't get the stubborn prick to agree. "What did you give him?"

"My room." She shrugged like it was no big deal. "He wanted a single. I had one, so I swapped."

"Oh hell no." Ford fumed, pacing the bathroom, running his fingers through his too-long hair. *No way. Absolutely not. No fucking chance could he agree to that. Just... no. Hell. Fucking. No.* Gabriella was not going to live with Hiro's sleaze of a roommate for the rest of the season. Ford groaned. Once Hiro got his own space, one season wouldn't be enough—he'd insist on it forever. And he'd be unbearable until he got his way. "You're not giving up your room."

"It's too late, Ford." Gabriella stepped in front of him, grasping his forearms and squeezing them. "I need to do this for you, Ford. Please let me. Go and see your man. The two of you are miserable."

"Gab, I can't." Ford shook his head, unwilling to let his friend—who'd already lived through hell—suffer any more, especially for him.

"Yes, you can. I'm a stronger person than I was when you saved me. I can look after myself now. You don't need to feel responsible for me anymore."

Leaning down to kiss her on her forehead, Ford took her into his arms. "Yet you feel like you need to repay me by doing this? You're my friend, I can't let you do this. Get your stuff into my room. You can take it for the rest of the season. I'll sleep in the double."

"Reef will be here in a few weeks. You two need your privacy."

"We can sneak around. Or I'll offer the holiday to my new roomie. You aren't staying with him. Promise me you won't, Gab. I don't like him, it'd kill me to know I let something happen to you."

Gabriella looked up at him, her eyes sad as she finally nodded. "Okay."

"Good. Now go and let me get cleaned up. I've got a plane to catch." Ford grinned unrepentantly as he stepped into the stall and whipped off the towel, tossing it on the seat as he slid the curtain closed.

Hot water cascaded over him as he scrubbed away the sleep and hangover from his body. Unable to wipe the smile from his face, Ford rushed through his morning routine. His stubble was thick enough to be a beard—he kind of looked like a hobo—but there was no way he was risking missing the flight to shave it off. After trimming it back a bit, he dashed from the shower room, finishing in less than ten minutes. Not slowing from his sprint down the freezing corridor, Ford slammed through his door and yanked out the case from the bottom of his closet. Pulling clothes off the hangars ready for him to wear, he paused, momentarily at a loss. "Um, shit. What the fuck do I pack?" he muttered under his breath as a soft knock at his door sounded.

"Can I come in, Ford?" Gabriella asked.

"I'm not decent, but yeah I could do with some help. I've got no fucking idea what to pack."

She closed the door behind her as she entered and motioned to the clothes in his arms. "Get dressed, I'll pack for you." Ford could have kissed her but he was too busy digging through the drawer in his closet. Picking up the first pair of matching socks and snug boxer shorts he found, Ford slid his underwear on under his towel and tossed it to the side. Jeans, a thermal shirt, and a sweater followed, and finally socks and boots, as his friend packed his snow gear and a few other clothes Ford took no notice of.

"Don't forget your passport."

Ford smiled and rummaged around the bottom of the same drawer he'd looked in earlier, holding it up in victory after plucking it out of the mass of black socks.

"I think that's everything. Got my wallet, keys, passport, ski gear. That's all the essentials."

"Good, now go. You're already late."

"Shit, I'm not even gonna have time to call him, am I?"

"No and don't do it while you're driving either. Oh shit, I almost forgot your boarding pass." Gabriella pulled out a folded piece of paper from her back pocket. "You're checked in already. Go straight to baggage drop off, but hurry. You're only just gonna make your take off time."

"I will." Ford took the paper from Gab's outstretched hand and hugged her tight. *"Ti amo, bella mia. Grazie."*

"Ti amo, anch'io." I love you too. "Now go, but please drive carefully. The roads are dangerous." Ford nodded at Gabriella's instructions and dropped a kiss on her head before snatching up his bag and dashing from the room.

THE INFLUX of people heading to the ski resort for the championships actually made things easier for Ford. Unable to speak a word of German, he wasn't looking forward to trying to find a way to get up the mountain. He needn't have worried. World championship flags donned the airport and arrows directed people to the shuttle busses travelling to the resorts. It made transit from the airport the easiest part of the journey.

Ford pulled out his cell checking the time. Again. It was dragging. He was so close, and still too damn far away. Mace reminded him that Reef had a few morning appearances lined up when he'd called—a promotional photo shoot, a modelling gig for one of his sponsors and an interview with Snowboarding Magazine. His man was uncontactable and completely clueless that Ford was only thirty minutes away from him.

Now on the home straight and packed like a sardine into the bus, Ford stuffed his cell back in his pocket. Unable to stifle his grin, he gazed out at the scenery as the bus jolted its way along the rutted road winding up the steep mountain. It was the first chance he'd had that day to breathe. He looked at the vista blanketed in white. The dark rock faces contrasted vividly against the dazzling snow and a calmness swept over him. And yet, the excitement starting to beat a steady pulse through him was amping him up too. They were past the line of the tall pines that crept part way up the slope, giving him an uninterrupted view of the rolling peaks ahead; the perfect canvass for shredding it on skis or a snowboard.

A prick of anticipation jolted through Ford. He could practically hear the roar of the crowd as they cheered on his man. And if he and Reef got to ski the mountain together a few times after the competition, it would be even better. Ford couldn't wait to feel the wind against his face as he flew down the slope, powder swirling around his knees as he crouched low and cut left to right, zigzagging alongside Reef.

The bus rumbled through the town and rolled to a stop in front of a giant timber and stone building. From the photos he'd seen online, Ford knew this was the base of operations for the Ski Federation and world championship contenders. Gravel crunched underfoot as he finally stepped off the bus and breathed in the cold mountain air. Impatiently, he waited for the driver to amble down the steps and open the luggage compartment. Ford would normally be polite enough to wait until the driver had unloaded his gear before dashing off, but not this time. He reached in and shoved aside the couple of bags on top of his and snatched it out, ignoring the grumbling of the other passengers and the middle-aged driver. "Sorry, excuse me," he repeated as he dodged past people, jogged up the steps, and pushed open the doors to the resort's main entry.

Ford's breath caught as he scanned the room and saw Reef, bent over and fishing something out of a big black bag. With a marker in his hand, he signed the jacket of the kid standing in front of him before fist pumping her and tossing the pen down again. Mace strutted across the lobby, coffees in hand, but held off passing the second one to Reef when he looked up and saw Ford standing there. With a nod and a smile, Mace stood back waiting for their moment.

Reef was slumped against the wall. Head hung low, he rubbed his temples, not even noticing Mace's return. He looked tired, stressed. Amazing. As Ford's heart beat wildly, he thumbed out a message on his cell.

Look up.

———

REEF'S CELL pinged with an incoming message. Digging through the bag at his feet he found it, opening the message from Ford.

Look up.

What the fuck? Look up. *Oh shit, look up.* Reef snapped his gaze up and searched the lobby, zeroing in on the man of his dreams as Ford ate up the space between them in long strides. Reef watched, stunned frozen as he met Ford's gaze. His laser focus set Reef on fire, the raw need electric. The charge in the air was palpable as an invisible current arced between them, drawing them irresistibly together and kick starting Reef's body into action. Launching himself off the wall, he damn near ran to Ford. It was a perfect *Baywatch* moment. You know, those slow motion runs along sandy beaches, the Hoff's perfect curls bouncing lightly in the wind? Yeah, it was one of those.

Reef snorted out a laugh at the thought as he threw his arms around Ford and held him tight, clutching onto him lest he disappear. He wasn't dreaming. Couldn't have been. It was too perfect, too... real.

"You're here. You're really here," he whispered into Ford's throat as the world around them fell away and the hustle and bustle of the busy lobby disappeared into the background. Reef's fingers found Ford's hair, as if they were meant to always be there. He speared them through the longer curls and breathed in his scent as he pressed his nose and lips to Ford's throat. "You're not a dream, are you?"

"I'm here, sweet. I'm here." Ford held him just as tight, wrapping him protectively in strong arms. His breath caught as every worry, every insecurity, every ounce of stress and self-doubt Reef had melted away, letting him breathe for the first time since he'd said goodbye to Ford a couple of months earlier. "Shhh, it's okay," Ford whispered when Reef trembled against him, unable to stop the tears now flowing. The murmured words soothed Reef.

"Ford," Mace interrupted loudly, clapping him on his shoulder. Reef pulled back and wiped his tear-stained cheeks with the back of his hand, putting a little distance between the two of them as Mace discreetly tugged him back. Much softer he added, "Our friendly neighborhood stalker has snapped a few shots of you two together. If you're planning on tomorrow's news being your coming out story, all good. Otherwise you want me to deflect?" Ford gave him the barest of nods, a slight tilt in his head. He and Ford had spoken about it before. As far as he knew, all the snowboarders on the circuit were straight; certainly none had come out. And while he and Ford weren't necessarily hiding, they were trying not to be obvious. Sometimes—like now—it was easier said than done. For the moment, he wanted the focus to be on his talent; he'd worked damn hard for his chance at number one. Most of all though, Reef didn't want to give Hailey the scoop – not with their history. But come the end of the season, all bets were off. He was coming out. So whatever Mace had up his sleeve to misdirect the reporter—

Mace stepped forward and shocking the shit out of Reef, he cupped Ford's face before pressing his lips to Ford's in a lingering kiss. Ford rested his hands on Mace's chest, pushing him away after a moment.

Reef waited, watching as they pulled apart, expecting jealousy to roar through his system, to make him act like a wild animal. It happened whenever he saw pictures of Ford and Gabriella together, but this time it never surfaced. Instead, his heart filled at the lengths his trainer and boyfriend would go to to protect Reef from having anything else to deal with.

"Huh, your lips *are* soft," Mace mumbled as he stepped back, surprise coloring his features. "Oh, God, I didn't just say that out loud."

Ford's bark of laughter had Reef smirking too.

"Yeah. You did." Reef shook his head. "Don't go getting ideas, Mace. Find your own man if you want one. This one's mine."

"C'mon, you've got thirty to get up on the mountain for your practice runs. Let's go get changed. Ford, you got gear here?"

"I do, man." Ford lifted the bag sitting at his feet and motioned to Reef to lead the way. Resisting the urge to take Ford's hand, Reef walked toward the bank of elevators.

As the doors slid open before them to an empty cart, Reef tugged Ford in and shot Mace a look. His trainer had already stepped away, either waiting for the next elevator or deciding to take the stairs to their room. The car began its smooth slide to the top floor until Reef hit the stop button and prowled toward Ford like he was prey. And Reef was ravenous, hungry to make Ford forget the taste of Mace's lips, to remind him he belonged to Reef. Staring into Ford's blue eyes, he took a step closer and Ford backed up, hitting the wall of the elevator. Another step forward and Ford was close enough to touch. But Reef didn't have the chance to reach out. Strong hands grabbed onto the front of his shirt and yanked him close. Crashing their mouths together, Reef moaned at the sweet glide of Ford's tongue against his own, tasting his man for the first time in far too long. They were all hands, lips, moans and gasps as they pressed their bodies together and made love with their mouths.

Ford pushed him back, switching their positions against the wall and took his mouth harder, deeper as he undulated against Reef in the sexiest fucking rhythm. Reef pulled back needing to draw oxygen into his lungs or risk either passing out or coming in his pants. Ford moved his mouth along his cheek and down his throat and Reef gasped a deep breath. The hot swirl of Ford's tongue and his nibbles on the spot that always sent Reef into a lust-filled frenzy had him punching his hips forward, desperate for friction. "Oh fuck," he moaned, long and low as Ford licked the place he'd worried with his teeth before biting down and sucking. Clutching his fingers onto Ford's shoulders, Reef panted, grinding his throbbing shaft against the leg Ford had pressed between his.

"Come for me, Reef. Gimme it. Fuck yourself on my leg. I wanna see you fall apart." Ford's sex-roughened words whispered in that dirty rasp of his, sent a zing of lust straight to his cock and had his balls drawing up tight.

"Oh God, Ford."

"Yeah, that's it." Ford's big hand cupped the back of Reef's head and tilted it further, exposing the tendons for his greedy mouth. His other hand travelled down the length of Reef's back, grabbing his ass and guiding the obscene grind Reef had going on. He couldn't stop even if he'd wanted to. His cock was an iron rod, throbbing and leaking a sticky trail of pre-cum into his underwear. He was riding the edge of sanity when Ford's fingers slid between his ass cheeks, pressing against his hole through the layers of material.

"Fuuuck," he moaned, jerking his hips harder against the thick thigh pressed between his own.

"Excuse me, is there a problem with this elevator? Are you in need of assistance?" a disembodied voice queried through the speaker next to Reef's head. His heart momentarily stopped then pounded like a heavy drum beat, the shock of the loud accented man making him jump out of his skin.

"Ah, no. No problem." Ford's voice, still rough from lust, was sheepish.

"Please be aware I am restarting the elevator. It is a nuisance to the other hotel guests during this busy time to stop them. Please refrain from doing so again in the future unless there is an emergency."

"Sure." Ford smirked at Reef as the car began moving again and the doors opened with a ding only a few seconds later. Quivering in his embrace, Reef was glad for Ford's support as he took a shuddering breath and tried to activate whatever remaining brain cells he had left—one or two if he was lucky—and marshal his legs into action.

A crowd of people gathered around the elevator doors grumbled as Reef staggered out, streaming in as soon as he'd moved out of the doorway. Mace, dressed in his ski gear, smirked at them from the back of the group. "Have fun boys?"

"Fuck off," Reef grumbled.

Mace chuckled. "I'll wait here for you, but hurry up. You've now only got five minutes before we need to be on the snow. You've only got an hour time slot where the mountain's yours. You won't be able to get back on until tonight when everyone has finished their sessions."

"Okay, dude. We'll behave." Ford wrapped his hand around Reef's and the feel of the fingers entwined with his own made his heart flutter. Reef looked across to him and smiled. *How the fuck am I lucky enough to have him here? Right when I need him. Right when I'm desperate.*

"How'd you pull it off, Ford? When we spoke last night you weren't coming. Was it bullshit?"

"No." He shook his head. "Yesterday there was no hope. Yesterday, Hiro told me to fuck off and stop asking him to swap shifts. I'd maxed out what Gab and Jose could take. All I needed was for him to take two, but the prick wouldn't agree." Reef stopped at the door to his— well, their—room and Ford cupped his face. "I tried, Reef. God I begged him." He shook his head. "Then Gab came bashing on my door at dawn and told me I was on the next flight. She gave up her room to get him to swap shifts."

Reef furrowed his brow in concern as he swiped the

card to get into their room and pushed open the door. "Where's she staying now?"

Ford followed him in and let the door close softly behind him. "She's in my room and I'm moving into Hiro's old room. She and I had singles, Hiro shared. The bastard wanted her to move in with his roommate, but there's no way."

Reef leaned against the back of the sofa, hands holding the cushions on either side of him. "I'm guessing he's a dude."

"Yeah, but it's not just that. There was a rumor a season or two ago that he raped a girl, but no one ever came forward, so it couldn't be investigated."

"Shit." Reef shook his head. "She's safe, yeah?"

"Yeah, she can hold her own, but I couldn't let her sleep in the same room as him."

"No way." Reef closed his eyes and blew out a breath. "I feel like a dick for getting jealous now. I'm an ass."

Ford smiled, the warmth and love in his gaze as he stepped between Reef's spread legs captivated him. "But you're my dick and I love your ass." Running the back of his fingers down Reef's cheek, Reef couldn't look away from the sincerity radiating in Ford's eyes. Pressing a lingering kiss on Reef's lips, Ford continued, "She's like the sister I always wished I had. I love her, but only as my sister. There's never been any attraction between us and that'll never change. I love you, Reef. I'm with you. Forever, remember?"

Reef couldn't help the smile that split his lips, the giddy happiness flooding his heart. "Forever."

"Come on, we need to get you on the snow. You've got a practice run to do."

CHAPTER SIX

"Okay, Reef. It's rolling," Mace yelled as Reef slid to a stop before Ford. Beanie, goggles, and a neck-warmer covered most of his face, except for his double-dimpled grin. Reef had had one of those goofy, mischief filled smiles plastered on his face ever since Ford told him he was his forever man. Ford knew his own grin matched Reef's exactly. Being together, doing the simple things like holding hands and kissing his man lifted his spirits, sent those gooey feels coursing through him until he wanted to dance around like a fool.

Ford reached out and knuckle-bumped Reef. "Can't wait to see you in action, sweet." Reef flashed a grin at him and turned, beginning his descent down the mountain. Knees bent, arms out wide, Reef picked up speed and cut a wide arc across the face, learning the fall of the slope. Ford stood, mesmerized, as Reef's talent shone through without having even reached the jump.

"Damn, he's impressive," Ford murmured out loud.

"Sure is," Mace replied, still filming. "Wait until you see the jump. He's kickin' ass, but it's stupid little things that are losing him points, things he worked on during pre-season training. And with him and Caden so close, those few points are losing him competitions."

"Tomorrow will be different. Wait and see."

"I hope so. I'm concerned about him and Momma Bear is worried too. You were right, he's putting himself under so much pressure." Reef zigzagged down the ski run, sending up sprays of powder as he turned, barely slowing down as he crisscrossed the face of the slope.

"Coach and I have spoken too."

"I didn't realize you guys talked."

"Yeah, often actually. They've been helping me get over the stuff with my parents. I've pretty much cut off contact with them and it hurts, you know?" Ford couldn't tear his eyes away from his man as Reef neared the man-made jump on the slope. Without hesitation, he angled the board ready to launch himself off it.

"What you and Reef went through was bullshit. Just hope it's smooth sailing for you now. Do whatever you can to make things easy, yeah?"

"Nothing for Reef is a chore, Mace. Whatever he needs I'll give it to him. Anything within my power is his. I love him more than I ever knew was possible. It's killin' me watchin' him so strung out." As Reef hit the jump, he flew high, spinning and flipping, grabbing on the board and kicking it out again. And still he soared, falling gracefully toward the snow. Dumbstruck, Ford could only stare slack jawed as Reef nailed the perfect landing, throwing his arms up and hollering when he'd slowed a little. "Holy fuck!" Ford exclaimed, grabbing onto Mace's jacket and shaking him. "Did you see that? Did you *see* that?" Reaching high above his head, fists clenched in victory, Ford shouted his praise down the mountain, whooping and cheering for his man.

FORD SLOWED to a stop in front of Reef after a solid run of perfect jumps. Hitting the last landing was the most spectacular. Tumbling and rolling, twisting and flipping through the air, Reef had straightened at the last possible second and nailed a flawless touchdown. Ford opened his mouth to speak, but nothing followed. He was utterly speechless, at a complete loss for words. What he'd seen Reef do on the slope blew his mind. Ford tried again, failing once more to get anything out.

"You okay, bunnykins?" Reef smirked, a wicked grin plastered on his face. He was riding the high of the adrenaline and a cockiness Ford had never seen before radiated from him.

Hot.

As.

Fuck.

He shook his head, trying to clear the puddle of mush his brain had turned into as the confidence Reef oozed short circuited every fragment of a thought before it could form in his head. Ford moved forward, cupping Reef's face as he gazed at his love, still trying unsuccessfully to communicate just how outstanding Reef was on the mountain. The warmth reflected in Reef's big browns had him falling even more in love with the man. Bringing their lips together, cold from the elements, Ford kissed him, sliding his tongue against Reef's bottom lip before thrusting inside. Ford let his body communicate everything his mind had been unable to do. Running his gloved hand down Reef's cheek, Ford pulled back resting their foreheads together. "I'm so incredibly proud of you, sweet. That was the most spectacular thing I've ever seen."

"Think I can win?"

"Without a doubt. But even if you don't, you're world class, Reef. The best of the best. You don't need a title to tell you that. You pulling off that jump, all of them... wow. Beyond amazing."

Reef snuggled into Ford's arms, nuzzling against his neck and Ford tightened his embrace. "Thank you. You have no idea how much I needed to hear that."

"Never second guess yourself. You're extraordinary. I'm so privileged to say I love you."

"I love you too, Ford." Reef's warm breath ghosted over Ford's throat as he spoke, sending a shiver of awareness through him. "Let's get inside."

THE THREE OF them skied toward the street as Ford followed Reef's beeline for the resort, Mason trailing behind them. The group of people gathered there were leaning against the protective railings either putting on, or taking off their skis and snowboards. Racks dotted the area, providing a barrier of sorts to the sidewalk and beyond that, the road. Reef stopped at one of the railings unstrapping the bindings on his board and Ford followed suit.

"Ford, my man," a familiar voice called out. "Good to see you, buddy."

"Hey, Caden. How are you?" He grasped the other man's hand and gave him one of those manly, one armed hugs.

"Come and get a drink with us. We're about to grab a bite to eat."

"I'm in, but I'm guessing these two wanna catch up," Mace piped in from behind Ford.

"Yeah, we're gonna excuse ourselves." Ford picked up his skis and set them and his poles aside just as Reef's stomach grumbled loudly. "Then again, eating at the restaurant will be quicker than room service. Let's get you fed, sweet." Reef's smile was shy as he leaned into Ford's side, clasping their gloved hands together.

Walking inside, they stacked the skis and snowboards up against the wall and made their way over to the sofas around the open fireplace. Reef flopped down, Ford settling next to him and Mace on his opposite side, Caden and his trainer sat on the other sofa. They ordered and within a few minutes, had steaming bowls of *Selchfleisch* in front of them. The flavors of the thick meat and sauerkraut stew burst on Ford's tongue as he spooned it into his mouth. Moaning, he cut off a piece of the pillowy dumpling and ate it before taking a long pull of the stein he'd been served. "Damn, that's good. I'm starving."

The bowls were cleared and they sat back on the sofas catching up, Reef cuddling into Ford's side. "Any ideas on the fundraising yet, Caden?" Mace asked.

"Nah, planking and ice buckets have been done. I'm outta ideas."

"Whatcha raising money for?" Ford wrapped his arm around Reef, pulling him closer.

"Breast cancer research. Any ideas?"

Ford nuzzled against Reef's temple and hummed in thought. "Lemmie think on it." The conversation took a turn again, meandering along—mostly with Caden giving Reef shit—when Ford had a lightbulb moment.

"Undie run," he blurted out.

"Huh?" Reef looked up at him from his spot snuggled into Ford's chest.

"Undie run. Challenge someone to do something crazy in their undies and record it—ski run or a bike ride, skateboarding, run down the street—whatever. If you don't take up the challenge, you make a donation. Between a few of the competitors, you've got to have a decent enough following to get a start on the hashtag trending."

Light flickered in Caden's eyes, an excited gleam sparking. The grin that spread told Ford he'd nailed the suggestion. "You're a brilliant man, Ford." Caden downed the rest of his beer and stood. "Right, I'm doing an undie snowboard run. And you lot are up next. Let's go."

"What? Now?" Reef sat up, indignant. "We're goin' to bed. I wanna get laid."

"Fuck each other's brains out after you've raised some money. Come on, up." Looking around the pub, Caden frowned. "Where is Hailey when you need her?"

"Thank God she's not here," Reef mumbled, leaning back into Ford.

Ford breathed in the scent of Reef's shampoo, dropping a kiss on his head. "Who is she, sweet?"

"Remember the reporter who was at Calgary Airport when you arrived? Her." Ford's growl had Caden and Mace smirking at him.

Caden looked apologetically at him and shrugged. "She's a pain in my ass, but I can pull a favor and get media coverage."

"So can half a dozen other reporters, Caden."

"She's the only reporter who'll get us coverage in America," Caden countered. Reef looked to Ford and nodded. His man was brave and, damn, his kindness and generosity for a good cause made Ford fall a little more in love with him. Ford squeezed him tight as Reef blew out a breath.

Caden's words got Reef's attention and broke the connection sizzling between them. "I owe you one, Reef. Lemmie call her and we'll head on up the ski lift."

TEN MINUTES later and they'd collected their skis and snowboards and were trudging up the kiddie slope, Hailey in tow with her cameraman. Snowflakes had just started to fall from the darkened sky, creating the most magical feel as they floated to earth, each one glowing ethereally when they drifted into the floodlit area. Ford hung back, tugging on Reef's hand until they were trailing the small group. Tiny flakes landed on Reef's hair, Ford brushing them off his eyebrow and running his fingers down Reef's cheek. Leaning close, Reef wound his arms around Ford's waist.

"I wanna kiss you stupid right now."

A shy smile slowly formed on Reef's lips, those dimples Ford loved appearing. "I'd love that." Ford leaned in and pressed their mouths together in a gentle kiss before Reef pulled back and walked up the slope again. Ford followed, grinning broadly, drunk on the quick taste of his man.

Already gathered around the top of the short hill, Hailey was talking, shifting them around so they were lined up. She slotted Reef in next to Caden, leaving Ford to join the end of the line next to Mason.

"Okay, when Jason gives the signal he'll start rolling and I'll introduce you and you can make a speech." Hailey looked at the cameraman and waited for his signal. It soon came and the journalist did her bit, speaking at the camera and handing over to Caden after introducing the fundraising effort.

"I'm Caden Lambert, World Champion Freestyle Snowboarder. A couple of months ago my mom died from breast cancer. Like Mom did, my baby sister has the mutated *BRCA1* gene, so she's at high risk for breast cancer, too. We can beat this disease, but only by doing more research, so I'm doing my bit and raising money through The Undie Run. Here's the challenge: if you're nominated, strip to your drawers, get your cell out and do something you'd never do in your undies. Then donate ten dollars to the National Breast Cancer Foundation. Or, decline the challenge and donate a hundred. Nominate someone else too and post your video online. Hashtag 'The Undie Run' and brag about it on social media. So here goes." Caden unzipped his jacket and stripped it off, tossing it aside before he tugged down his pants. In his boxer shorts, his pants around his ankles, he spoke, "I'm doing The Undie Run in the snow and I'm challenging my friend, Reef Reid."

Reef stepped up and quickly stripped off his jacket, unzipping his pants before dropping them too. "I'm accepting Caden's challenge to do The Undie Run." Reef nominated the next person in line and she followed, doing the same thing. The camera finally landed on Ford who grinned and unzipped his jacket. "I'm accepting The Undie Run challenge too. I'm nominating far and wide. Riccardo and Angelo Di Pasqua in New Zealand and Gabriella Di Pasqua in Italy."

Everyone else had already set off down the slope, but Reef waited for him as Ford tugged down his pants. Unlike the snowboarders, who were struggling with their feet spread, Ford didn't have the same problem. His skis made it easy. But that hardly eased the bite of the cold which hit him like a tsunami.

"Fuck me, it's cold." Ford shivered, teeth chattering as a

gentle breeze chilled him to the bone. Touch him and he'd shatter to pieces, frozen solid like he'd been dunked in dry ice. He wasn't the only one who was fucking freezing, either. Reef's lips had already turned blue and he was shuddering as if the earth was moving below him. "Go, sweet. Get down the hill. You need to get inside."

Reef dipped his head in a shaky nod. Dammit, Reef would get hypothermia if he wasn't careful. *Shit. Whose stupid idea was it to strip? Oh, yeah, mine.* Bundling his jacket under his arm, Ford quickly caught up to Reef on the slope, bracing himself against the barest puff of a breeze as they made a beeline for the end of the run.

———

GODDAMN, IT'S FUCKIN' freezing. Reef's breath caught as the gentle wind buffeted him, but he was nearly there. Nearly at the bottom of the slope where he could put his clothes back on and warm the hell up. Caden owed him big time for this. And Ford had better be ready to get in a steaming hot shower with him.

Missing Caden's high five as he slipped on his jacket, Reef stopped and held out his hand clasping his friend's, before pulling up his pants and undoing the bindings holding his feet onto the board. "Now we're off. See you tomorrow."

"Thanks, man, I appreciate it. See ya tomorrow."

"All good." Ford shook hands with Caden and clicked his feet out of his skis.

AS REEF SWIPED his key against the door, Ford crowded him from behind, breathing warm puffs of breath on his neck as he nibbled a line up Reef's throat. Dropping his head back on Ford's shoulder, Reef moaned. "Sweet, open the door," Ford growled in his ear, the deep timbre of his voice going straight to Reef's cock. Turning the handle, he let Ford push them through the open doorway and headed straight to the attached bathroom.

Ford situated Reef against the counter and stripped off before stepping behind the panel of glass to turn on the shower. Reef rubbed the growing bulge in his pants and bit his lip. Damn, the man had one hell of an ass. The commanding way he handled Reef, maneuvering him into place and utterly dominating him, was hot as fuck. His breath caught at Ford's unexpectedly gentle movements. Slowly unzipping his jacket and slipping it off Reef's shoulders, Ford's gaze never left his own. Reef's heart flip-flopped in his chest.

When Ford dropped to his knees to unlace Reef's boots, Reef gripped his thermal shirt from behind his head and tugged it off. Watching his man on his knees before him, heat smoldering in his eyes, Reef sucked in a breath. Need raced through him, his dick grew impossibly hard.

The room had steamed up; clouding the mirror and shrouding them in a warm haze, sheltering them from the outside world and all the stresses of it. Desire arced between them, sparking like electricity in the humid air.

When both his boots were off, Ford reached up and curled his fingers under the band of Reef's briefs, tugging them, together with his ski pants, slowly down his legs. Leaning close, Ford laid soft open-mouthed kisses on Reef's hip and nearer to the patch of hair at the base of his now-straining cock. Nuzzling him, Ford grasped Reef's ass cheeks and squeezed, moaning as he did. It set fire to Reef, need erupting within him. Hauling Ford to his feet, he crashed their mouths together, their tongues tangling hungrily as Reef speared his fingers through Ford's hair. Body against body, the hard muscular plains of Ford's chest and abs pressed together, their hard cocks sliding against each other had Reef gasping for breath and fighting to get closer at the same time.

Ford's strong fingers curling around his hips and tugging him into the shower had Reef falling into him. Eyes closed with their mouths joined, Reef trusted Ford to guide him. Cold tiles pressed against his back, Ford's hot and hard muscles against his front. The contrast, like day and night, made Reef shiver in delight. He hummed when the hot water hit his skin, adding another sensation to his over-stimulated nerves. Ford sucking on his throat, that spot which always took him to the edge of sanity and his big hands mapping every inch of Reef's body within reach, had him moaning incoherently.

The weight and heat of Ford's body disappearing had Reef cracking his eyes open. But his man hadn't gone far. Reaching for the shampoo, Ford squirted some out and lathered it in his hands, then slid his strong fingers along Reef's scalp, massaging him. Reef's eyes fluttered closed and he hummed. He needed both sides of Ford—the part of him who cared for Reef like he was the most precious thing on earth, as well as the side of him who wouldn't hesitate to jump Reef and ride him like a rodeo cowboy—and damn did his man deliver. Hot water streamed over Reef's head, washing away the bubbles from the shampoo and after a few beats, Ford's hands were working his shoulders.

"Turn around, Reef." The voice in his ear, gravelly from desire, had Reef moving quickly. Crossing his arms and resting his forehead on them, Reef relaxed, letting Ford take care of him. When those strong hands hit the knot of muscle in his shoulders again, Reef's knees almost buckled. Pain and pleasure coursed through him.

"Oh, *God*," he moaned. The warmth of Ford's body, his breath against the shell of his ear, those magical hands that could send him into orbit and the hard cock resting between the cheeks of his ass had Reef shuddering. Want and need pounded through him like the hammering of his heart. Along his arms, under them, down his back and lats, over his ass and down his legs, Ford massaged every muscle, every sore spot in Reef's tired, stressed-out body, leaving him whimpering for more and begging him to stop all at the same time.

Ford turned him and started the same firm massage on his front. Blinking his eyes open, Reef focused on his man. Pupils blown wide, his heated gaze seared into Reef. Riveted him. He was being watched, preyed upon. Hunted. And he fuckin' loved it. Tugging Ford closer by his shoulders, Reef joined their lips in a hungry kiss. Swiping his tongue against Ford's bottom lip, he moaned as Ford thrust his into Reef's mouth and ground their cocks together in a dirty slide. Sensation shot to his balls, drawing them up close as a tingle began at the base of his spine.

Only when he was lightheaded did he pull back for breath, but the movement of his hips didn't slow. Grinding against each other, all soapy and wet, Reef writhed in Ford's embrace. His man bit down on his lower lip and Reef shuddered in his grasp, his grip tightening in the wet curls at the back of Ford's head.

Reef widened his stance when Ford nudged his knee between his legs and shivered again as Ford danced his fingers slowly down Reef's side and over his ass. Soapy digits curled around the inside of Reef's leg and brought it up, hitching it around Ford's hips. Reef's head fell back and he moaned long and low when Ford ground against him. Hard heat scorched him, need igniting every fiber of his being.

"*Fuck.* Ford, I need you."

Ford gripped the leg Reef had hitched around his hips and held tight, then reached down to grasp Reef's other and lifted him with ease. Clutching tight, Reef wound his legs around his man's waist, erasing any sliver of distance between their bodies and joining their lips together in a fierce mating as Ford effortlessly stepped out the shower.

Ford's bruising grip, the stroke of their tongues, brush of lips, every moan sent him higher, closer to ecstasy. As if he could read his mind, Ford strode straight to the bed, falling onto it with Reef still in his arms, pinning him down. Chest to chest, every part of their bodies were aligned.

Reef reached out to the side table snagging the bottle of lube he'd stashed there. Ford licked his throat before biting down on his lobe and whispering to Reef, his tone a dirty as fuck rasp, "Wanna watch you use that on yourself, sweet. Wanna get up close and watch you come on my face as you fuck your fist and I lick you." Reef abandoned the lube, needing to stop the orgasm he was racing toward. Gripping the base of his cock tightly, he grunted as his shaft twitched. Reef bit down hard on his lip and groaned as his back arched and his feet scrambled for purchase on the bed.

"Get inside me, Ford. Now." Reef ground his teeth together and hissed out, "Don't wanna come without you in me." There was no messing around, no more lead up or foreplay. Reef watched, wetting his lips with his tongue, as Ford slicked himself in lube and rubbed his coated fingers over Reef's hole, pressing inside. Reef sucked in a breath and bore down, Ford's digits sliding inside him. It'd been two months. Two long months since he'd had Ford inside him and even the small connection sent Reef spinning. Coming home and flying high all at the same time. He was tight; the twinge of pain crept along his spine as Ford scissored his fingers.

"Relax, sweet. I don't wanna hurt you."

"Need to feel you, Ford. Need the burn." Ford stilled and looked at Reef, his brows furrowed.

"Reef—"

"Ford, please. I'm ready. Just go slow to start."

Ford pulled back until he was kneeling between his spread legs. Reef missed the stretch of Ford's fingers immediately but he didn't have to wait long. Ford reached under his knees, hitching them over his arms and leaned forward, pressing his cock against Reef's hole as he sought entry. They both hissed as Ford pushed in past the tight ring of muscle and he fell forward onto his elbows, bending Reef in half. Holding steady, the tension vibrating off Ford while he waited for Reef to adjust was palpable.

Sweat beaded on his forehead, Reef's corded muscles strained.

The burn was sharp and sweet, a reminder of what he'd missed—Ford.

A drop of sweat ran down Ford's temple and Reef lunged up in a half crunch licking the salty liquid away. Ford bucked, pushing in further, then he froze again. The burn had turned. No longer painful, instead it was something far more erotic. Reef couldn't wait any longer. He needed to be filled, to be marked and claimed by Ford again. With the cotton sheets against his back and Ford's big body pressing against his front, Reef used Ford's arms as a swing and rocked. He pushed down, impaling himself on Ford. Ford's cock slid in deeper, tunneling against the bundle of nerves, which never failed to put him on the edge. Reef cried out and bucked, seeking out the pressure on his prostate again. Digging his fingers into the hard planes of Ford's back, Reef curled more, pushing Ford in to the hilt, needing more.

Desperate for him.

Ford grunted and pulled back before slamming forward again, bending Reef until his knees were at his ears. Ford's powerful thrust had Reef shouting out, begging him to go harder, faster. With snap of his hips, the bedframe punched against the wall and their bodies slapped together. A sheen of sweat slicked their still wet bodies and grunts and moans filled the air as they climbed toward the precipice of a monster orgasm.

Lost in their own world, focused on Ford, Reef almost missed the incessant banging on the door. But like an annoying buzz in the back of his mind, it wouldn't stop, bringing Reef back into himself. He paused for the barest of moments, but with Ford's concentration zeroed in on him, his man halted mid-thrust. The interruption was enough to dash away the quickening at the base of his spine. "WADA, Mr Reid. Open up, please."

Ford heard it too. "What the fuck is WADA?"

"World Anti-Doping Agency. I'm being drug tested." Reef's arms fell to the bed and he closed his eyes. "Fuck." Disappointment lanced through Reef, reality intruding and dragging him back. Stress weighed down again like an anvil. For one moment, he'd been able to disconnect, to forget where he was and what he was doing. But it wasn't meant to be, their moment stolen by a doctor in a white coat.

"Hey, it's okay." Ford kissed him gently, moving his arms and letting Reef's legs drop to the bed. "Take a minute. I'll let him in and get him settled. Come out when you're ready." Ford pulled out and gave Reef a small smile.

"I'm sorry. God, this couldn't have happened at a worse minute."

"Oh, it so could have. Another thirty seconds and I would have been watching you blow. Getting interrupted during that would have been a tragedy."

"At least I would have come," Reef muttered sullenly.

"Sweet, you're gonna come—"

"Mr Reid, competition rules require you to undergo a drug test. Open the door."

"Coming. Jesus, hold your horses," Reef shouted, watching Ford as he climbed off the bed and snagged the shirt Reef had tossed on the floor when he'd changed earlier. He didn't bother putting it on, instead holding it in front of his privates he strode out the bedroom to the door. Reef couldn't help the small grin tilting his lips as he ogled the best ass on the planet as it, and the fucking hot man it was attached to, strode out and gave him a much-needed moment to compose himself. The buzz of his impending orgasm had died down, leaving Reef needy. Ford's absence, on the other hand, left him cold.

"Hi, please come in. Reef will be with you in a moment," he heard Ford greet the WADA doctor.

"Thank you. I'm Doctor Montgomery." Reef's sore muscles protested as he pulled on a pair of sweat pants and walked out of the bedroom. The doctor had his hand outstretched to Ford and his man was reciprocating, almost connecting their palms before snatching his hand away. The doctor's eyebrows hiked up and he regarded Ford as he wiped his hand on the shirt he was still protecting his modesty with.

"Shit, sorry. I'm Ford Wallace, Reef's boyfriend. I um... lube. Sorry, I won't shake hands." He flushed red, babbling to the doctor.

"Why don't you put some clothes on, hon," Reef interrupted the awkward conversation. Directing his question to the doctor, he asked, "Piss test or blood test?"

"Urine sample only this time, Mr Reid. You know the drill, yes?"

"Yep." Reef showed his passport to the doctor and signed the forms he had ready after the doctor had checked his identification. Once he'd finished the paperwork, the doctor gave him two sample jars and followed him through the bedroom into their attached bathroom. Their ski gear lay discarded, items haphazardly thrown after being stripped from their bodies and the air was still humid from their steamy shower. Kicking clear a path, Reef stepped over to the toilet. It was humiliating having someone watch you take a piss; definitely one of the less glamorous aspects of his job, but if he wanted the title, he had to do it.

Reef sealed the two jars, bagged them and attached the sticky security labels to each, making sure to sign both before handing the bags to the doctor. After washing and drying his hands he walked the doctor to the door.

"Thank you, Mr Reid. Results will be communicated via email. Enjoy the rest of your evening and good luck for tomorrow."

"Night." Closing the door behind the doctor, Reef leaned against it.

"Come back to bed, sweet. Lemmie love on you." Ford held out his hand and Reef reached for him, twining their fingers together as they walked to the bedroom.

"Lube on your hand, huh?"

Ford grimaced. "Yeah, sorry. Brain to mouth filter wasn't working."

Reef shrugged. It was no big deal. He honestly didn't give a shit what the good doctors of WADA thought about his sex life. As long as his drug tests were clear—and there was no doubt they would be—he was all good.

Standing at the edge of the bed, Reef slid his arms around his man and drew their bodies together, resting his head on Ford's shoulder as he hugged him close. "I've missed you, hon. God, so much."

"Me too, sweet." Ford dropped a kiss on Reef's temple and squeezed him tighter. Standing there, just the two of them together was everything Reef needed. Being wrapped in Ford's arms was like coming home, reconnecting with the other half of his heart. Reef pulled back and gazed into those blue eyes that had captivated him from the moment they'd met.

"I love you, Ford."

"And I love you. Always."

CHAPTER SEVEN

FORD CARESSED Reef's cheek and inhaled his scent. Damn the man did things to him. He couldn't resist him, didn't want to. He kissed him, slow and soft, their lips melding. Breaking apart, he sucked in a breath but Reef's skin was too tempting. Ford nuzzled close again and dropped a line of kisses along his cheek. He hummed when he licked Reef's throat, tasting him, his lips and tongue caressed stubble that was just long enough to be soft. The sheer masculinity of his man's tight body had Ford's cock throbbing. Ford ran his hands down and under the waistband of his man's sweats—the muscles in Reef's back flexing as he moved—to cup his ass and massage the perky globes as he ground their shafts together.

Reef kissed his ear and Ford rolled his head to the side, giving his man better access. The puff of breath against Ford's throat had him breaking out in a shiver. Joining their lips again, he worshiped his man, their tongues gliding and stroking until they were both gasping for breath. He remapped every inch of Reef's body with his lips as he fell to his knees and dragged Reef's sweats down. Ford kissed up the length of each of his legs, nuzzling his hips and the fucking sexy 'v' leading down to the patch of hair at the base of Reef's cock. The soft skin of his sack beckoned and Ford laved it with his tongue, loving on his man. With a groan, Reef widened his stance, giving Ford more room to play.

"How are you feeling, sweet? You sore?" Ford licked the length of Reef's cock, tasting the drop of pre-cum on the tip as he ran his fingers down the length of Reef's crack, pausing over his still-lubed hole. Reef's moan and the shameless way he pushed back onto Ford's digits had him taking the head of Reef's cock into his mouth and sucking while he teased his entrance.

Ford stood when Reef's hands under his arms tugged him up. He reclaimed Reef's mouth again, kissing him slowly as he guided him onto the bed.

"Come inside me, Ford. I need you." Ford couldn't wait a second longer. Slicking up his cock with lube, he did exactly what Reef begged him for—slow and steadily making love until both of them were a sweaty mess of quivering exhausted muscles.

"SO, Mace, where'd you sleep last night? We didn't hear you come in." Ford stood behind Reef, his arms wrapped around his middle as they waited in the competitor's tent at the top of the ski field. He held him close as they watched one of the other competitors do his run. The announcer's voice filled with excitement as he commentated the jump. The colorful flags flapping in the air and the cheers of the crowd created a festival-like atmosphere on the steep mountain, despite the heavy cloud cover marring the skies and taking the temperature down a few degrees. Dressed in full cold-weather gear, Ford was toasty, his warm breath dissipating in a puff of steam as he exhaled.

"Caden's room."

"What?" Ford whipped his head around to face Mason. "Caden? Are you serious?"

"It's not like I gave him any tips, Ford. He's got his own trainer. He doesn't need me. We had a few more drinks and he offered me a place to crash to give you two some space."

Ford's grip tightened on Reef. "Did you know about this, sweet?"

"Yeah, of course." Reef leaned into Ford. "Mace told me over breakfast when you were getting us coffees."

Mace was defensive—his back straight and gloved hands fisted by his sides—he stepped closer. Through clenched teeth, Mace seethed, "I'm not hiding anything, Ford."

"Are you okay with it, Reef?"

"Ford, calm your tits. We went upstairs, crashed together and got woken up when the WADA drug doctor came knocking. Then we crashed again. Caden was still asleep when I ducked out this morning and came to wake the two of you up. That's it, man."

"Yeah, okay." Ford nodded, conceding Mason's point. He knew logically Mace was good people, but damn if those protective instincts didn't kick in where Reef was concerned. "Fair enough." They fell silent, watching the next competitor take his run. This guy was number three in the world championship rankings, but a mile behind Reef on points. He pulled off a pretty impressive counter-clockwise fourteen-forty—a triple spin that had him landing smoothly. Cheers went up through the crowd and Ford yelled out along with Reef and Mace. There was no way number three was going to close the gap on the two frontrunners with that sort of jump. Not today. Not when Reef had pulled off the mother of all practice runs the day before.

Caden was up next. As he was lining up, Ford studied the other man. Mace did too. Reef, on the other hand, leaned his head back on Ford's shoulder and took a deep breath, letting it out slowly. Ford nuzzled his throat through his neck warmer, gently biting the tendon there. Reef's shiver had him smiling as they turned their attention back to the world champion. Caden's warm up routine was completely different to Reef's. Reef meditated and focused, blocking out the crowd. Caden worked himself up like a WWF wrestler, playing up to the crowd and encouraging their cheers and whistles. The buzzer—giving Caden the go-ahead—punctuated the cold, clean air and he took off, making a beeline for the steep jump.

"His line is off." Mace watched him like a hawk as he hit the ramp. "He was too far to the left. Clean landing's gonna be hard to pull off." The world champion spun and flipped, grabbed the board and did some more. Ford lost count of how many he did—four, five maybe—before losing height and hitting the snow hard. Caden stretched out his arm to steady himself, digging up a deep gauge in the snow as he struggled to get upright. Rotating the board into the mountain and using his arm as an anchor, the momentum had him tipping up. As quick as he'd started, he turned the board again, managing to avoid face planting the snow and staying upright. But a messy landing like that was going to hurt his point score.

"Good jump, but the landing sucked. He did well to hold it the way he did though," Ford murmured.

"He'll lose ten points for that landing. Reef, if you can pull off the jump you did yesterday, you'll be ahead on points for the championship."

Reef tensed in Ford's arms and Ford squeezed tighter, nuzzling his throat as he spoke. "Shh, its okay, sweet. Forget the competition. Forget the points. Let your body do its thing. You've trained for this. You've got nothing to worry about."

Reef's hum, a low sexy rumble, dragged Ford's thoughts back to the hot as fuck massage he'd given Reef that morning. Every touch they'd shared, every glide of oiled-up skin, had turned him on more. He couldn't stop, murmuring every filthy desire in Reef's ear as he slowly fucked him into the mattress. Ford's breath caught and he moaned softly, his shaft thickening as the memories bombarded him.

"Your cock stickin' in my ass like that is gonna have me thinkin' about gettin' bent over, when I should be thinkin' about jumping."

A wicked smile split Ford's lips as he imagined doing exactly that. *The cold will be a bitch.* "Doin' it out here'd have my foot-long shrinking to a six-incher."

Reef laughed, playfully elbowing him in the ribs. "Foot-long? You wish." Turning his face into Ford's, Reef gave him a quick kiss. "I'm up soon. I need to go and get ready. Wish me luck."

Ford momentarily tightened his grip on his man, holding him close and nuzzling into his throat, before stepping away. Reef smiled at him, his brown eyes lighting up Ford's world. "I love you, sweet. Good luck." Ford watched as he exited the protection and privacy of the shelter erected on the mountaintop, moving into the competition area.

Reef was strapping into his snowboard and going through his pre-jump routine while Ford watched the next two competitors fly high. Both were crazy good, picking hard jumps and managing to land them with ease. The scores were so bloody close and ridiculously high. Nerves flipped in Ford's gut. Could Reef pull it off? *Absolutely.* But it was going to have to be a near perfect run, or there was no way he'd win.

And then it was Reef's turn. Ford so desperately wanted to go to him, give him one last hug, tell him he could do it. He watched as Reef shook out his arms and stretched his neck before tilting his head up to the sky. The sun was weak, barely piercing through the cover of clouds, but that didn't seem to matter to Reef. A grin split his lips. The confident, sexy swagger radiating from Reef had Ford mesmerized.

"He's different today," Mace murmured. "More settled, self-assured."

Ford didn't have any words to respond. He was focused on Reef, on his smile. Ford was absolutely not swooning. Well mostly. Giving him the thumbs up, Ford watched as Reef spun, pointing his board down the mountain and beginning the fast slide to the jump.

"Perfect line, Reef. Perfect," Mason encouraged under his breath. "Come on, you can do it."

Ford held his breath just as Reef hit the ramp and flew high. Time moved in slow motion and sped up to light speed all at the same time. Entranced, Ford couldn't have ripped his gaze away from Reef even if he wanted to. The jump was all spins and tumbles, perfect arcs and air like Ford had never seen before. The spectacular jump Reef pulled off in practice paled in existence to the one he was in the middle of.

He started to fall toward the slope and Reef pulled out of the spin. Arms out wide and legs bent, he smoothly touched down on the snow. It wasn't until Reef's whoop tore through the silence that Ford realized the crowd was quiet. But it didn't take more than a second for them to erupt into cheers and whistles. He looked across at Mace who was slack jawed too.

"He did it," Mace whispered. He met Ford's speechless stare and yelled, "He fuckin' did it!" Ford choked out a cry and hugged Mace hard. Heart hammering in his chest, hands shaking, Ford was overwhelmed with pride and love for Reef.

"Let's go see your guy, hey?" Mace asked as he pulled back and smiled at him. Ford nodded and didn't hesitate to pick up his skis and snap into them. Mace was only a second behind, strapping into his snowboard as Ford grabbed his ski poles. They tore down the mountain, dodging the few people who'd attempted the hike up to get a better view. Most of the spectators were gathered at the base of the ski run behind the crowd barrier. Wind against his face, snow under his skis and the sheer joy of seeing Reef pull off a superb jump had Ford giddy and grinning like a fool as he cut back and forth down the slope.

By the time Ford had passed through the opening in the barrier and skied over to Reef, Mace was right beside him. They threw themselves at Reef, sandwiching him between them as they hugged and laughed. "You did it, sweet. You've won it!" Turning to the crowd, Ford lifted Reef's arm and yelled, "You're lookin' at the next World Champion right here!" The spectators went nuts, chanting, "Reef, Reef, Reef," whistling and hollering their encouragement and Reef beamed.

"It's not in the bag yet, hon, but this feels damn good."

Mace gripped his shoulders looking into Reef's eyes. "You've got it in you, Reef. This jump proved it. You've got the competition. Now the championship's yours to win too."

"Good jump, man," Caden called out from nearby as he

trudged over holding his snowboard, and held out his fist to Reef. Instead of bumping it, Reef pulled him into one of those back-slapping hugs.

"Sorry about your first jump, dude. Make up the points on your second run, yeah?"

Caden shrugged his shoulders. "Don't think I've got any hope of catching up with your points even if you blow your second jump."

"Hey, they haven't even announce—"

"Congrats, Reef. Sick run, dude," the guy doing the announcements for the competition called out over the loudspeaker. He was American and sounded more like a surfer than someone who you'd find on the snow, drawing out each of the vowels as he spoke. "We've tallied up the judges' points. By a unanimous decision, the score awarded to Reef Reid for his first jump of the day is a perfect 100. That puts Reef in the lead for competition points ahead of Adriano Bertucci in second, and in third place, Zhen Kwek."

Reef's eyes bugged out and he looked from Ford to Mace. "Did he just say perfect score?"

"He did." Mace nodded and Ford grinned wider. *Perfect score. Fuckin' awesome!*

"Okay, lads, let's move it back up the mountain ready for your second run." A lady with a cockney accent herded them toward the chairlifts. "Oh, and Reef? Congratulations, lovey. Well done."

"Thanks, Margaret."

———

PERFECT FREAKING SCORE. Reef shook his head and tried unsuccessfully to wipe the grin off his face. But he had to. He needed to get in the zone again, pull himself together and concentrate for a few more minutes. He was strapped in, waiting for the buzzer so he could start his run, but he was jumping out of his skin.

Ford appeared in his line of sight and gripped his biceps gently. "Sweet, close those eyes and take a deep breath. Center yourself."

Reef let his eyes slide closed and he tipped his head back and let the energy of the big sky seep into him. "That's it. Long, slow breath. Focus your mind." He let Ford's deep rumble guide him, calm him as he relaxed and hit his Zen.

Ford's grip on his arms loosened and when he let go, Reef opened his eyes. Ford was standing next to him. He didn't speak a word, but his presence grounded him and was everything Reef needed. "Thank you," he whispered.

"Any time, sweet. I love you."

"Love you too."

The buzzer sounded. Reef took a deep breath and pushed off, cutting through powder as deep as his calves. All thoughts of his earlier jump evaporated as his mind zeroed in on the jump before him. Like a guidance system, his mind's eye plotted out the line to follow. Reef's vision tunneled, his focus on the jump absolute. The cheers of the crowd quickly faded, the rustling of the powdered snow the only noise penetrating his concentration. Even the cold rush of the wind hitting the only exposed part of his body—his face—faded from his awareness.

A blanket of pristine white slope lay before him. His polished board cut through with ease. Crouching more, he picked up speed. Leaning forward, knees bent and arms down by his sides, Reef adjusted his trajectory to hit the ramp square on.

Connecting with the ramp, the momentum propelled

him forward, up the launch point and into the air. Weightless; Reef lived for those brief seconds when he was flying. This was why he was a snowboarder. Defying gravity, just for a moment in time, his adrenaline kicked in, the endorphins spinning around his body. It gave him a natural high better than any chemical induced one could ever be—well, Reef thought so anyway.

Arching his back, Reef kicked off the first backward tumble. Again and again his vision filled with grey sky, white snow. Three flips. Then four. He pulled out of the spin and grabbed his snowboard, his other held high above his head. Kicking the board out to his side, Reef finished off with a classic skateboarding move, then straightened. Arms held out wide to steady himself, he dropped the final few feet onto the snow. Knees bent, he touched down. It took a moment for his brain to come back from that zone—the all-consuming Zen which bordered on orgasmic whenever he got mad air. He was on the slope. He landed. He was upright, still skiing.

He'd done it. Pulled off another of the most complex jumps he'd ever mastered. But he hadn't just pulled it off, he'd nailed it. Joy surged through him, those happy vibes doing a damn party in his heart and head. He knew, without a doubt that whatever anyone else got on their run, Reef had won the competition. Both fists raised in the air, he let out a whoop and soaked up the cheers, the celebrations from the die-hard fans.

Zig-zagging to the spectator area, he shifted his weight onto his heels slowing to a stop and unbuckled his bindings. Freeing himself from his board, Reef planted it upright into the ground and strode over to the spectators. Grinning, he took the American flag off the big, burly dude holding it and man-hugged him before wrapping it around his shoulders.

Wearing the red, white, and blue, Reef high-fived as many of the fans as he could reach.

"Reef, Reef, how does it feel to have pulled off that jump?" Hailey Watts, the tour reporter asked, holding a microphone in his face.

"Surreal. Mad. Freakin' awesome," he gushed excitedly. "Like chocolate chip cookies, coffee, and sex all rolled in one."

"Right on." Hailey smirked at him and continued. "Is this the start of the tides turning for you this year?"

"I hope so, but only time will tell. The competition is tough, the toughest it's ever been. I worked hard in the off-season so hopefully I can keep going like this, but I respect the hell outta the other competitors. None of them are gonna give it up easily."

"Thanks, Reef."

Before Hailey could start her wrap up, Reef interrupted, "Momma Bear, Dad, this one's for you. Love you both." Flashing the peace symbol, he grinned at the camera and walked toward his board, pulling it out of the snow.

"Reef, you freakin' legend!" Mace shouted as he and Ford skied to a stop before him. Waddling up, still strapped to his snowboard, Mace hugged him hard and slapped him on the back. "Well done, my man, well done. You were amazing."

"Incredible, sweet," Ford's voice sounded behind him. Mason stepped back and Ford wrapped his arms around Reef, holding him close. "I'm so damn proud of you." Cupping his face, Ford leaned their heads together. "God, so proud." Reef closed his eyes and relished his man's touch for the brief moment it lasted.

As they stepped away from each other, Reef asked, "How'd I score, Mace?"

"It's gonna be in the high nineties. You've got this, bud."

The five-minute wait for the point score was interminable. Uncertainty shrouded Reef's celebrations. He watched, distracted, as his team— Mason and Ford— laughed it up with Reef's fans. Heart pounding and his palms sweaty, his gut churned. Reef knew there could only be so many outcomes with a successful jump, but not knowing made time crawl to a snail's pace. His future—his fate—was literally being determined by a handful of people. The judges' decision would mean the difference between a win or a placing. Everything coalesced to this point—this turning point as the reporter had put it—the years of training and travelling, competition after competition, the sacrifices he'd made. Was he the best or not good enough?

"We have the judges' scores for Reef Reid's run. Ninety-eight, man. He's on fire and officially the winner of the Austrian competition. No other competitor can beat him. Congrats, man."

Reef closed his eyes and let the words wash over him. Relief was the overriding one. He'd done it. It wasn't the first competition he'd won, but it was the most important. Or at least it felt like it was. Reef had hit his lowest point days ago. He might as well have been drowning, struggling to keep his head above water and steal a breath while his emotions and the stress swamped him. Now he was on top of the world. This win was the reassurance Reef needed to get him through this competition and restore faith in himself. Scores of ninety-eight and a perfect one hundred didn't come along every day. He was good enough to win the championship. He'd proven that to himself. Now, like Mace said, he just had to show the rest of the world.

A grin tugged his lips and he couldn't stop the bubble of laughter even if he wanted to. Opening his eyes, Reef caught Ford's gaze and his man nodded, giving him a smile, his eyes full of warmth and love. *Why are we hiding?* Suddenly, giving Hailey the exclusive story didn't matter anymore. Sure, she'd fucked him over when his girlfriend had cheated on him and made him look like the bastard. But he was over it. Did it really matter if she got the jump on the story over his other journalist friends, if doing so meant avoiding Ford's touch when it was the most important?

"Let's get you inside and get some food in you, Reef." In a lower voice, Mason added, "You're starin' at Ford. It's obvious there's something between you."

"I'm not sure I care if everyone knows, Mace."

"You want the press at the moment to be about your skills, not about who you're sleeping with. You'll get a lot out of this win, but she's got the power to undermine it. You've seen what she's capable of first hand. Don't give her the chance. Ford understands. He's got your back."

"Not everyone's homophobic."

"That's not what I'm saying, dude. There are some who are, but you don't want them as sponsors anyway. What I am saying is that she'll turn the focus away from your skill to your sex life. You've been through that once. Don't set yourself up to do it again."

"Is everything okay?" Ford stepped up beside Mace, looking intently at Reef.

"Yeah, hon. Mason's reminding me why I don't want the reporter to find out we're together."

"Sweet, I'd give almost anything to be able to kiss you stupid right now, but I won't. What you did up there took a hell of a lotta skill. Give it fifteen and pics of you jumpin', of you kickin' ass'll be all over the web. Recognition for everything that you've done to get here. If I kiss you? Everyone'll forget what you just did. It'll be a by-line in your coming out story. You deserve more than that."

Reef sighed and shook his head, his shoulders slumping. The shine of the win was tarnished by the back of the closet he was sitting in. "I hate this, hate not being myself and sharing this with you."

"So let's go inside where we can get some privacy." Ford nodded toward the resort and gave him a wicked smile. Reef knew exactly what'd be happening the moment they got that privacy.

CHAPTER EIGHT

GOING inside the main doors to the resort was a stupid freaking idea. They should have snuck in the back and climbed the fire stairs to their room. The big screens were set up in the bar relaying live jumps of each of the competitors. People spilled out into the open lobby area watching the telecast and Reef was dragged into the fray before he'd even had the chance to really step through the door.

With the heat turned up and so many bodies in the club, he'd soon had to strip off his jacket and toss it to the waiting bartender. Bottles of beer were thrust at him and the back-slapping continued. It wasn't only just fans though, he recognized some of the sponsors and promotional reps of the merchandizing companies there too. Mace encouraged him to network, introducing Reef to a select group of the big wigs. And yet, as good as it was speaking with them, all Reef could do was surreptitiously look for Ford because, well, he was nowhere to be seen. As he'd been whisked away, Reef caught glimpses of Ford pushing through the crowd to get to the bar, but he hadn't spotted him after that.

It'd been hours since they'd walked through the doors, the competition long since ended. Music was pumping through the speakers and as the complete cover of darkness descended, the lights had dimmed, creating more of a night-club feel than a bar in a hotel lobby. Exhausted, Reef stole away, ducking into a dark corner in the hopes of catching a break from all the back-slapping and schmoozing. He was starving. He rubbed his grumbling belly as a familiar arm wrapped around him from behind and a warm body pressed into him. Ford's big hand splayed against his abs pulling him closer as he kissed Reef's throat softly. Leaning back against him, Reef sighed.

"I ordered us some food an hour ago, sweet, but with so many people here it's taking a while. Should be here any minute though."

"I love you." Reef turned and buried his face in the crook of Ford's neck. Standing side on, he wrapped an arm around him and cuddled close. "Wanna get outta here?"

"I'll get the food sent up. Let's go."

———

THE MAN who entered the elevator with Ford and the one standing opposite him was like two different people. As soon as those doors closed, it was as if a switch had flipped. Eyes hooded, Reef stared at him hungrily. And like the good prey he was, Ford was ensnared.

Trapped in Reef's aura.

Pinned by the man stalking him.

Reef stepped forward, aligning their bodies. The barest shake of Reef's head let Ford know to drop the arm he'd been reaching out. Dominance rolled off Reef in waves. And it was hot as fuck. Ford's breath shallowed out and he curled his fingers around the bar behind him in a white-knuckled grip. He couldn't look away even if he'd tried. Heat flushed Ford's skin and anticipation burned through him. The electricity between them was palpable, like the sparks of a tesla coil. And when the arcing bolt of energy connected, it would consume them. Ford couldn't wait to leap into the fire, to feel the flames of desire licking his bare skin while Reef fucked him into oblivion.

Reef shot his arm out to hold open the doors and tilted his head toward the entrance. *When did the elevator stop?* Ford took the hint, exiting fast. The lock flashed green after Reef swiped the key and Ford sucked in a breath. Anticipation thrummed through his veins. He'd barely stepped a foot inside before Reef was on him, twisting him around and plundering his mouth as he pushed Ford up against the wall. The cool hard surface at his back was a heady contrast to the heat of the barely restrained man plastered to his front.

Reef vibrated with a wild desire that had Ford's erection achingly hard. Tearing their mouths apart, Ford only had time to suck in a breath before Reef claimed his mouth again. With a frantic clashing of lips, their tongues delved and dueled, rediscovering the contours of each other's mouths. His heartbeat thundered in his veins, his entire being focused on another in a way it had never been before Reef.

Pinning him with his hips and bracing those lean arms on either side of Ford's head, Reef caged him in. But it wasn't close enough for Ford. Too many clothes were in the way and he needed to touch his lover's warm skin. Needed the intimacy of their connection.

Slipping his hands under Reef's thermal shirt, he splayed his fingers against Reef's sinewy back and pressed his palms over the dimples above his ass. Reef's moan and the buck of his hips had Ford exploring more, desperate for some friction against his throbbing dick. Moving to Reef's sides, he ran fingertips over Reef's lats and obliques, memorizing each bump and valley in his body as their mouths dirty danced together. Reef's hiss was like music to his ears, his shudder like food for his soul. Ford trailed his fingers up Reef's chest to his pebbled little nipples and plucked them as he kissed his man stupid.

This time it was Reef who broke away. Breath heaving like he'd run a marathon, his pupils blown wide and with kiss-swollen lips, Reef rasped, "Boots." He didn't need to say more. Ford knew exactly what he was being told. Sliding down the wall, Ford crouched and yanked off Reef's boots. He tore off the thermal socks Reef wore and massaged Reef's feet. "Up," Reef ordered. Without hesitation, Ford stood and kicked his Chucks off. Reef's hands were on him, yanking his jacket off his shoulders. Ford's thermal shirt followed suit a moment later.

He shivered; it wasn't from any chill in the air.

His lover appraised him hungrily before wrapping long fingers around Ford's cock. Joining their mouths again, Reef teased and tormented him to the edge of sanity. Balls drawn tight, precum soaking a spot in his black Calvin Kleins, Ford's hips punched forward into Reef's grip.

He moaned, the sound a desperate rasp even to his own ears.

"No coming without me." There was no playfulness in Reef's tone as he drew his hand away. It was a demand—one Ford was expected to follow.

Already on the brink, he gripped the base of his cock and squeezed hard, desperate to stop the orgasm that came barreling toward him with Reef's words. Looking up into

Reef's warm brown eyes, Ford suddenly felt small. But those few extra inches Reef had on him weren't the reason. The man had presence, stop the traffic charisma, and when he let it out to play, Ford was putty in his hands.

A knowing smirk tilted Reef's lips, as he brought his face close to Ford's ear and whispered, "Get us naked, Ford. I wanna fuck you." Ford's lids fluttered closed and he squeezed his dick harder, this time praying to the snow gods that he could stop himself from coming. Taking a deep breath, Ford opened them, and popped the button and fly on his pants before pushing the offending clothing off his hips. His movements quick, he reached for Reef's thermal shirt and pulled it off. Tossing it aside, Ford curled his fingers under the waistband of Reef's pants, reveling in the warmth of skin against hard muscle. Touching him, being there with him in that moment was everything, love and lust, and the simple perfection of their connection wrapping around him like a warm blanket.

He undid the fastening and lowered them, dropping to his knees to help Reef out. He wanted to worship every inch of him, to show him all the emotions swirling around in his chest. Ford closed his eyes and pressed his lips to Reef's hip, to the thatch of curly hair at the base of Reef's cock. He breathed him in, all musk and man. "Suck me, hon," Reef begged, his tone husky.

Ford took him to the root in one pass. As he pulled off, he swirled his tongue around Reef's veiny shaft. Laving his mushroom-shaped head and the slit leaking pre-cum, Ford loved on him. Over and over he sucked him down deep. Fingers tightening in his hair had him looking up to see Reef mouth 'up' to him.

The moment he stood, Reef crashed his lips down on Ford's overwhelming him with the erotic attack. Ford melted into him, loving the way Reef molded his stance—a knee between his own pushed his legs apart, his hands pinned above his head. Reef broke their kiss only to tease Ford by licking a line from his jaw to his ear, then getting downright frisky with the lobe. Exploring it in the same way he'd done to Ford's mouth before nibbling his throat, he sucked a bruise into his skin.

"You marking me?" Ford panted, loving the idea of having a tangible reminder when their weekend ended.

Reef hummed. "Damn right I am."

Burying his nose in Ford's pit and inhaling deep, Reef let loose another of those contented hums. And didn't that just send the gooey feels in Ford's chest fluttering around like a kaleidoscope of butterflies. His man loved on every inch of him. He licked and bit down on Ford's bicep, sending a shudder through him. He couldn't help it, his senses were on overdrive. With each touch, each caress, Reef had his muscles twitching and shivering deliciously. His mouth around Ford's cock made him gasp for air. Tight muscles swallowing around his shaft, had him trembling with the intensity of being rocketed to the edge. Ford buried his fingers in Reef's hair and gave into his body's instinct, thrusting into the warm wet cavern. All too soon his mouth was gone, replaced by cool air as Reef moved down and laved Ford's balls, licking until they were drawn tight against his body. Each swipe of his tongue shot fireworks through Ford. He was close. So close.

"Reef," he begged, not knowing whether he wanted to be tossed over the edge into the abyss of rapture or for Reef to stop so he could regroup and steady himself. He didn't get the chance to decide. Reef spun him to face the wall, manhandling him like he weighed nothing. Cheek pressed to the cool surface Ford moaned, the crazy need to come coursing through him. When Reef's warm breath ghosted over his ass, he ground his hips against the drywall, desperate for the friction.

"Uh uh, none of that, Ford." Reef jerked him backward.

Instinctively, he reached out seeking purchase on the smooth surface as Reef pressed a hand between his shoulder blades, bending him forward and kicking open his legs. He was presented to Reef like a Vegas-style buffet, ready to be devoured. And Reef took full advantage, pressing his tongue against Ford's high sac, licking over his taint and around his hole in one fell swoop. Ford would have been embarrassed by the lascivious whimper he let loose if Reef hadn't heard it before. Hums from Reef and his own moans and grunts filled the air. An erotic symphony. Who needed music when their sounds were such a turn on?

Ford had been close before, but this edging was a new kind of sublime torture. Spearing tongue and fingers into Ford's channel, Reef loosened him then pulled back to flick his rim and drive Ford insane. He never wanted to come down from the high. He uttered, 'Oh God, oh God,' far too many times to count.

Ford moaned when Reef pulled away and the bastard teasing him laughed. He couldn't help the growl from erupting, reduced to grunts like a fucking caveman as frustration rolled through him. "I've got you, bunnykins. Hold tight for me." The sound of Reef lubing up was illicit. The *schlick...*schlick... schlick* sending a shudder of anticipation through Ford.

Reef's strong hand was on him again, holding his hip steady while teasing Ford's needy hole with his lubed up cockhead. It was normally him topping Reef and that was fucking-fantastically amazing, but when Reef went to town on him, Ford flat out pined for the man's dick in his ass. But

Reef was teasing him, not giving him the drug he craved like an addict. "Fucking do it, Reef." His aggressive growl was more like a whine, the tone begging. "God, please. Please."

The fucker chuckled again, but pressed home slowly and stretched Ford's hole around his thick shaft, not stopping until he was buried to the hilt. Their simultaneous shouts ricocheted around them as Ford reared back, arching against him. With arms wrapped tightly around him, Reef held him steady.

"Oh fuck, yeah. Look down, Ford. See what I see."

Breathing through the initial intrusion, Ford let Reef's words ground him. When their meaning sunk into his lust-addled brain, he turned his gaze down. The sight set off a full body shudder. *Fuck.* Ford stood on tiptoes, his feet slightly turned in, as his ass adjusted to the hot as fuck impaling. His body was strung as tight as a bow. His hard cock jutted out, heavy with desire and weeping pre-cum. Reef's feet caged his, planted flat on the floor with his knees slightly bent. The other man's taller stature gave him enough height to drive into him, hard and deep with every thrust. Reef had one arm wrapped around his waist, the other hooked under Ford's arm, clutching his shoulder.

Their legs were the perfect contrast and yet, the ideal match—Ford's thicker muscle and dark hair against Reef's leaner, wiry frame and fair hair. It was so masculine. So fucking hot. Never in a million years would he have predicted his soul mate would be a man, but there was no way he could deny how his body had instantly recognized his heart.

"Tell me to move, Ford," Reef rasped, his hot breath against Ford's ear. With one hand, he reached back, tangled his fingers in Reef's mussed up hair and held tight. Then gave one short sharp nod. Reef pulled out slowly, almost all the way before driving back in, sliding every inch of his cock against Ford's super-sensitive prostate. Ford lit up from the inside out, grunting with the motion. Their bodies glistening with a sheen of sweat, slapped together over and over again, careening them toward rapture with every move.

Reef could play his body like a finely tuned instrument. Ford's cock was so hard it hurt and he needed the contact, the warmth of Reef's hand to ease it. "Reef," he begged.

Reef bit down on Ford's shoulder and at the same time, he grasped his cock. One pass of that lubed-up hand, one more thrust tunneling Reef's hard shaft against the bundle of nerves buried within him and every muscle in Ford's body coiled then seized. Fireworks lit behind his closed eyelids.

The tingle at the base of his spine, the one that had been constantly building since their elevator ride, exploded through his body. Ford didn't recognize the animalistic growl he let loose as ropes of cum painted the wall in front of them. For the longest time the orgasm pulsed through him. Gasping for breath, Ford held on for dear life as Reef pistoned his hips back and forth. His man pounded the fuck out of his prostate until Ford keened and Reef let out a strangled shout, pressing deep while pulses of heat pumped into Ford.

———

CUDDLING WITH HIS MAN, he was the little spoon. Reef loved how Ford always gave him exactly what he needed, loved how he always *knew* what he needed. But loyal, strong, protective Ford also had a kinky side that he let loose sometimes just for Reef. He smiled, remembering every touch between them the night before. But the noise blaring from his alarm said they didn't have time for a repeat. They were both flying out in a few hours, their weekend together at an end.

"Think if we ignore it long enough I won't have to leave you?" Ford's voice was rough with sleep, the words mumbled into the crook of Reef's neck.

"Let's run away together. No one would look for us on a tropical island."

Ford nuzzled his ear and nibbled on the spot that always got Reef going. "As long as you wear a pair of sexy little trunks and I get to take them off you whenever I want."

Reef grinned, turning his head to give Ford more room to play. "Mmm, the ones that look like my underwear? Deal."

Ford moved suddenly, propping himself up on his elbow and hovering over Reef. Reef rolled onto his back and Ford shifted his weight, lying mostly on top of him. "Should we? For real. At the end of the season? My cousin, Conner, is finishing up his active service. Maybe we could go visit him. It's a two or three hour flight from home."

Reef smiled. The idea of being together again at the end of the season always did that. It didn't even matter that he had no idea which home Ford was referring to. "I'd love to. Where's he based? France? Greece?"

Ford looked at him, brows knitted in confusion for a moment, before a slow smile spread across his face. "Connor lives on the Gold Coast. He's Australian. Queenstown's my home, as long as you'll be there with me. Otherwise, it's wherever you are."

Reef pulled Ford closer and pressed their lips together in a slow kiss. Shifting his weight, he moved between Reef's legs and lined up their semis.

Banging on the door interrupted them. "Hope you boys are decent, you've got company," Mace called through the door.

"You and whatever company we have need to fuck off for a bit," Ford yelled back. "We're busy."

"Nope, you don't have time. Stop jackin' off and get in the shower. We've got an official breakfast to attend and unless you've forgotten, a few flights to catch."

"Yeah, yeah," Reef muttered. "I need to go to that breakfast. I have to get my check and do a photo shoot with the event sponsors. Sorry."

"Don't be. It's okay." Ford nodded reassuringly, cupping his face and kissing him again. "I'll have you all to myself in a few weeks for Christmas."

"It's an age away."

"Nope," Ford chastised. "It'll fly by. You'll be doin' what you love on the slopes and I'll be being my usual heroic self." Reef couldn't help his snort of laughter. And Ford's wicked grin as he preened himself had Reef chuckling harder.

"You're a dork."

"But you still love me."

"Without a doubt." Reef pulled him in again and kissed him slowly.

"Guys, knock it off," Mason's exasperated voice sounded from behind the closed door. "Reef, priorities man."

"You need to get laid, Mace," Ford muttered while he nuzzled Reef's nose with his.

Mason let out a frustrated huff. "Fuckin' tell me about it."

GOODBYES WERE NEVER EASY, but that one especially sucked. He and Ford had clung to each other until
they'd both had to leave and the whole time they did,
Mason had sat there brooding. Reef hated seeing his friend
so frustrated, but a long-haul flight in cattle class was no
place to talk about whatever was bothering him. So, instead,
they sat in silence as Reef laid back in the reclined seat and
closed his eyes. His smile was easy. Even though it was
short, those couple of days with Ford had recharged
his soul.

"I like seeing you happy, Reef."

"And I'm here if you decide you want to talk about why
you aren't."

"Would you and Ford mind if I came to Italy with you
for Christmas?"

"As long as we don't share a room, he'd be happy to have
you there with us. I would too. I was thinking I might even
ask Caden to come. His dad's spending it sailing with his
sister. I don't know why, but Caden won't go."

"He gets seasick," Mace replied quietly.

"I didn't know that." Reef looked at his friend and
trainer. There was something going on with him. He
seemed distracted. And if Reef had to guess, he looked
confused, troubled. "Mace?"

"Yeah?"

"Seriously, I'm here if you want to talk."

He nodded and gave Reef a weak smile. "I'm not ready
yet, but yeah, I'll take you up on it. Now get some sleep. You
look wrecked."

THE LITTLE AIRPORT at Mammoth Mountain, Cali-
fornia was about the biggest contrast you could get from

LAX. And what a relief that was. LAX was insane at the best of times, but a delayed landing had them sprinting for the shuttle so they could get to their connecting flight in the terminal across the other side of the airport. They were already close to missing it when security stopped him, demanding he submit to a full explosives check. He'd skidded to a stop at the gate just as it was being locked, Mace pleading with the attendants to give him a couple more minutes. They'd only just been allowed on the flight. So, by the time they'd arrived at Mammoth Mountain, Reef was tired, hungry, sick of planes, and sore. Cue the violins.

Stretching out the kinks in his muscles, he saw his reflection in the shop front windows. Reef's whole outfit had seen better days. His jeans were faded, threadbare at the knees and his Henley had holes in it. Even his boots were scuffed. The only new clothing he wore was his beanie —care of his sponsor. He looked like a bum. No wonder LAX security had picked him out.

His slow walk to exit the terminal, obviously wasn't fast enough for Mace, his trainer calling out, "Come on, dude. We've got a cab rather than a bus. And don't forget to call Momma Bear. She'll have my ass if you wait."

"On it." Reef pulled his cell out and flicked off airline mode, brought up his contacts and dialed Momma Bear.

"Hi, honey. How's my boy?" Just hearing her voice made him smile. God, the woman filled his heart with love. He adored her.

Even he could hear the smile in his voice when he responded. "Good, Momma. I've literally just landed at Mammoth."

"You're not driving and talking are you? I'll spank that behind of yours if you are."

Reef laughed, shaking his head. "No. We're walking to the cab now. And really? A spanking?"

"I'll tell Ford. If I don't spank you, he will." She paused a moment before adding thoughtfully, "You might enjoy that though. Unless you're helping put Mr Kleenex's kids through college, fasten the chin strap on that helmet of looove. Mhmm."

Reef choked out a laugh, blushing furiously. He brought his hand to his heated face and shook his head. Still laughing, he replied, "You have no idea how much I've missed you, Momma Bear."

"Be safe, Reef. You know how those jumps you do scare me."

"I will, Momma. Love you."

"Love you too, Reef."

He hung up his cell and jogged to catch up with Mace who was already helping the cab driver load their luggage.

"You're blushing like a bride. What gives?" Mace asked as Reef slid his board bag in.

"Momma Bear talkin' to me about safe sex." Reef blushed again and laughed. "Tellin' me to fasten the chin strap on my helmet of love."

"Oh, that's fuckin' gold." Mace laughed as he dropped the final suitcase into the cab. "I can only imagine how many rubbers you and Ford would go through." He held his hand up. "Actually, don't answer that."

Reef's blush intensified and Mace stopped him from turning away with both hands to his biceps. "Wait, what's that look for? Don't tell me you guys aren't fucking. I won't believe that shit."

"Ford and I both got tested. We stopped using condoms a few months ago."

"Serious?" Mace looked incredulous.

"It was a big step for us. Neither of us had ever..." Reef shrugged, not really knowing what to tell Mace.

"I'm happy for you, man. You've found the love of your life, you're on top of the world and you've got me as a buddy. What more could you want?"

Reef laughed. "Come on, dumbass. Let's go. You need to feed me. I'm starving here, wasting away to nothin'."

DRIVING down the main street of town, Reef looked out the windows. Cute little coffee shops, bars, ski shops and souvenir holes in the walls were typical around every ski resort town, but Mammoth had this great theatre company which ran cabaret shows a few nights a week. As they passed it, the costume shop got his attention. "Holy shit." Tapping the driver on the shoulder, Reef asked, "Hey, man, could you stop the cab. I've gotta check out the costume shop."

"What the hell for?" Mace asked

"New Year's Eve costume party." Reef grinned, excitement coursing through him. He had an idea, a bloody brilliant one as Ford would say. Hopefully they'd have what he wanted. "You'll need one too if you're coming."

"I'll swing by after I've eaten. Weren't you starving?"

"I can wait." Turning once again to the cab driver, he asked, "Can you pick me up from here in, say, an hour?"

"Sure, dude." He nodded.

CHAPTER NINE

FORD BEAMED AT THE TEXT. His man had done it. He'd kicked ass in the competition at Fenway Park in Boston. It was a hell of an achievement too, especially after the injury to his knee at Mammoth Mountain. He'd lost that competition, but they'd all been more worried about what it meant for the rest of his season, his career, rather than the points from that one comp. He hadn't done so well in the next meet either, coming eighth. But he'd picked right up again by the third competition after his injury healed, finishing in equal second. Ford shuddered. Every time he thought about Reef getting hurt, it made him feel sick.

"SHUT UP. SHUT UP," Ford yelled over the hubbub of the bar. It was the same one they always went to, so no one was surprised when Ford pointed to his man being televised live on the sport's channel. "That's Reef." He watched as Reef turned his face to the sky and stilled. The commentator was babbling on about his killer year; Ford knew all of Reef's

statistics—they rocked. He'd be a monkey's uncle if Reef didn't have the championship in the bag.

Reef's takeoff was perfect, a solid run down the steep slope to the jump, launching him into a high arc. The camera followed his course, and Ford held his breath as he watched Reef execute flips and tumbles with a finesse he was in awe of. But then in a flash Reef was falling.

Plummeting out of the sky.

Crashing out.

Landing hard on the snow and clutching his knee.

"Oh, God. No," Ford cried, his voice cracking like thunder around the pub whose patrons let out a collective moan. Dread settled over him, sitting heavy in his gut as he watched Reef writhe in agony on the snow. He needed to get to him and help him, like Reef had done for Ford more times than he could count.

Helpless. Ford was utterly helpless. There wasn't a single thing he could do to lessen his man's pain, reassure him, to hold him when Reef needed him most. The fear of what the injury meant for Reef and his career, the pain and the heartbreak of watching it unfold before his eyes manifested itself physically, like a rusty spear piercing his heart. Ford's hand automatically went to his chest, rubbing the ache there to no avail. Gab slipped her smaller hand into his lending him comfort.

The camera panned, showing the fluttering flags and zeroing in on the commentator's worried face. "No," he breathed, willing the camera operator to zoom back in on Reef. The only thing Ford could do was watch uselessly from the other side of the world. But he watched on, seeing the movement of the announcer's lips and yet, not hearing a word. Every worst case scenario that could come from the *injury flashed in his mind's eye as he waited for the visual to confirm Reef was being cared for.*

His cell rang in his ear. When did I call Mace? *No answer. Over and over he rang, one call after another and no answer.*

Ford waited, his gut twisting. He watched. And he prayed to the snow gods, something Reef would do if he wasn't in excruciating pain. Finally, the camera locked onto Reef again. He wasn't alone anymore. Mace was with him, on his knees behind Reef, holding him, shouting to someone off screen. Where the fuck is alpine rescue?

It took a lifetime for the team of medics to pull up on the snowmobile, towing a rescue sled behind them. Any sign that Reef's injury wasn't as bad as he feared would be a welcome sight, but there was nothing obvious from the video feed.

The lifetime it took mountain rescue to tend to Reef was nothing compared to the eternity before he got a call from his man. Hours had passed before his cell rang. Groggy from the painkillers he'd been given, Reef's words were slurred, but just hearing his voice was enough to calm Ford a little. Not enough to stop him flying over to him—that happened later when Momma Bear called, assuring him that they were on their way to Reef.

Gabriella nudged him, bringing him back to the present —to his spot at the little table in the alcove of their favorite pub, the one with the perfect view of the TV so he could watch Reef's competitions. Pointing to the cell in his hand, Gab asked, "Good news?"

Ford couldn't wipe the grin off his face. Reef's knee had held up well over the competitions since his injury and this win was well deserved. "The best. He won." Ford's smile widened as his chest filled with those crazy, fluttery cartoon love hearts he got when he thought about Reef, and how proud of him he was.

Gab shrieked, and threw her arms around Ford. "*Fantastico.*" She stood and stepped onto the chair she'd been sitting on. "Hey, listen up," she shouted. "Ford's boyfriend just won the competition in Boston. He's gonna be snowboarding's World Champion." Arms up in the air she let out a whoop and jumped down off the wooden seat.

A cheer went through the small crowd of people gathered at the pub. They'd watched Reef on the pub's big screen so many times he now had his own loyal fan club there. Alfonso, the owner of the bar and Gab's new boyfriend, grinned and gave him the thumbs up before turning away and going back to work. It was only a moment later that he brought over a tray of beers for their table. Ford would never normally drink any liquor when he had a shift the next day, but one wouldn't kill him or anyone else.

"On the house." Alfonso waved away Ford when he pulled out his wallet to pay for the drinks. "Congratulations to your man. I bet he's happy."

His man would be celebrating the win for a while yet, so Ford held off calling him. "I'd say so. Haven't spoken to him yet, but he's had a rough few weeks. He's done so well keeping it together."

"I'm just glad we're still cheering him on." Alfonso picked up the empty tray and leaned against the chair Gab was sitting on. Smiling down at her, he tucked a lock of hair behind her ear and looked back at Ford when he spoke again.

"You and me both. It ripped him apart when he wasn't sure whether he'd be able to finish the season."

"It ripped *us* apart having to listen to you freak out about it," Gabriella teased. He wasn't *that* bad. Well he was, but Ford didn't need to admit it to them. They'd seen his meltdown first hand. Not being there when Reef needed him wasn't easy, but the results of the MRI were the best they could have been. Reef's injury was, although painful, a minor strain and thankfully, not a season-ending ligament tear.

"Bloody bird." Alfonso shook his head.

"Even now when I watch the footage, I can't believe it happened." Ford ran his fingers through his too-long curls, still shocked over how the bird had appeared out of nowhere in the middle of Reef's jump.

"Totally a freak accident," Gabriella added.

"I don't know how many times I've watched the video. The damn bird just pops into the frame. One minute Reef was kickin' ass and the next he was fallin' out of the sky."

"Stratford?" Ford's blood ran cold hearing the all too familiar voice. He turned to look at his mother and saw the instant she noticed Gab's arm snaked through his and the familiar way she leaned against him. It didn't matter that Alfonso was standing close to Gab too, carding his fingers through her long hair. His mother's eyes lit up and her smile turned almost predatory, as if she'd locked in on fresh meat and was zeroing in on them. Ford's stomach churned. Instinct told him to get away, to yank his arm away from Gabriella and get the hell outta Dodge, but he didn't. He couldn't. Frozen to his chair, he opened his mouth to say something, anything, but nothing came out. *Why is she here?*

"Have you forgotten your manners, Stratford?"

Ford's voice finally made an appearance. "Ah, hello Mother."

"Hello, Stratford. Are you going to introduce me to your lady-friend?"

"Gabriella, Alfonso, meet my mother." Ford's words were clipped, devoid of any emotion. It amazed him that he sounded so calm and collected, when inside the anger and hurt threatened to consume him like the wash of a tidal wave.

"Pleased to meet you Mrs. Wallace." Gabriella stood and held out her hand to shake his mother's.

"My dear, it is lovely to meet you. How long have you and my son known each other?"

"Mother," Ford warned.

Gab placed a hand on his shoulder and squeezed, smiling down at him. He'd told Gab everything—about his parents' rejection and how much of a toll it took on him. He'd questioned his identity because of them. How could he be good enough for Reef when he came from that DNA pool? Would he turn into his father and end up a callous prick? Or would it be his mother's cold-heartedness he mastered? He'd nursed many a soda until it was warm and flat as he tried to work through his jumbled thoughts. And Gab would let him get it all off his chest and then kick his ass after he'd poured his soul out. She had a knack of putting things into perspective, making him realize being 'good enough' wasn't a destination—it was something he'd work on being every day. But in the meantime, Ford would love Reef with everything he had in him. And that's how he knew Reef was the one—he made Ford want to be good enough for him, in love and in life.

"I've known Ford for years. He's like another big brother to me. We're so happy he's found love with Reef."

Way to go, Gab. Ford smiled. His friend did well setting his mother straight whose pursed lips now imitated a cat's ass. It was priceless. "Oh. I thought—"

"I know what you thought, Mother—"

"I want you happy, Stratford."

"No, you don't. You want me to fit into your square-assed mold. But I won't do it. I'm not leaving Reef."

"But think of your future. You have a beautiful woman here who clearly adores you. Why not choose to be with her?"

"Because apart from the fact that she and Alfonso are together, she's like my sister. We're not romantically involved and we never will be. I'm bisexual, Mother, and I'm in a relationship. With a man. It's not gonna change. I love him. Either accept it or don't, I don't care." Ford stood, the chair scraping against the floor of the bar. The noise echoed through the quiet space. As he looked around, Ford saw each group of patrons quickly look away, going back to their conversations.

"Stratford, wait—"

"No, Mother, I won't. I'm gonna go and call my man and celebrate the fact that he's one step closer to winning the world championship."

"Aren't you going to ask me why I'm here?" she called as he stalked away. That made him pause. *Why is she here?*

With his back still to her, Ford asked, "So, tell me, Mother. Why are you here?"

"Your father needs you."

His shoulders dropped and he shook his head. "Forget I asked. I'm leaving." Ford took another step.

"He's sick, Stratford." Her tone was pleading, bordering on desperate. *Is something wrong with him? Or is she full of shit?* He didn't want to care, but hell, the man was his father. What if he were truly sick?

"What's wrong with him?" he asked quietly.

"He wants you to come back. I do too."

Ford whirled around on her, shocked. That shock

turned to anger when he looked closely at her and realized
she was lying. Eyes hardened, emotionless, she stood before
him. Her body language screamed smug satisfaction. She
thought she had him, that he'd cave and drop everything to
rush to his father's non-existent sickbed. *Fuck that.* Ford's
anger erupted like a volcano. How dare she try to manipu-
late him. And why? So they could control him, get him
under their thumb? Fuck, he hadn't been that person in over
a decade. And who the fuck said someone was sick when
they weren't?

He pointed at her as he took a step closer. Towering
over her petite form, Ford curled his lip in disgust as he
clenched his teeth together so hard he was surprised he
didn't crack a tooth. His voice wavered as he hissed, "*You*
were the ones who drove me away. All you had to do was
accept me, accept us. But you didn't do that, did you?" His
body shook with barely restrained anger. It pissed him off
that the hurt, the pain, was still so raw. The little boy who
lived inside him just wanted his parents' love. The realist,
the cynic, knew it wouldn't happen unless Ford gave up
someone far more important to him. For what? Their condi-
tional approval? It'd be taken away the next time they
thought he fucked something up. The whole farce broke his
bloody heart. He was ashamed that he couldn't be stronger,
that he couldn't stop them from hurting him again and
again, that the love of his life had been affected as much
as Ford.

He dashed the tears leaking from his eyes and tracking
down his cheeks with the back of his hand. Ford's voice
broke when he whispered the next words. "You hurt me,
dammit. You took away my family. You *left* me." The anger
at his mother and the disappointment in himself welled up.
Emotion choked him, leaving him a shaking mess as he

forced out the words that needed saying. "I'm your son and you don't even love me enough to keep me. All I asked was for you to get to know him. To open your heart to the possibility I might be happy. Why couldn't you do that? Why couldn't you love me enough for that?"

Ford turned into Gabriella's welcoming embrace. She held him tight, her touch comforting, while he buried his face in her shoulder and cried. "Why can't you accept me, Mother?"

"Your father wants to retire, Stratford. You need to come back and step into the family practice."

Ford pulled back and glared at her. *Who the fuck is this monster?* "No." He shook his head. "No. Absolutely not." His voice sounded brittle.

Gab rested a hand on his arm, drawing his attention to her. Her concern for him was obvious. Brows pinched together and her lips a thin line, so different from her usually unflappable grin. She was one of his closest friends, the sister he never had but had hoped for as a child and now, as an adult, wished for. "Let's get you out of here, Ford." He nodded, taking a deep breath to try and steady himself.

"Don't you walk away from me again, Stratford. It will be the last time you do." Ford couldn't believe her cold and utterly emotionless ultimatum.

Gabriella whirled on her and pointed. Her voice shook with rage, her expression reflecting the look of loathing he'd only seen once before—on his parents' faces when he'd introduced them to Reef. "I've had enough of you, you evil bitch. How dare you come here and hurt him again. You and that piece of shit husband of yours stay away from him."

"Who do you think you are speaking to me like that?" his mother shot back, her stance rigid, unyielding.

"His family. And unlike you, we all love him unconditionally."

"Madam," Alfonso interrupted, motioning for the door. "A cab will arrive in a moment to take you wherever you want to go. You can wait for it outside. You aren't welcome here anymore."

"You cannot eject me." Ford almost laughed at her sense of self-righteousness. Of course his mother would think she'd be in the right here.

"I can and I just did. No one hurts my family." Alfonso's hand on his shoulder and Gab's strong and steady embrace had warmth seeping back in through the cold that had chilled Ford to his bones.

"Let's go, honey." Gab patted his belly comfortingly, and steered him to the door, leaving his mother in their wake. He was moving like an automaton, completely numb, not snapping back to his senses until the cold blast of air hit his face. He stopped walking and turned, taking in his mother standing there in the main bar area, a rocky island in a sea of friendly faces. He wasn't hurting anymore, he realized. He only felt pity for the woman whose actions had driven him away. It was definitely her loss, not his.

"Gab and Alfonso are right. Reef is my family. They are too. In case you cared, Mother, I'm happy, happier than I've ever been before. You made your decision, now I'm making mine. Don't bother coming to see me again. This is goodbye."

"Stratford."

He shook his head and turned away, walking out the door, head held high.

"Call Reef, honey," Gab implored. Ford already had his cell out, bringing up Reef's number. His man's face lit up the screen, peaceful in sleep. He'd taken the picture at two in the morning. Reef had been fast asleep curled up on his chest but Ford hadn't been able to close his eyes. He'd lain awake for hours holding him tight, running his fingers up and down Reef's smooth back, never wanting to let go.

The cell rang twice before he heard Reef answer, "Hey, bunnykins." Reef's voice was a little slurred. Not drunk, just tipsy. He was happy. Ford could hear the smile in his voice.

"Hey, sweet. You did good, you know that?"

"I fuckin' rocked it, Ford. The jump, the landing... I did it, hon. I'm so close, I can taste it."

"You've got this, Reef. I know you can do it."

"I wanna come home, hon." Reef's voice was quieter, the background noise having dropped away too. The longing in his tone slayed Ford.

"Soon, sweet. One more competition then we'll be together." Ford wrapped his arm around himself. Even though he had his friend next to him, holding him tight, he'd never felt more alone. "God, I can't wait. I'd give anything just to hug you right now."

The pause on the line was telling. Reef could see straight through him. He suddenly sounded a lot more sober when he asked, "What's happened?"

"My mother decided to pop in for a visit." Ford relayed his conversation with her to Reef and sighed. "I'm sorry, you should be celebrating and here I am unloading on you."

"Stop right there, Ford. You've been through hell and back at their fuckin' hands. I need to be there for you, hon. What's the point if we don't stick together?" Another pause and a question asked much quieter this time. "You don't wanna split, do you?"

"God, no," Ford said in a rush. "Never."

"I'll be with you again soon okay, hon. I love you, your

friends and family—Momma Bear, Coach—do too. They adore you. You're an amazing man and your parents are total dumbasses. Driving you away is totally their loss, not yours."

"I know, I just needed to hear you say the words. I love you too, sweet. Always. Now go party."

"I'll have a few shots for ya."

"Call me when you're doing karaoke. I need a laugh."

"Fuck off, I'm good at it." Reef's indignant tone had Ford smirking. Reef really wasn't good. His singing was atrocious and the dance moves... God, so nineties.

"When the Back Street Boys reunite and add another member, you'll be their first choice."

"Hell yeah," Reef shouted out, then in what sounded more like a caterwaul than singing added, "Backstreet's back. Alright!"

Ford snorted out a laugh. "You just did the John Travolta move, didn't you?"

"You just don't have an appreciation for classic dance moves."

"You're a dork." Ford grinned.

"But you love me."

"Totally do." Ford's smile turned boyish as the warm fuzzy feels went fluttering around his heart. "Go have fun, sweet. I'll talk to you tomorrow." They said their goodbyes and Ford hung up, grinning. Without fail, Reef did that, made him smile and lifted his spirits. If he was going to dwell on it, he'd ask why his parents couldn't see that. But Momma Bear and Coach could, and that was good enough for Ford.

CHAPTER TEN

REEF STEPPED off the bus and enjoyed the feel of solid ground beneath his feet. He didn't think he'd ever arrive at the place Ford made his home for the northern winter. Getting to the little village tucked away in the Italian Alps had been a challenge, but, *wow,* so worth it. Ford told him Santa Caterina di Valfurva was beautiful, but looking around, the sprawling vista before him was breathtaking. The quaint little village was perched precariously on the steep mountain terrain, in the valley between the two converging mountains. Surrounded on three sides by towering peaks and age-old pines—their branches heavily laden with snow—the village was largely sheltered from the wind blowing a gale at the peak. Swirls of white curled up and out over the precipice. The blue sky stretched out above, marred only by puffy white clouds floating along, carried by the current of wind. It was charming, romantic. The perfect place for he and Ford to spend the holiday season wrapped up in each other.

A gust blew through the parking lot, making Reef wish he had his ski gear handy rather than crammed into the luggage currently stored in the bottom of the bus. Jeans and a thermal shirt weren't enough to keep him truly warm, but apart from his beanie and scarf, it would have to do. Winding it around his neck, Reef rubbed the cold from his arms as he waited for their packs to be unloaded from the bus.

"THE HOTEL'S OVER THERE, MACE." Caden pointed out.

"Geez it's pretty here, isn't it?" Mace mused as they walked along the salted path. "So, what's Ford up to this afternoon?"

"He's working, but I'm gonna head over to say hi. Wanna get some food later?"

"Sure." Caden nodded. "Food here better be an improvement on that shit of a resort we were just in."

"Fuckin' awful, wasn't it? So damn greasy."

A high-pitched squeal had Reef wincing as he looked around to see who was making the god-awful noise. Then he spotted her, standing just off to the side. "Oh. My. God. You're here!" Another squeal. "Ford's gonna go nuts."

"Huh?" Reef asked. "You're talking to me?"

"Yes, silly." She smiled. "You're Reef, right?"

"Yeah. I'm sorry, who are you?" Reef was confused, totally bewildered by the woman now standing before him, jumping out of her skin with excitement. She wasn't Gabriella. He'd spoken to her and seen enough pictures of her to know this blonde haired lady with a Scandinavian accent wasn't Gabriella.

"I'm Svetlana. I'm part of the cheer squad."

"Oh, hey," Reef replied excitedly, suddenly understanding. Holding his hand out to hers to shake he added, "This is Mason, my trainer, and Caden, my—"

"Your number one rival and the man who's goin' down."

The shocked look on Caden's face as he dropped his outstretched hand was comical. Svetlana laughed and leaned in closer to Caden saying, "You're actually my favorite, but you can't tell Ford Reef's frenemy should win."

Caden barked out a laugh. "I like you. You should come with us when we get some supper. I'm sick of bein' outnumbered."

"Come to Alfonso's later. We'll all be there. Food's really good."

They waved goodbye as Svetlana sashayed off and they picked up their luggage again and staggered over to the hotel. Reef left his bags with concierge and after getting directions on which way to head, left Caden and Mace to finish checking in.

Anticipation bubbled within him. He barely contained his excitement as he marched up the steep incline toward the imposing four-story building at the top, a ridiculous grin plastered on his face. The giant skier painted on the side of the timber and stone structure was the only indication that it was the gateway to the chairlifts and international competition standard ski slope.

Turn right at the building and follow the road further up the slope. You can't miss the giant, red cross on the wall.

Reef saw the first aid office as soon as he cleared the side of the building at the base of the slope. An ambulance was parked outside the open roller door, its back doors wide as a man and woman maneuvered a gurney into the building. Reef quickened his pace, dread gnawing at his gut. It wasn't like he could do anything to help—if anything, he'd be in the way—but he would be there for Ford. He needed to be.

Boots crunching on the gravel, Reef jogged the final few yards to the door marked 'entry' and pushed through. Warmth instantly surrounded him, defrosting the frozen strands of his stubbly growth as he stepped over the threshold. He hadn't realized how much the temperature had dropped just by moving the few hundred yards up the mountain until he was faced with working heaters. A little boy sat on a sofa in the corner of the room coloring in. The top part of his ski-suit hung loose around his waist, while calm voices sounded from another room somewhere in the structure.

Reef closed the door behind him and a bell tinkled. Ford's familiar voice called out from the open door. "We'll be with you in a moment. Take a seat while you wait, please."

He didn't answer, instead sitting down next to the boy. "You okay, bud?" Reef asked.

"Yeah, me mom's back there," he replied in a strong Australian accent, pronouncing the 'o' in mom more like a 'u'. "She's come off 'er snowboard and popped out her dodgy shoulder."

"That's not good."

"She's done it before. She was right once the doc got it back in."

"You from Australia?"

"Yeah. We're 'ere on holidays for Chrissy."

"What's Chrissy?" Reef asked confused.

The boy looked at him like he'd grown two heads. "Ah, der, it's Christmas."

"Oh." Reef laughed. "Yeah, pretty stupid that I didn't guess."

"Okay, Shane, your mom's... Reef?" Ford stood in the doorway drying his hands with some paper towel, his mouth open. Reef flashed him a quick grin and cocked his head to the side motioning for Ford to continue. "Sorry, yeah. Um, your mom's ready to head down to the hospital in Bormio. You wanna ride with her in the ambulance?"

"Um, where's me dad? I was gonna go with him."

"He's just up on the beginner run getting your sister now that her lesson's finished. He said he'd meet your mom —and you, if you go with her—at the hospital. If you'd rather stay with him, I can take you up to the beginner slope once your mom's in the ambulance."

"I can take him while you finish up if you like," Reef offered.

The relief on Ford's face had Reef wanting to take him in his arms and hold him tight. He looked exhausted, frazzled. "That would be amazing. Take my jacket though so you aren't cold." Ford plucked a red ski jacket off a nearby hook and walked it over to Reef. Holding it open at the collar, Ford smiled at him. It took everything in Reef not to kiss his man. *Why aren't I kissing him? Screw it.* Reef closed the space between them and kissed Ford chastely on the lips, whispering, "Hi bunnykins."

"Hi." Ford smiled at him, his gaze full of longing as he draped his jacket over Reef's shoulders. Ford's spicy scent surrounded him as Reef slid his arms into the sleeves and pulled the zipper up. Leaning in, Ford kissed him again. "I'm so glad you're here. I've gotta go, but I'll be free soon." Ford motioned back to the open doorway.

"Go, I'll come back." Reef turned to the young boy. "Shane, yeah?" When he nodded, Reef continued, "You know where the bunny run is?"

They walked out of the first aid office together and the boy, who was probably eight or nine, pointed up the slope to an area bordered by two rows of flags. "S'up there." Shane pointed. They had barely stepped between the flags before Shane's father spotted them, and with a little girl in tow, slowly skied over.

"We were on our way to come and get you." He held out his hand and said to Reef, "Thanks for bringing Shane over. Is Miranda in the ambulance yet?"

"She was being loaded up as we left. I'm sure she's on the road now."

"Great. Thank you for looking after her. I'll get these kids off to the hospital now."

"Hope she's okay."

"Yeah, she'll be right. She's strong as a bull."

THE BELL tinkled again as Reef closed the door to the first aid office behind him. He turned to see Ford leaning against the doorframe, his eyes travelling slowly up his body. Ravenous. That was the only word Reef could think of to describe the heat in Ford's slow perusal. And his man wasn't alone. It had been a long couple of months since those few stolen days in Austria. So much had happened since then, he couldn't even begin to list them. But everything was good—no great. Everything was fucking great. He'd managed to hold onto his second place spot on the world rankings despite nearly being wiped out altogether by an errant endangered hawk and the world championship was still within reach. A hair's-breadth separated his and Caden's scores. But at that moment, Reef couldn't care less. How could he when the man of his dreams was stepping toward him with a sexy swagger?

"I wasn't expecting you for a few more hours." Ford fingered the zipper of his jacket, licking his lips as he tugged it down, letting each tooth slip through the slide as Reef's breathing accelerated.

"Earlier bus," he rasped, pulling off the grey beanie adorning his head and tossing it toward the sofa. Running his hands up Ford's strong arms Reef paused as Ford pushed the borrowed jacket off his shoulders. Dropping his hands, he let it fall to the floor. Ford sucked in a breath as he ran a palm down Reef's lean chest, his eyes following the trail of his fingertips. Reef couldn't tear his eyes away from Ford's lustful gaze as he drank him in. The world around them disappeared when their focus zeroed in on one another.

Ford was his alpha, his omega.

He was Ford's ying, his yang.

Their very existence irrevocably intertwined.

Fated to be.

Ford curled his fingers under the waistband of Reef's jeans, causing his breath to hitch. And then he was moving, being tugged forcefully into Ford's arms, wrapped in the glorious warmth and strength of his man. Reef pushed his hands into Ford's hair, as their lips crashed together. On a moan, Ford thrust his tongue against Reef's. Rediscovering. Devouring.

The tinkling of the bell at the door had them stumbling apart. Reef's heart beat frantically, an erratic tattoo pounding heavily in his chest. Out of breath, he and Ford's gaze didn't break until a throat being cleared distracted his man. His cheeks heated, a blush staining them as his friend —Gabriella was unmistakable—grinned at him like the Cheshire cat. "I believed you when you said you had chemistry, but Ford, *mi amore*, you were holding out on me. You two don't have chemistry. You have fireworks."

"Reef, Gab. Gab, Reef."

"Hi." Reef smiled, hesitating. Gabriella laughed and pulled him into a tight hug, kissing both his cheeks. *"Ferito il mio amico e io a calci in culo."*

"Non mi farà male," Ford replied, the words rolling off his tongue like a freaking pro.

Reef's dick hardened instantly. *Holy smokes Batman, what a turn on.* "Wait. You speak Italian? What did you say?"

Ford laughed. "Of course I speak Italian, I live here half the year. Gab said if you hurt me, she'll kick your ass and I told her you wouldn't."

"I'll deal with you later." Reef pointed at Ford. "I expect a fuck-load of dirty talk in Italian from now on. I'm as hard as a fuckin' fence paling." After adjusting the boner which had sprung up, he turned to Gabriella and sobered. "I'd never hurt him Gab. He's everything to me. I love him more than life itself."

The smile she gave him was blinding and the hug fierce. "Good, because I love seeing my friend so happy. I want him like that forever."

"I love seeing him happy, too." Ford's arms snaking around his middle had Reef relaxing back. He didn't ever want to move. This was his spot in the world—leaning against Ford's chest, feeling the vibration of Ford's deep voice against his back and his strong arms caging him in.

"Ya know, I am in the room with you."

Reef nuzzled his head against Ford's before kissing him in response.

CHAPTER ELEVEN

REEF SNUGGLED DEEPER into Ford's embrace, his head resting comfortably on his man's shoulder and an arm and leg tossed over Ford holding him close. The early morning light of Christmas Day began to peek through the window, the blinds doing a shitty job at keeping both the warmth in and the light out. The bed was lumpy and the room draughty too, but it didn't matter. He was with Ford. Warm under the covers, content and alone. Ford no longer had a roommate, thank God —what an absolute clusterfuck it was when roomie decided to butt into their first night together.

Reef kicked the door closed, it banged loudly as they fell onto the bed together. Ford kissed the ever-loving fuck out of him, the taste of whiskey on his breath. They tore at each other's clothes. When he couldn't stand the barrier between them anymore, Reef rolled, pushing Ford onto the mattress. He stood and toed off his boots before shucking off his jeans and underwear while Ford did the same. With his man naked and wanting, his cock leaking pre-cum onto his belly, the temptation to taste every inch of Ford was too much. Beginning at his throat, Reef nibbled and licked, tasting his way down to the v between Ford's hips, studiously avoiding Ford's cock and skipping to the soft skin of his upper thighs instead.

"Fucking get on with it, Reef," he growled. "Suck my dick. Make me come."

"Uhuh," he mumbled. "You're not coming until I'm buried so deep in your ass, my cock'll hit your tonsils." As Reef lifted his weight, sliding down more, Ford flipped over, presenting his ass to Reef. The sight greeting him nearly had Reef blowing before he even got inside. A black plug stretched his hole wide. Reef moaned and licked around the edge of it, using his fingers to wiggle it around and torment his wanton man. Ford's muffled shout pushed Reef beyond the limits of sanity and restraint. There wasn't a single hot blooded man on the planet who could resist a sight like that— his lover spread out before him, ass in the air begging to be claimed. Foreplay became a distant memory. His dick couldn't handle waiting even a second longer. He needed to be inside Ford.

Like yesterday.

Yanking on the plug, he pulled it out and tossed it aside. Ford's hole stayed slightly open, the invitation for Reef to slide into ecstasy impossible to refuse. And who was Reef to resist? Slamming home, Ford scrambled for purchase, his back bowed and he shouted out again. The lube from the plug gave him just enough slip to bottom out and he drove into Ford with mindless force. Hooking his arms under Ford's pits, he hung on and rode his man like a cowboy on a prized stallion. And Ford was one damn fine stallion.

Except Reef was gonna last longer than eight seconds.

Probably.

Their bodies slapped together, Reef's grunts mixed with Ford's moans. The sheen of sweat on Ford's back called to

Reef, tempting him to taste. Bending down, he brought their bodies together. The move had Ford reaching back, threading his fingers into Reef's hair as Reef licked a path up his neck and back down, biting down on Ford's shoulder.

Drunk and horny, he was sure he wasn't the only one edging. Reef was so close, clawing at the end goal, his orgasm barreling toward him as he drove in and out of Ford. And that's when he felt it. A cold hand. On his nuts. Reef froze. Am I imagining things? But then it was Ford's turn to freeze before he bucked Reef hard and shouted, "What the fuck?"

Reef flew off Ford, being tossed aside like a ragdoll as his man jumped up out of bed like he'd had a hot poker shoved up his ass. He watched as the discarded butt plug bounced in slow motion when Ford switched on the blindingly bright light. Roomie-from-hell—Reef couldn't remember what the fuck his name was—was sitting naked in their bed, his boner deflating by the second as he looked between them, then at his hands, horrified.

"What the fuck do you think you're doing?" Ford boomed pointing at fucking-idiot-roomie.

"Fuck, I'm sorry, man. I thought I could make it better for you and your girl. You know, join in, turn it into a three-some. Have all of us get off. But fuck, Ford. Whatcha doin' with a dude? That's fuckin' gay, bro."

"Shut the fuck up, dipshit," Ford spat back.

"You ain't doin' that—" he pointed, moving his finger in a circle at them, as he continued, "in my room."

Anger flared in Reef at the violation perpetrated on his man—on them. Outrage welled up and spilled over like water escaping the floodgates of a dam. "Doing what? Fucking?" Reef growled, standing up and moving over to his man —yes, his man—Reef wrapped a hand around Ford's cock, slowly jacking him off. "Actually I'm pretty sure we were.

Ford, you think we were fuckin'?" Reef pulled Ford's body closer with his free hand and crashed his lips to Ford's. The need to mark him as his own had Reef's animalistic possessiveness blazing to life. But one kiss brought him to his knees. Every instinct switched instantaneously from 'fight' to 'mate'.

Ford broke their kiss, gasping for air. In no more than a whisper, Ford rasped, "Yeah, sweet. We were definitely fuckin'. You were lodged so deep in my ass, I could feel you hitting my tonsils."

What roomie did after that, Reef had no idea. He was so lost in Ford that the world could have ended at that precise moment—a giant ka-boom—and he would have been completely clueless. The brush of material against his arm and the noise and cold of the door opening let them know he'd left, and they hadn't seen him since.

Reef smiled thinking back to the laugh he and Ford had shared after that night. He'd never for a second thought that he was so possessive, that it would manifest with Reef putting on a damn show, but what do you know?

"What's got you laughing so early in the morning?" Ford mumbled from above him, his voice rough with sleep. Reef had laid in the same position all night—Ford on his back, his arm wrapped around Reef's shoulders as Reef half laid on top of him, curling into his side.

"Just us, hon." Reef smiled wider and lifted his head to look into Ford's eyes. "Merry Christmas."

"Merry Christmas, sweet." Ford squeezed him tight, rolling onto his side so they were facing each other and sharing the pillow, their faces only inches apart.

"I got you something small. You wanna open it?" Ford's eyes lit up. Reef chuckled and rolled over, stretching out to reach the small package he'd wrapped and placed by the side of the bed. Reef was nervous. It took him weeks to get the right present and he still wasn't sure. He handed Ford the box.

Ford took it and sat up, cross-legged on the bed. Reef mirrored his pose, the covers falling down around their waists as he watched Ford slide a finger under the tape, slowly opening it. *Oh God, he's one of those people who saves the wrapping.* Placing it gently to the side, he pulled the lid of the box up and slid out the glass bauble Reef had had made by a glass blower in Boston. Painted on the inside of the glass was a snowflake, its intricacy surprising even Reef when he'd seen the finished product. Written in script below were the words: "Our First Christmas". In it, there were tiny half-inch square photos Reef had painstakingly cut up and slipped inside. Each one of them was different, a whole lot of them together and some of their favorite places and things they'd shared.

His man stared at the gift, blinking twice before he looked up at Reef. His voice tinged with wonder, he asked, "The photos are of us?"

"Every one. One for each day we've known each other, for each experience we've shared. Sorry, it's probably corny."

"It's fuckin' amazing, Reef." Ford leaned in and cupped his cheek, kissing him softly before nuzzling at his temple.

"I thought maybe we could get a small tree to hang it on next year." Reef pulled back and looked Ford in the eyes, hoping, wishing he'd want the same—maybe get a little apartment together, make it their own. But he was jumping ahead of himself. He was a pro-snowboarder who travelled non-stop during the northern winter.

"Yeah. Yeah, I'd love that." Ford nodded making Reef

smile, those ridiculously gooey and sweet feels coursing through his veins.

Ford pulled a package from behind his back and handed it to Reef. "Your turn. This one definitely is corny, but..." Ford shrugged.

Reef grinned. "Shut up, Ford." Ford looked embarrassed, a pink tinge staining his cheeks. Seeing it had Reef reaching out and grasping his hand, closing his fingers around Ford's. He gave them a quick squeeze before he turned his attention to the rectangular box Ford handed him. His stomach flipped, anticipation making him antsy as he slowly lifted the lid and paused. He was shocked. In the best possible way. Lying nestled in the navy blue velvet covered case was a key on a black leather chain shaped into a word 'home', and two silver dog tags hanging off leather bands. He ran his fingers over the letters engraved in bold, block lettering on the tags—

You're the snow on my mountain
The beat in my heart

ENGRAVED THROUGH THE middle of both tags was a line—no two—that looked to Reef like a heartbeat. But it wasn't quite right. There were two peaks and valleys with every beat.

"Ford... I don't..." Reef shook his head closing his fist around the tags. He couldn't believe what he was seeing. He was speechless, blown away, but Ford must have mistaken his reaction for dislike. Reef moved on instinct untangling himself from the bedding. Words weren't going to be enough—he needed the contact with Ford to make him understand. But, Ford had already looked away.

Reef straddled his legs, grasping Ford's hand. "Ford—"

His man wouldn't look at him. Shoulders slumping, he blew out a breath. The devastation in his posture shredded Reef. In a broken whisper, he replied, "It's okay, you don't have—"

Reef shot out his hand, grasping Ford's chin and turning his face toward him. He pressed two fingers of his other hand over his lips. "I love them. You're giving me a home." Reef was *not* crying. He was not such a dork that he was going to cry over a present—even if it was one as thoughtful as Ford's. No one had ever done anything so amazing for him before. Sure, he received hand knitted stuff from Momma Bear all the time, but that was different. She was his mom. The best present Addilyn, his ex, had ever given him were the cuff links she'd lifted from a shoot which Alexander Skarsgard had worn. Nope, the tears escaping from his eyes were because he suddenly had something in them. Yeah, not even the most gullible of people would believe that, but that was the story Reef was sticking to. "And these are handmade, aren't they?" His question was more of a statement but Ford answered nonetheless.

"They are."

"What's this?" Reef asked of the lines intersecting the two.

"Our heartbeats. Is that dumb?" When Reef shook his head, sniffing as he wiped his eyes again, Ford continued. "Remember after the fire at the pub in Fernie? When the docs hooked you up to the heart rate monitor for observation, I took a pic of the printout. Then I did the same with mine. I had no idea what to do with them, but then I thought of this."

"They're really close."

"Yours is the slightly slower one. You're a bit fitter than me. You've got a slower resting rate." Ford pointed out tracing the lines with his fingertips.

"I love it, hon." Reef slid his arm around Ford, his fingers spearing into the sleep-mussed curls there and shuffled up his legs further, straddling his lap. With the other hand, he reached out and plucked the dog tags out of the box. "I love them. Can I have this one?" He showed Ford the one he wanted. "I kinda like being the beat of your heart." Ford nodded and Reef dropped the tag he wanted onto his leg so he could fasten the leather band of the other one around Ford's neck. When it was done, he patted the tag where it sat half way down Ford's chest. "And you've given me luck on the mountains; you're my snow. You should definitely have this one."

Reef watched Ford scoop up the leather band lying on his leg, unfasten it and bring it up to Reef's neck. Ford growled, a low rumble in the back of his throat. "I like seeing you wearing this. Mine."

"Yours." Reef tugged on the leather band hanging from Ford, eliminating the space between them. Lips against Fords, he murmured, "And you're mine, too." Bodies pressed together wasn't enough. It was never enough. Reef needed Ford. Needed to feel him moving above him, inside him. Making love to him. And that's exactly what Ford did, loving on every inch of him as the weak winter sun rose higher in the sky.

———

CHRISTMAS LUNCH in Santa Caterina was always celebrated by the mish mash of the friends gathered from far

and wide that Ford called his family. Looking around
Alfonso's bar, which he closed for the day so he could celebrate with them, Ford took in the decorations he and Reef
had helped the others hang. Tinsel was taped to every wall
and reflected the flickering tea-light candles placed on all
the unused tables surrounding them. The candles, the
roaring fire in the stone hearth in one corner of the alcove
and in the opposite one, the white Christmas tree lights,
created an ambience that was intimate, warm.

"It's romantic," Reef murmured. "I've never had a
Christmas like this. Usually, those of us without family
close by, end up in some chain hotel eating a buffet and
getting drunk on cheap champagne and egg nog."

"You've got no choice on where you go now. You'll have
to come here every year for Christmas or Gab'll kick
your ass."

"Just Gab?" Reef asked, leaning into his embrace.

Ford shrugged and grinned. "I'll just stalk you." He
wiggled his eyebrows until he was sure he looked like an
insane asylum escapee. "After all, I'm your number
one fan."

"Dumbass." Reef laughed, tightening his grip around
Ford's waist. Ford pulled his man closer, dropping a kiss on
his jaw as they held each other.

Christmas carols started playing in the background and
Gab, with Alfonso following close behind, appeared in the
doorway leading into the bar from the kitchen. "Aww, aren't
they adorable?" She snickered, earning her a playful one-
finger salute from Ford as he captured Reef's lips in a soft
slow kiss. Ford's all-time favorite scent—outdoors and man
—overtook his senses. He moaned softly, the sound
captured in Reef's mouth as his man took over the kiss,
deepening it.

Pulling back, the other smells around them permeated Ford's psyche once more – the fresh pine from the Christmas tree and the delicious aromas of the feast Gabriella's mom, Palmira, was whipping together in the kitchen. The fiercely independent woman drove up to the village the day after Reef had arrived and she hadn't left the commercial kitchen in Alfonso's bar since. She'd been cooking for days, but it was her labor of love.

Ford watched the goings on before him while everyone buzzed about. He and Reef stood in front of the fire, his arms firmly in place around his man. Ricky, Gab's oldest brother and Ford's friend from New Zealand, pushed open the rear entrance door, his arms piled high with more logs for the fire. Alfonso took the two steps needed to get to Ricky and held open the door for him, almost at the same time Mace stuck his head in the front entry. Reef waved him over as Mace held the door open for Caden. Dressed casually, they looked comfortable in each other's presence, being greeted like family by Gabriella and Alfonso when they'd crossed the bar. Ford smiled. Warmth spread through his chest. These people were his family. It meant more than he'd ever realized to have their support.

The only no-shows were Angelo, Gab and Ricky's other brother, and Trent. Ford knew his friendship with Angelo was solid, but as much as Trent had pissed him off while he and Reef were together in Queenstown, he missed him. Trent was part of the family of friends Ford had built around himself. He knew he needed to sort things out with him, he just had to figure out how.

"You're awfully quiet, hon." Reef's murmured comment, had Ford snuggling in closer.

"I'm thinking about Ang and Trent. Wondering what they're up to."

"Do they normally come?"

Ford nodded. "Yeah, they've been best friends for a decade. Absolutely inseparable. Ricky moved to Queenstown and Angelo followed a few months later. He'd only been in Queenstown for a month when he and Trent met. Trent's not real close with his family, so they always head over every year."

"How many years have they missed coming back?"

"It's the first time. I can't help but think it had something to do with me. Trent and I haven't really spoken since he barged in on us that first night we spent together. But if that's the reason, it's pretty damn childish."

Ricky interrupted their softly spoken conversation, volunteering the answer as he plucked the last piece of bark off his sweater. "Trent couldn't get time off work; he offered to stay so I could come home. He wanted Angelo to come too, but Angelo wouldn't leave him,"

"Why not?" Reef asked.

"Dunno, but Angelo was pretty adamant that he was gonna stay with him."

"Angelo is Trent's person." Gabriella supplied as she and Alfonso joined them by the fire. Gab handed a glass of red to Ricky and shook her head, looking at them like she were stating the blindingly obvious.

Fashionably late, Gabriella's father, Frank, and his arm candy, Lourdes, entered the bar with a flair that had Ford rolling his eyes. Frank marched straight over to the tree, setting down the gifts they'd brought with them with the others piled under it, then happily embraced his children, Ford and each of the partners and friends. In stark contrast to Frank's back slapping man-hugs, Lourdes air kissed each cheek, the scent of her cloyingly sweet perfume lingering in the air long after she'd moved away.

Ford jumped at the opportunity to get the ball rolling on the food, crowding behind Ricky when Palmira called for him. Reef was hot on his heels too, followed closely by Mace and Caden. Ford's eyes bugged out when he got a look at the banquet spread out on the stainless steel top. Turkey, pork, and lamb roasts awaiting carving were laid on serving platters, pasta in a great bowl, two different kinds of soups in terrines, the ladles hanging from hooks on the lids and steamed and sautéed vegetables on covered trays filled most of the counter, leaving just enough room for a bread basket, the size of a bucket, filled with freshly baked bread rolls.

"Holy shit," Reef breathed, in unison with Caden. Ford grinned. Palmira's 'simple Christmas dinners', as she liked to call them, still had that effect on him too.

"I'm never leaving," Caden added. "Palmira, will you marry me?"

"No way." She laughed. "You couldn't keep up."

"Believe me, if you put food in front of me like this every night, I'd clear the plate."

"In bed, *bello vista*." Ford smiled at her compliment—and calling Caden good looking was about the biggest compliment Palmira would give to someone. She patted his shoulder as she walked past, smiling innocently at him. "You couldn't keep up with me in bed. My men are stallions."

Caden's shocked expression—eyes wide open, mouth agape—was comical. Reef snorted out a laugh as he and Mace cracked up.

Mace wrapped an arm around Caden's shoulder and patted his chest. In true Mace fashion, he blurted out, "That's fuckin' gold."

"Mama, please," Ricky begged. Mace wrapped his free arm around Ricky's shoulder and cackled with glee.

"Shut up, Mason," Ricky grumbled, making the other man laugh harder.

"*Andiamo,*" Palmira ordered, this time squeezing Caden's ass playfully.

Two trips and they'd cleared the kitchen, filling the table with the dishes of home cooked goodness. Alfonso ushered Palmira into her seat at the head of the table while Ford poured the rich red wine into her crystal goblet and Reef placed one of the hand baked bread rolls onto her side plate before passing the basket down the table. Ford caught Palmira's approving smile at his man and Reef's beautiful smile back at her. Warmth bloomed in his chest. That acceptance, that love, was a damn good feeling.

"I think your man's won her approval," Mace whispered to Ford.

"Yeah, I'd say so, but I never doubted that she'd see the good in him." Ford couldn't help but think of his own parents and their reaction to Reef. Disgusted, he shook his head and clenched his jaw tight.

"Hey, dude, relax," Caden said from across the table, pointing to his white knuckled grip on the cutlery. "You're gonna bend Alfonso's silverware."

"Sorry," he mumbled, placing them gently on the table and smoothing out the white tablecloth. "My asshole parents have that effect on me."

Reef turned to him and threaded his fingers through Ford's. Leaning closer, and lowering his voice, Reef murmured, "Fuck 'em, Ford. It's their loss."

"Reef's right, brother," Ricky chimed in. "You've got family all around you right here. Don't let them bring you down."

"Yeah." Ford smiled. "This is a celebration." Raising his glass of red, he called out, "To the best kind of family you can have." He looked at Reef. "The ones you love," and turned his gaze to survey the table, "And true friends."

A chorus of, "here, here," and "*salut*," echoed around the room from the others at the table.

"Merry Christmas everyone." Ford smiled. *Yeah, this is it—the good life.*

ONCE THEY'D CLEARED the table, Ford followed the others into the kitchen to start washing dishes and scrubbing down surfaces. Palmira was at the sink, hot water multiplying the bubbles from the commercial grade dishwashing detergent she'd generously poured in. Gloves up to her elbows and wrapped in an apron that was far too big for her, Palmira was already furiously scrubbing away at the tiramisu tray.

"Mama, sit down. We've got this," Ricky ordered, frustrated as he placed the few plates he was carrying down.

"Listen to Ricky, Mama. You've worked too hard today," Gab added.

"No, no. Sit down, you enjoy your time off." Ricky's growl at his mother's insistent response had all of them sidestepping. It wasn't the first time in the Christmases they'd shared, that Ricky had forced his mom to get off her feet. This time he just picked her up and carried her over to the sofa, dishcloth still in hand. The sparkle of laughter in Reef's eyes and Caden's bugged out stare had Ford laughing. "This is normal, lads. We've had more than one water fight when Palmira hasn't wanted to leave the kitchen."

"There was the gelato fight of 2008 too," Gab added, smirking.

Alfonso chose charm over brawn, bringing over a steaming cappuccino with a plate of the melt-in-your-mouth almond biscotti Ford loved so much. Reef's snort of laughter clued Ford into what was going down. Turning just in time, he watched as Palmira snuck up on her eldest son and flicked him on the ass with the towel. Ricky yelped and jumped back, glaring good-naturedly at his mom.

"I'm definitely in love with you, Palmira." Caden grinned.

PALMIRA EXCUSED herself shortly after she'd finished her coffee. Mace hopped up, instantly offering to walk her back to her hotel room next door. It was cute seeing him and Caden practically falling over themselves to impress her. Like the perfect gentleman, Mason helped her into her coat and placed her hand in the crook of his arm before leading her out onto the icy sidewalk. Frank and Lourdes left within moments of Mace and Palmira, leaving the six of them— Ford and Reef, Gab and Alfonso, Caden and Ricky—to wait for Mason to come back.

They'd long since migrated onto the sofas near the fireplace, enjoying the bottles of Campari Alfonso had pulled out. Ford sighed, nuzzling into Reef. The night cocooned them and the fire, which they'd stoked into a roar, was the only light left in the pub. He was warm and comfortable with Reef sitting between his legs, cuddled into him and his closest family surrounding them. Ford was happy. And tipsy. It might have been the alcohol talking, but Caden looked pretty damn comfortable in his seat between Mace— who'd returned and now had Caden leaning against him— and Ricky, whose arm was stretched out along the back of the sofa, his fingertips brushing Mason's collar. Gab and

Alfonso were wrapped up together, in their own little world too, enjoying the rare day off they had with each other.

Reef's eyes were closed and the sigh he breathed out was pure bliss. Even though he was perfectly comfortable where he was, the only thing Ford wanted was to have his arms wrapped around Reef under the warm covers of their bed. "Want to head home, sweet?"

Reef opened his eyes slowly, blinking as he woke up. "Hi." He nodded, smiling shyly. "Sorry, I fell asleep on you. Yeah, let's go."

They stood and hugged everyone goodbye. Gab lingered, cupping his face between warm hands. "Ford, I'm so happy for you. The more time I spend with him, the more I adore him."

"Hey," Alfonso protested playfully. "What about me?"

"What about you?" she shot back, flashing him a wicked grin.

"I'm leaving, children. Squabble when I'm gone." Ford shook his head and rolled his eyes. Then he smiled softly. "He's pretty damn special."

"You ready, hon?" Reef handed Ford his coat and grasped his hand after he'd slipped it on.

"I'll see you before then, but don't forget the New Year's Eve party is a costume party."

"We're sorted." Reef smiled sheepishly. "I think. I haven't showed Ford what I got for us yet."

"Is it still okay for us to come?" Caden asked.

"Absolutely, the more the merrier." Alfonso nodded, smiling. "You sorted for costumes? I'm going into Bormio the day after tomorrow to get some supplies. You can come if you need to pick one up."

"We've got superhero costumes." Mace looked pretty satisfied with himself with that explanation.

"Lame," Reef teased.

"Superhero costumes aren't lame," Ricky added defensively. "That's what I'm wearing too."

Ford smiled as he watched the banter between the three of them while they collected their jackets and rejoined the group to say goodbye.

"They're good together, aren't they?" Reef murmured to him. "Well, not good together like *that*, but...you get what I mean."

"Yeah. They are. Like they've been friends forever."

"Come on." Reef nudged him and they waved their goodbyes as he followed Reef's lead out of the bar. As the cold air hit his face, Ford looked up to the sky. Fat snowflakes fell around them. He focused on Reef once more and pulled him close. Snow was landing on his hair and shoulders. Ford brushed away a flake that landed on Reef's lapel before sliding his hands down Reef's chest back to his waist. He was totally smitten, gone. And he fuckin' loved the thought of it. He'd never experienced the all-encompassing love he had with the man before him. It was the first Christmas they'd spent together and it was the first time Ford was completely at home, like he knew exactly where he was meant to be right at that moment. There was no other word for it—it'd been magical.

Reef leaned forward, brushing a sweet kiss over his lips. "Merry Christmas, Ford."

CHAPTER TWELVE

THE NEW YEAR'S Eve party was in a few hours, and Reef was still struggling with the damn nail polish. "Urgh," he groaned. "Fucking shit." He tossed the balled up cotton wool, wet with remover and now tarnished black, into the wastepaper basket. Why the hell hadn't he decided on a costume which didn't involve tackling the impossible task of putting on nail polish?

The door to Ford's room opened and a tired but gorgeous sight walked through. Something had shifted in his man over the last few days. He was lighter. He laughed more, the stress he'd been under seemed to have disappeared. But as he took a breath, he cringed. "What is that god-awful smell?"

"Hi, Reef. How are you, Reef? What did you get up to today while I was working, Reef?" he teased Ford.

"Shut up and kiss me." Ford stepped closer and pulled Reef into a tight embrace. Ford's strength was obvious—even through the heavy and soaking wet ski gear—as he wrapped strong arms around Reef and held him against his body. "You look fuckin' hot."

"You like?" Reef had shaved off his stubble for the first time in weeks and wore his normally unruly hair slicked back. He was surprised how different he looked doing that, especially after he'd lined his eyes with the heavy black kohl. Black nail polish was supposed to finish off the look, but he couldn't get the bastard on. His hands were too damn shaky and every time he tried applying it, he made a mess.

Ford didn't answer him, instead kissing a line down his throat and sucking on the soft skin under his ear. Reef shuddered in his hold, moaning softly as Ford slipped cool fingers under his tee. "How was your day, Reef?" Ford murmured against his flushed skin.

Reef had no words to respond, all he could manage was a garbled moan as Ford pinched his nipple. Through heavy-lidded eyes, he fumbled for the zipper on Ford's jacket, noticing for the first time the crimson stains splattered down the front of it. He snapped out of his desire-drunk state, instantly focusing on his man.

"What the fuck, Ford?" He ran his fingers over the stains on the jacket, before Ford grasped his hands firmly.

"It's okay, sweet. It's not my blood," Ford reassured him.

"What the hell happened?" Reef squeezed Ford's hands before he pulled them loose and wrapped his arms around his man. He needed to feel him close, to have the physical reassurance as well as Ford's words. His job wasn't dangerous—in the 'you could get shot or mugged' sense—but Ford's experiences as a paramedic hadn't been without death and pain. The thought he could be suffering again almost brought Reef to his knees.

"There was a fight on the slope. Some dumb ass wasn't watching where he was going and hit a beginner. She was hurt and her partner flipped out and tried to beat the crap out of the dude. He had bloodied knuckles and his girlfriend got a laceration on her face. It's a mixture of both of their blood from treating them. Luke, the new guy, sorted out the other dude's broken nose."

"Are you okay? Were you hurt?" With one hand tangled in the curls at the base of Ford's neck, Reef cupped Ford's stubbled cheek with the other and leaned forward, resting their foreheads together.

"I'm fine. I wasn't hurt at all." They stood there, holding each other tight, Reef's eyes closed as he breathed in his man.

"You never told me what the smell is," Ford commented.

"I'm trying to put nail polish on, but I can't fucking do it. How do girls do it without making a mess? I'm not even gettin' it on my nails."

"Sit down, I'll help you." Ford stepped out of his ski gear as Reef rifled through his closet for a pair of sweats he could put on. Finding the last clean pair, he tossed them on the bed, taking Ford's gear and bagging it up for dry cleaning as Ford dressed again. Curling up on the bed with his man, Reef held out his massacred nails for painting over.

Ford snorted out a laugh. "Jesus, you did make a mess of them. Lemmie work my magic." Ford painted them with a perfectly steady hand, covering every part of his nail without catching any skin. He moved quickly, finishing one hand, then the other in a matter of moments. With a complete coat done, Reef blew on his nails, keeping his fingers straight as he shook them dry.

"You gonna tell me what our costumes look like?"

"Gimme a minute and I'll show you." Reef grinned at him and pointed to the polish. "Do your nails first." Ford rolled his eyes and smiled, complying with Reef's direction before he'd even finished asking—or telling, really.

Reef touched the tips of his fingernails, testing whether the black lacquer was still tacky. It was good enough. He unzipped the suitcase still lying on Ford's former roomie's bed, and pulled out the purple plastic bags containing their costumes and boots. Suddenly nervous, he bit his lower lip as butterflies danced around in his gut. *Damn nerves.* Reef had no clue how Ford would take his idea, but it was too late now. Reef tried to get Ford to choose a back-up costume, but it was futile. As soon as he told Ford he'd been inspired by a picture hanging in the costume store, Ford wouldn't hear of changing it.

"Will we be able to get into the party if we aren't dressed up?"

"Yeah." Ford nodded. "But we'll be the only ones there without a costume on. Believe me, there's nothing you could choose that wouldn't be good to wear. The costumes are normally pretty outrageous."

"Okay then." Reef's attempt at confidence sounded flat even to his ears. He pulled out the thigh high shiny black stiletto boots he'd bought for himself and laid them out.

"Fuck me, they're hot," Ford murmured from behind him. Reaching out, Ford picked up the jumble of leather straps Reef had chosen for him. "What's this?"

"A harness. That's part of your costume. As well as these." Reef pulled out a pair of black leather shorts about the same shape and size as Ford's Calvin Klein boxers, fishnet stockings and a pair of ankle boot style stilettos. "These too." From a separate bag, he pulled out a black knee-length trench coat as he said, "Topped off with that. Whatcha think?"

"As long as you're wearing those," Ford pointed to the thigh-high boots, "I love it."

"Mine's a little different, but yeah, I'm wearing them."

Reef upended the bag onto the bed. He'd chosen black leather briefs, a black marching band jacket and the boots. Yeah, it was cabaret, but he'd instantly imagined him and Ford when he'd seen the picture.

"Get dressed, Reef. I wanna see you in your getup."

Reef stripped off his sweats, and standing naked in front of Ford, he snatched his briefs off the bed and went to put them on. *Oh fuck. No.* Reef held them out before him, then flipped them around. They weren't briefs. It was a fuckin' jock strap. "Shit. Dammit. Fuck." Reef's voice rose in panic with every word he spat out. "I grabbed the wrong fuckin' package."

"What were you supposed to get?"

"Underwear like what I wear, not a fuckin' jock strap. My ass is gonna be hangin' out everywhere." Reef ran his fingers through his slicked back hair, probably messing up the strands he'd painstakingly styled with a year's supply of product.

"Wear your underwear instead. It'll be dark. No one will notice." Ford had started massaging Reef's shoulders as he murmured soothingly into his ear, but it was no good. He wanted to jump out of his own damn skin. How could he have screwed up his costume so badly?

Reef shook his head. "I don't have any clean ones. I went commando today and I haven't had a chance to do any laundry yet—I've been helping Alfonso all day."

"Okay. Um... What about swim trunks?"

He shook his head again, his shoulders sagging. "I wear board shorts."

"Okay, what about a pair of mine?" Ford asked helpfully, giving his arms a squeeze.

Reef pulled away and started pacing the small room. Those butterflies that were doing a dance in his gut before were spinning around out of control, like he had a class-fucking-five hurricane going on. "You checked your underwear drawer lately?" He didn't mean to snap at Ford, but he was stressed, freaking out about...well everything. Why the fuck had he acted on impulse? Ford stepped closer and rubbed his arms, dropping a kiss on his shoulder. Reef rubbed his face. "Your drawer is empty too. I looked this morning—I was gonna steal a pair then." He held out his hands, palms up and tried—really tried—to calm down a little. He wracked his brain, trying to think up a solution, any solution. But nope, nothing. Nada. He was gonna be bearing his ass to his friends. *Way to go, Reef.*

"Let's swap jackets. I'll wear yours and you can put mine on. No one will ever know."

Like a lightbulb had been switched on, Reef smiled. "Yeah," he replied brightly, handing Ford his jacket, but immediately realized the problem. "Fuck. It'll hang off me. Your shoulders are broader than mine."

"Lemmie call Alfonso. Maybe he's got a jacket I can wear and you can still wear mine." Ford rummaged around on the bed until he found his cell under the mass of plastic bags and dialed Gab, knowing Alfonso would be running around doing last minute prep.

Reef zoned out listening to their conversation until Ford tugged him down onto the bed next to him. "Okay, Gab. Thanks for that. We'll see you in ten." He dropped the cell on the bed and pulled Reef into his arms.

"What's the verdict?"

"Alfonso has a jacket that might fit. Gab's bringing it over, but she said that Alfonso would actually appreciate you wearing the jock strap. She's got him a costume that has his ass hangin' out and he's over in the bar freakin' out too."

"He'll be behind the bar though. No one will see him."

"Alfonso'll be waiting tables all night." Ford laughed. "Can't wait to see what it is—Gab's cackling like a hyena."

Reef smiled and slid on his sweat pants. "Come on, go have a shower so you can get dressed. Then I can help you with your fishnets."

FORD HAD JUST PULLED on his shorts—and what a damn fine look it was—when the knock at the door sounded. Reef opened it and Gab grinned before him, stepping in as he held it open for her. "*Ciao*, Reef. Here, try this." She held out the hangar with a black jacket. Reef slipped it on. It was a little big around the shoulders but not too bad. Running his fingers along the hemline, Reef groaned. It was too short. The bottom of his ass would still be hanging out. He shrugged it off and held it out to Ford.

Ford slipped it half way up his arms and shook his head. "Nope, already too tight. Don't worry, sweet. I'll wear a coat and take it off when I get there. You can go in mine."

"You know what? Fuck it. I'm gonna wear what I chose. So what if my ass is hangin' out? You'll just have to dance behind me. Me and Alfonso'll give 'em something to look at."

"Atta boy." Gabriella playfully patted him on the ass as she took the jacket Ford was holding out to her and she went to the doorway. "Nice fishnets, Ford. They're sexy."

Gab left and Reef picked up the harness holding it out for Ford. Slipping it over his shoulders, Reef buckled it up and wrapped his fingers around the leather, tugging Ford closer. Placing a lingering kiss on his lips, he pulled back just as Ford tried to deepen it. "Do me now."

Ford's eyes darkened as Reef shucked his sweats. A bolt of lust lanced through him and any hope that he'd will his semi down enough that he could slip the jockstrap on, fled. It covered him, but he didn't exactly want to be sporting full wood. He threw on the marching band jacket and reached for the thigh high stilettos. Ford was on him, gently taking the boots out of his hands. Just the brush of his fingers had Reef's breath catching.

"Let me," Ford rasped, as he fell to his knees. Reef watched with heavy-lidded eyes as Ford unzipped them and held the shoe open for Reef to slip into. Once he'd put on the boot, Ford straddled him, pressing his heavy balls against the arch of Reef's foot and leaned in, running his tongue up Reef's calf and thigh as he zipped it up. Reef moaned as his man kissed and nipped his way up the inside of Reef's leg to the edge of his jockstrap, and gasped as warm breath ghosted over his throbbing erection. Pulling back, Ford went for the other boot and repeated the process until Reef was mindless with lust, desperate to tug himself out and breach the lips of the man panting before him.

Ford stood and Reef crashed their lips together, sliding his tongue into Ford's open mouth to plunder him. He towered over Ford with the shoes on, but even still, they were a perfect fit together. Hands in Ford's hair, Reef ground his aching cock against the hard planes of Ford's belly, eliciting a strangled cry of such desperation from Ford that Reef nearly blew on the spot.

"You have no fucking idea how sexy you are, Reef. Fuck me, I wanna bury myself in you so bad."

"I wanna ride you like a fuckin' pony. Hold this harness and fuck you cross-eyed."

Ford sank down onto the bed and dragged Reef with him, until he was straddling his man. Desperately grinding together, they moved in practiced strokes, nearing the edge of delirium with every move. The mattress rocked beneath him, creaking with each thrust of his hips. Reef's supplies for the party were strewn all over the mattress. But Ford's hand on his cock was the only thing Reef could focus on. He mimicked Ford's pose, reaching into the hot as fuck leather shorts his partner wore, seeing stars when Ford rubbed his thumb over Reef's crown, slicking the pre-cum steadily dripping from him.

———

THEY WERE a little past fashionably late to the party. They smelled like sex and Reef was walking a little awkwardly, but Ford didn't exactly have any regrets. Seeing Reef in the barely-there jockstrap and damn those boots, well, he went insane with lust. Lying back on the bed, bone-less after his monster orgasm, Reef had fussed over him until his heart almost burst with all the sweet feels. After wiping him down and readjusting everything, Reef had straddled him, darkened his eyes with black man-liner and helped him put his stiletto ankle boots on before pulling him up. He must have been wearing a goofy smile, because Reef let out a snort of laughter, saying, "You look thoroughly fucked."

Ford had hugged him close, whispering, "Nah, just in love." But as corny as it sounded, it was true and everything was pretty damn perfect because of it.

FORD MOTIONED for Reef to go through the door into the pub first, getting a good look at those long legs—looking even longer in four inch heels—encased in shiny black leather. Heated air blasted them, warming them after their dash from the cab to the door. It wasn't snowing—it wouldn't have been so cold if it was. Nope, the one night where they both went outside wearing next to nothing, the weather didn't want to cooperate, deciding to dump sleet on them. A howling wind and an icy sidewalk had Ford clutching onto Reef in the hope that if his man slipped, he wouldn't break an ankle and destroy any chance of the coveted world championship.

"Here goes nothing," Reef uttered nervously, as the door closed behind Ford, blocking out the storm. Moving to slip off his heavy coat, Ford could see the movement of Reef's Adam's apple as he swallowed.

Placing a hand on his chest, Ford stopped him before stepping behind Reef and slipping it off his shoulders. With an arm wrapped around his waist, Ford murmured, "Your costume is perfect." Before handing it to the cloakroom attendant. With a ticket in hand, Ford directed Reef into the main room of the pub. It was already packed, every table and chair occupied, and as the strobe lights flickered on and off, Ford could see that the dancefloor was full of writhing bodies. Their relaxed sports bar had been utterly transformed into something out of a fantasyland, each costume more elaborate and risqué than the last.

"Looks amazing in here, doesn't it?" Reef yelled over the noise.

"You and Alfonso did a great job setting up. Well done, sweet."

"You finally made it." Alfonso greeted them with a smile. Wearing a broad white Stetson, white chaps and cowboy boots, Ford watched as Alfonso pulled Reef first, then him, into a quick hug and pointed to the back of the room. "The others are up the back. Come, I'll take you over." When he turned, Ford suddenly understood Gab's comment that Alfonso would be grateful if Reef wore a jockstrap. Walking around in ass-less chaps, he was in exactly the same boat as Reef—butt hanging out for the world to see. He couldn't help his chuckle at his friend's expense.

"Keep your eyes up top, Ford. This one's mine," Gabriella teased as she joined him, slipping an arm through his. Ford's chuckle turned into a full on laugh as he got a close look at her. Purple sparkly unicorn head worn like a hat, a mane flowing down her back and a skimpy corset and skirt with furry knee-high boots, Gab was clearly the horse that her cowboy would be riding later that night.

"Tell me you have a tail." Ford leaned back, checking out her ass, and sure enough a long purple tail swished behind her with every step she took. "Your costume rocks, love."

They joined the table in the corner—close to the bar but far away enough that they weren't crowded and private yet only a few steps away from the dancefloor. It was the best in the house. Gab held out her arms and Ford hugged her, kissing both her cheeks before she held him at arm's length and gave him the once over. "You look hot." Once she got a look at Reef, her eyes bugged out. The slow perusal had Reef blushing, visible even under the muted lights of the bar. "*Madre di Dio, che è sexy.*" *Mother of God, that's sexy.*

"*Non è lui. Non riesce a tenere le mani di dosso.*"

"Tell me that was something dirty you just said," Reef murmured against his neck, warm breath whispering over his skin as he wrapped his arm around Ford's shoulders and pulled him close.

"Gab called you sexy. I said that I can't keep my hands off you."

Reef moved against him, swaying to the heavy beat of the music as Ford held him close. He spotted Caden first, weaving his way back through the crowds from the bar to their table. Holding a few glasses high, he dodged people dancing and the others vying for his attention. He wasn't low on attention from the fairer sex, but it was as if he had blinkers on, giving only the briefest of smiles to everyone as he passed.

"Hi guys." Caden placed down the glasses and held out his closed fist for Ford to bump his against, then thumped a hand on Reef's back. "Nice costumes. Kinda Rocky Horror."

"Not the way I'd describe it, but yeah, okay."

Ricky stepped up after Caden, carrying pitchers of beer, with Mace following close behind balancing another stack of glasses. The three of them looked like they'd coordinated their costumes—Mace as always was the infallible good guy—the Captain America of the trio; Caden was Bucky, the kinda damaged but always loyal mate. Dressed in World War military gear, he filled it out nicely. Ricky, kind of predictably, was Iron Man—fave hero of his tech mad, kinda-geeky-but-looks-like-a-jock friend. Even before Ford had understood his own sexuality swung both ways, he'd watched the movies, read the comics and seen the gay fan art. He'd wondered about Captain America's past and present friends and the energy that passed between them. It was kind of hot thinking about the three men together and watching Ricky, Caden, and Mace—even though they were only playing the roles in store-bought costumes—he could easily picture a level of intimacy between the three of them. They... fit.

THE DRINKS FLOWED and he perched on a bar stool with Reef in his arms. Ford relaxed back and enjoyed the moment, watching Reef laugh with his friends, Gab dancing with one of the girls they worked with and Alfonso running around looking after everyone, yet still making time to stop by every few minutes to check on them. There was only a few hours left in the year and looking back on it, Ford smiled. He was happy, so damn happy. After all the shit that had happened—the avalanche, the fire, his parents and the shit storm there, Coach quickly coming around and becoming his pseudo-father just like he was Reef's, and Reef...well, Reef was everything in his crazy world.

"Sweet, let's dance," he murmured in Reef's ear. When Reef turned to him and smiled, Ford knew without a shadow of a doubt that he'd spend every New Year's Eve for the rest of his life exactly where he was right at that moment —in Reef's arms. Holding hands, Ford followed his man onto the dancefloor. Bodies crowded around them, writhing as the beat permeated every cell of his body. Reef's body against him, his leg between Reef's, his arms around his man's waist and Reef's hands in his hair, Ford surrendered and let the music, the moment, guide the sway of his hips. Reef's lips on his, their connection—pure and perfect— resonated through him even deeper than the music.

Ford had long since shucked his jacket and as the first strains of *Sucker for Pain* sounded, Reef teasingly slipped his jacket off his shoulders, tossing it toward the table. Ford swallowed, his mouth suddenly dry from the sight of his man's lean body—arms above his head, face tilted up with his eyes closed and his hips swaying in a seductive beat. His skin shone with a sheen of sweat and dressed only in the barely there jock strap and those damn boots had Ford's semi rock solid in an instant. He watched enraptured as Reef reached out to him, curled his fingers over the leather harness and dragged him closer. The words from the song

—*being a slave to his games*—had Ford reaching out and pinning Reef to him, sliding his leg between Reef's and grinding his cock down on tight muscle. He swallowed Reef's moan, capturing his lips with his own and as their tongues delved and danced, their bodies moved in a rhythm scripted just for them.

Reef broke away, spinning in his arms and pushing his ass back against Ford's erection. Reef slid one of his hands into his hair and the other gripped his ass. Ford held on tight, letting his man lead as he explored the sensitive skin of Reef's throat and shoulder with his lips. Ford hummed as the saltiness of the beads forming on his man's neck hit his tongue. Reef bucked in his hold, grinding harder against him. Moving incessantly, rocking against him, Ford responded, thrusting his hips in a seductive roll. It was as if he was inside Reef, memories of how his dark channel gripped him—so hot, so tight—sent him careening toward an orgasm of epic proportions. Reef slipped his hand between them, deftly undoing the tight shorts and freeing his aching erection. Ford shuddered, unable to control himself anymore as the heated skin of his cock nestled between the globes of Reef's perfect bubble butt.

Mindless with lust and in the middle of a dancefloor in his friend's pub-turned-nightclub, Ford gave in to instinct and turned Reef's face, capturing his mouth with his once more. Reef opened to him and pushed back harder against Ford's erection. His cock slid sensuously along Reef's crack, lubricated by the copious pre-cum leaking from his slit. Ford slid his hand low down Reef's belly, feeling the cum gutters leading to his man's rigid shaft. Curling his fingers under the waist band of Reef's jockstrap, his fingertips brushed the thatch of trimmed hair at the base of Reef's cock, sending a spark of need through Ford.

"Fuck me, Ford. Rub your dick on my ass until you blow right here on this dancefloor. Show everyone in here how fuckin' hot you are when you come," Reef growled against his lips, panting hard as they moved together.

The craving for Reef and the hot-as-fuck words he whispered had Ford riding the edge of ecstasy. Insane with the need coursing through him, Ford was powerless to stop from falling over the edge. His breath caught as Reef rolled his hips, pushing back hard so his cock slid the full length of his crack. "Oh yeah," he moaned. "Fuck I'm gonna come right here too. Show them, Ford. Show me how much you want me. How you own me. Mark me as yours."

Ford shuddered as fire ripped through him. He let out a choked cry as streams of thick white cum pulsed out of his cock, coating his abs and Reef's back. He held tight as his legs turned to jelly and breath sawed in and out of his lungs.

"Wanna come in your mouth, hon," Reef moaned, resting his head on Ford's shoulder as he pushed Ford's hand down to his cock. Fingers in Reef's jock strap, he wrapped them around his man's iron hard shaft. Ford bit down on the sensitive spot on Reef's throat that always made him writhe from his touch.

"Want to finger fuck you and suck you deep down in my throat." He canted his hips forward, Reef's ass cradling his softening dick, as his cum slicked the way. Reef's wanton moan was all he needed to hear. Guiding him off the dance floor, hand still gripping Reef's cock, Ford led them toward the men's room, but they didn't get that far.

Reef pointed to the short corridor leading to the office and basement where the kegs, wine, and crates of liquor were stored. It provided hardly any privacy, certainly not enough to love on his man the way Ford wanted to, but the way Reef dragged him into the alcove, there was no way he was going to wait until Ford could get him in a bedroom. Pushing him face first against the wall, Ford dragged his cum down, slicking Reef's hole before he pressed two fingers in. He watched enraptured as Reef thrust back, swallowing more of his digits before pulling back and impaling himself again. "Need you, Ford," he gasped.

Ford didn't wait for more of an invitation. Pulling his fingers out, he wiped off as much of the cum on his belly and Reef's back as he could, slicking his fingers with the viscous liquid. He spun Reef around. His breathing heavy, Reef's pupils blown with lust, he gripped Ford's harness and pulled him close, possessing his mouth with his own. Ford broke the kiss and slowly dropped to his knees before him, licking a path down Reef's taut abs as he went. Tugging aside Reef's jockstrap, he wrapped his lips around Reef's crown and flicked his tongue over the slit as he pressed his fingers against Reef's ass. Reef came hard, gasping as his body locked up, clenching hard around the digits Ford had buried deep inside him. Ford tasted him, relishing each pulse pouring into his willing throat.

He let him go as the twitching in Reef's dick finally subsided and it began to soften in his mouth. Ford stood on shaky legs, the shoes not helping things and leaned forward into Reef's embrace. Hugging his man tight, their breaths mingled as they stared into each other's eyes. Reef smiled and it lit up Ford's world.

"I love you, hon. I can't tell you how grateful I am for it being *you* on that mountaintop."

"I love you too, Reef. You're my world, everything to me." Ford leaned in and kissed him, their lips slowly melding together as the DJ announced the countdown was five minutes away. A quick detour via the bathrooms to clean themselves up had them rejoining their friends a couple of minutes later. Ford wrapped his arm around Reef and held him close as their group shouted out the numbers together. When the digital display hit zero, Ford turned to his man. "Happy New Year, sweet."

"Happy New Year, Ford," Reef murmured as they kissed and saw in the new year in the best possible way.

CHAPTER THIRTEEN

"So, how's the fundraising going?" Reef asked Caden as they sat on the steps of the resort waiting for Ricky and Mace to meet them. Tendrils of warmth wrapped around him as the cloud cover lifted and the sun's rays shone bright, reflecting off the pure white snow and sparkling like twinkling diamonds. The ozone smell from the fresh dump the night before invaded his senses, invigorated him as much as the view.

It was a perfect day compared to the blizzard which kept them inside for the better part of the week since the New Year's Eve party. Even though the ski fields were closed and roads impassable, Reef hadn't complained too much—he and Ford had enjoyed a few long lazy days in bed, curled up together watching movies. But being cooped up for so long had started to make him stir-crazy, fidgeting and pacing constantly. Now that the ski fields were open again, he was itching to get out there. Two foot of snow had to have fallen and knowing that untouched powdery perfection was so close was doing his head in. And even crazier was his promise to Ford that he wouldn't get on the slopes until his shift had finished and Ford could join him. His man hovering over him in bed, tickling him had finally done the trick and Reef had given his promise.

"Fundraiser's goin' pretty good. We've raised quite a bit and the hash tag is starting to trend. The videos online are getting a stack of views too. It's not viral yet, but it's growing, so that's what's important."

"It's a good thing you're doing, Caden." Reef knocked his shoulder into his friend's playfully. Looking at Caden, he marveled at how much the man had changed. Or maybe it was him that had changed. At the end of the previous season when they'd last toured together, Caden was a pain in his ass. The constant ribbing and non-stop reminders that Reef was always losing to him had rubbed Reef the wrong way. He could handle losing, but when the winner was a bad sport, it sucked. There wasn't any of that constant sense of one-upmanship anymore and it'd completely transformed their dynamic. Reef now counted Caden as a friend rather than a competitor.

Caden shrugged and smiled sheepishly at Reef's compliment before his gaze shifted and held. The change in Caden's demeanor was instant and when Reef followed his line of sight to the sidewalk, he spotted Ricky and Mace walking together, talking and laughing. Reef eyed his friend thoughtfully. Unless he was getting it completely wrong, Caden's gaze was full of longing. As far as he knew, Caden was straight, but hey, more unexpected things had happened than a guy turning out to be bi.

"Hey, sweet."

Reef startled at the sound of Ford's voice. He didn't expect to see him for a while yet and Ford had totally snuck up on him. Caden forgotten, Reef turned his attention to Ford as his man dropped down on the step next to him and wrapped an arm around Reef. Leaning in for a gentle kiss, he hugged Ford back.

"You're early." Reef smiled.

"I missed you." Ford flashed a grin at him when Reef rolled his eyes. "Actually, Alfonso came to see Gab and they were pashin' and I was a third wheel, so I ducked out a few minutes early. Hiro can deal with the horn-dogs when he gets there for his shift."

Mace and Ricky stepped up and Caden was instantly on his feet, moving toward them. His friend was awfully eager. He huffed out a laugh. Who was Reef kidding? He was too. "We all ready?"

"Yeah, dude. Let's shred it." Ricky tossed the comment over his shoulder, the three of them already walking away together. Reef slipped his hand into Ford's and they followed, loping up the hill toward the mountain base where they could catch the chair lift up to the sweeping ski fields.

When Ford's cell started ringing, he fished it out of his pocket. "Hey, Dale. How're things?" Ford tilted his cell away from his mouth and whispered to Reef, "Director at The Remarkables." Reef wasn't eavesdropping, but he couldn't help overhearing that they were looking to fill some positions at the resort.

"Everything okay?" Mace asked as Reef joined their group at the entrance to the ski field, Ford standing off to the side wrapping up his conversation.

"Yeah, all good. Ford's got the director from New Zealand on the phone. He's looking to fill a few positions next season. Apparently they want to hire a few people to stick around for a while so they don't have to keep re-training their ski instructors."

"God, being a ski instructor would be a dream job, wouldn't it? No travelling, no living outta suitcases."

"Sure would." Reef nodded.

Ford rejoined them and they walked toward the ski lifts. "No worries, I'll let you know if I come across anyone who'd be good. See you." Ford hung up his cell and pocketed it. "Sorry about that."

REEF STRAPPED INTO HIS BOARD, as he and Ford waited for the others to get off the ski lift. Standing at the top of the mountain, clear blue skies stretching far above them and a blanket of virtually untouched white below, Reef took a deep breath letting the calm of the mountain seep into his bones. A light breeze caressed his exposed skin like silk. Ford stood to his side, his eyes closed, head tilted up. "I get why you do this every time you do a run."

"It's my church, you know?" Reef pulled off his beanie and rubbed his gloved hand over his mussed up hair. "The snow, the cold, the freedom... I'm connected to something bigger out here, like the snow gods are part of me. I come here to worship nature, life, us. Everything."

"I get it." Ford took his hand and Reef turned to face him, a small smile tilted his lips. "But it's never been perfect until now. Until you were standing next to me." Ford raised his hands, cupping Reef's cheeks and kissed him, a slow melding of lips. The love that filled him was tinged with melancholy, both of them clinging to every moment they had together.

Resting his forehead against Ford's, Reef couldn't help his sigh. He was brilliantly happy, but the noise that came out sounded sad even to his ears. "I'm not gonna be here much longer though. Two days and I'm on tour again."

Ford slipped his arm around Reef's waist, drawing their bodies together. It was awkward with him on a snowboard and Ford on skis but they managed to wrap their arms around each other. "The season's half over, Reef. We can make it the rest of the way and then we'll have the off season together." Ford smiled as he dropped a kiss on Reef's cheek. "A few months without interruption."

"Yeah." Reef nodded. "It's gonna suck until then though." Ford squeezed him tighter and Reef couldn't help but kiss him, brushing his lips softly over Ford's.

"Come on, guys," Ricky called out, pulling them from their intimate little bubble. He smiled at Ford. It didn't matter that he was leaving in a couple of days. He planned on making very good use of the short time they had left together. Starting with skiing the powdery slopes of Santa Caterina di Valfurva.

Ford shifted his weight and took off down the slope and Reef followed close behind. Soft powder rustled around his knees as the wind rushed against his face. His waxed up board was almost frictionless. Sliding down the slope, cutting through the deep snow with his man and their friends was a rush. The warmth of having found his place in the world spread through Reef's chest. This was living. Loving. It was the life he'd dreamed of having.

The contours of the ski run undulated and lifted under him, the natural unevenness of the ground mostly smoothed over by the thick covering of snow and ice. The picturesque mountain-scape before him was awe-inspiring. Towering peaks glittering with their pristine white covering, the ice catching the soft rays of the winter sun and hundred year old pines, their branches heavily laden with powder. The old trees lined the edges of the ski field proper, marking out the safer zones for inexperienced skiers.

Changing the angle of his board, Reef cut behind Ford, zig-zagging across the mountain as they whipped down it, the five of them in a conga line. Dominating the slope, Reef watched Ricky holler and whoop his way down first, Caden, then Mace following and he and Ford bringing up the rear. Reef couldn't wipe the grin off his face and let out his own whoop as Ford turned and flashed a smile at Reef. He was in fuckin' heaven doing this run. Free from the pressure of competition he relaxed, enjoying the ride. *Feel the freakin' love.* He sounded like a hippy, but that wasn't too far from the truth with his upbringing. His natural high rocked it hard.

As the ground levelled out, Reef threw his hands out and skied into Ford's arms, sending them both spinning around. Laughing, Ford held him tight before planting a hard kiss on Reef's lips. "What a rush. Let's do that again," he panted out of breath.

"Hell yeah." Reef laughed.

———

IT'D BEEN five long weeks since Reef had held Ford in his arms. Since he'd kissed his man. Touched him. And it was fuckin' torture. Sixteen days and they'd be together for the last competition of the season.

Three hundred and eighty four more hours.

He just needed to get through the rest of the meet in Sapporo. But Reef was struggling, totally miserable actually. The loneliness was killing him. Jet lag from the long flight to Japan and a broken night's sleep didn't help either. *Damn doctors from the World Anti-Doping Agency.* He'd never understood why the drug tests were done at such crazy times. A blood test at two in the morning the night before a competition was insane. And having the mother of all head colds didn't help. Reef groaned. Everything—his head, his throat, and all of his muscles—ached, the exhaustion and uncontrollable shivering adding to his misery. He just wanted to sleep. It wasn't fun being sick, it was knocking him around a hell of a lot more than usual.

Reef sighed, his exhale heating the thermal neck warmer he'd pulled up around his face. A shiver passed through him and he huddled into Caden more. They weren't the only ones standing together, trying to use each other's body heat to warm up. One of the Aussie competitors, a Canadian and a German guy were standing in a tight-knit circle to their side, but nothing was working. The shelter the competitor's tent provided them at the top of the slope was useless and the weather was getting worse, visibility dropping as fast as the howling wind was increasing. From this spot on the mountain, you could normally see the white-capped peaks surrounding the slopes, stretching up to meet the blue sky high above. Today's view was an even shade of grey above and white below his feet.

He didn't want to be there which sucked. He loved Japan. Sapporo was a fantastic city—great clubs, food to die for and beautiful slopes close to the city center. By this stage in the season, he was normally in party mode. Keen to celebrate, he'd often walk the city in his downtime, immersing himself in Japanese culture. Last time he was there he'd checked out a few Tea houses and spas and at night he'd dragged Mace to the famous karaoke bars in the city center. But he was over it: over the competition, the travel, everything. He wanted to go home to Ford's place. No, to *his* and Ford's place. To their bed. Despite feeling like shit, he cracked a smile.

Twenty more days until they were there.

Things weren't all bad. He was close, so damn close to something he'd only dreamed of. Winning the world championship had been an impossible dream even a year ago and now he was in the lead. It wasn't a big one. If he messed up either of the two remaining heats, he'd lose. Precious championship points rested on his performance on the mountain and Reef would be damned if he gave up a win, no matter how much he'd rather be sleeping. Or doing almost anything else, anywhere on earth, other than where he currently was. Freezing his nuts off, waiting for his run down the treacherous mountain was not Reef's idea of fun.

He looked outside the tent, studying the landscape before him. The weather was turning, worsening even in the half hour he'd been standing there. Sleet was now falling in sheets around them, the powdery surface of the naturally formed ramp having long ago turning icy. A gust of wind howled through the air, buffeting hard against him. It rendered the thermal layers of protection and thick ski gear Reef wore completely ineffective.

"Dude, I was warmer doing The Undie Run." Reef's voice, scratchy from his sore throat, barely carried to Caden and he felt, rather than heard, his responding chuckle. The honey and lemon concoction Mace had fed him earlier could have had razor blades in the damn thing and apart from tasting awful, did jack shit to sooth the pain.

The announcer's voice boomed over the speakers nearby introducing Caden as the next person to jump. He pulled back making Reef instantly miss his body heat. "That's me."

"Good luck." Reef winced, the words tearing his throat apart. He didn't watch Caden's jump. He heard enough of the announcer's commentary to know that he'd nailed it, but struggled on the landing. He expected that when it was his time to finally take his jump, he'd be doing exactly the same thing, but first, two of the competitors huddled in the group next to him had their go.

Mace skied up beside him and unclipped his boots from the snowboard bindings. "Reef, you're up soon."

He nodded his response, groaning when even the small movement hurt more places than he cared to list.

"You still feelin' like shit?" Another nod in response, accompanied by a full-body shiver.

"Reef, bud, I know this is the end of the season and every point counts, but you have to be realistic. If you're too sick to compete, you need to pull out."

"No." His voice came out as a croaky whisper. He may not be able to talk, or move without discomfort, but there was no way in hell he was missing this competition. The Tylenol he'd taken earlier had worn off. Once he topped it up, he'd be fine.

"Okay, but you can deal with Ford." Mason smirked at him when Reef shot him a glare. The bastard had him there. Shit would hit the fan if Ford thought he was too sick to compete and truthfully, he didn't have the voice to argue the point with him.

Reef clutched his throat as he forced out the words. "Feel like shit. Lemmie jump then I'll sleep."

"The rest of the day in bed. Chicken soup and more honey and lemon." Mace raised his eyebrow, waiting for Reef's response.

"Whatever. Fine." He shook his head, clenching his teeth together to stop the groan leaving his lips. Another shudder passed through his body, this one more violent than the last. He was fucking freezing. Mace moved in front of him and peeled off his glove, his eyes full of concern. Lifting Reef's beanie up, Mace pressed his hand against his forehead, making him sigh in relief, the coolness a balm to his raging fever.

"Reef, man, you're really sick. You're burning up."

He didn't have the energy for a response, instead, he rested his head on Mason's shoulder, using his friend and trainer for warmth and maybe a little support to hold himself up. At this rate, he'd just ask Mace to roll him down the mountain.

"Last chance to pull out, Reef. You sure you can do this?"

He nodded. "Gonna have to. It'll be bad form if I pull out of the last jump for the day."

"Come on then, let's get you strapped in." Mace led him to where the competitors' snowboards were neatly stacked, reaching up to the highest shelf to pull the bright green snowboard down. Reef leaned against the racks hoping against hope he could pull off at least a mediocre jump.

He was up next. Mace had managed to get him strapped in as the announcer's voice came over the PA system. *"Now, the dude you've been waiting for. He's the current point leader for the world championship, Reef Reid."*

Reef groaned and pushed off, skiing out of the tent. Hand up in the air, he waved to the die-hard crowd he knew was gathered along the sides of the slope near the landing zone. He couldn't see them but he was being televised on big screens. He knew they'd have the perfect view.

He'd jumped like this before—bad conditions, sick—it was nothing new when you lived and breathed cold weather. He just needed to suck it up and get it done. Stopping at the top of the mountain, Reef looked down the steep gradient, following its fall to the jump platform. He took a deep breath and prayed to the snow gods. *Keep me upright. Give me a safe landing.*

The buzzer sounded, indicating the beginning of his run and Reef pushed off. Pointing his board down the slope, he relaxed into the moment. A no frills jump wouldn't get him huge points, but it was the best he was going to do. *If* he could do it.

Ice crunched under his board, the powder having long since blown away in the gale force winds. Reef powered on, gathering speed at a ridiculous pace. Hurtling over the jump, he sailed into a high arc. The takeoff, the air, the flying—it was the reason snowboarding was his life. This time though, the sleet hit his face like hundreds of tiny needles piercing his skin. The wind roared through him, chilling him to his bones. Visibility was shit. But he'd trained for this moment. Pulling off complex jumps was one thing—you needed a hell of a lot of talent to do it—but winning the world championship was as much about consistency as it was flair. Reef had practiced long and hard to get to this point. It had to be enough to get him through.

Grasping the front of the board with his right hand, his left held out high for balance, Reef kicked his left foot down and twisted. He did a perfect three-sixty degree spin in the air, then another. He dropped his grip on the board and straightened, priming his body ready for the difficult landing.

The shitty visibility and the headache from hell that was currently pounding out a rhythm in his brain, threw out his depth perception. Reef hit the icy surface before he was ready, his board slipping wildly. Cartwheeling his arms, Reef struggled to stay upright. Dropping into a lower squat, he turned, using gravity to steady him and slow his slide.

He'd made it. He'd pulled it off. A grin spread across his lips and he lifted his arm in victory, punching the air. Muscles aching and throat burning, Reef waved to the cheering spectators huddled at the edge of the run. On a good day, he'd stop and talk to them, shake hands and take as many pictures as they wanted, but he didn't stop to socialize. His hotel room—his bed—was calling his name.

The warmth from the roaring fireplace in the building at the base of the mountain surrounded Reef as soon as he stepped through the door. He scanned the open plan area looking for a quiet corner. There weren't any. The sofas near the fires were jam-packed and most of the tables were full too. He wandered over to a small table with a lone chair and dropped into the seat. His energy completely sapped, Reef was grateful for the space the fans and other competitors gave him when he rested his head on crossed arms on the table. His eyes drooping closed, Reef relaxed. Sleep was begging him to succumb to it.

Mason's voice and his hand on Reef's shoulder startled him awake. Disoriented, he couldn't figure out why everything was orange.

"Come on, Reef, let's get you back to the hotel. You didn't even get your goggles off before you fell asleep." He touched his face and looked down at his still-gloved hand. Gripping the fingers in his teeth, he yanked each glove off, before lifting the goggles away from his face. His beanie and neck warmer were quickly stripped away and tossed aside too. Face uncovered, Reef breathed easier, but the exhaustion that had set in was overwhelming.

He struggled to his feet and took a tentative step away from the table. His movements were sluggish, pained as he made the short walk through the building to the waiting busses. It was an hour long trip down the mountain to the hotel in Sapporo where they were staying and the sooner Reef made it to bed, the better.

Mason was behind him as he alighted the bus and

collapsed into the seat immediately behind the driver. "Get settled and I'll look after our gear, okay?"

"Wake me up when you need me to do something," Reef mumbled, already falling asleep again.

THE BUS LURCHED from side to side, jarring Reef out of his slumber. His head bounced against the window he was leaning on, but the bus was quiet and warm, the rocking quickly lulling him into the darkness once more.

IT WAS dark and there were hushed voices, a lot of poking and prodding. He was sinking, drifting underwater. The voices were garbled and distant, and the resistance against the small movements of muscles was strong, like he was fighting the tide. He struggled, lights flashing in his sore eyes until a strong hand pressed down on his pec and Ford's whispered voice called out to him, calming him. He stopped fighting. He was safe. Darkness enveloped him again, blessedly washing over him.

REEF BLINKED his eyes open to a darkened room. He was lying down, stretched out on white sheets, a gloriously cool compress on his forehead. The last thing he remembered clearly was getting on the bus. *Huh.* His surroundings were familiar. *Where am I?* He looked around and saw Mace sitting asleep on a striped armchair next to the bed. The hotel had those seats. They must be there. *Thirsty.* God, he needed a drink.

He moved slowly, rolling to the side and groaned in pain. His head hurt. Reaching out, he picked up the bottle of water on the side table and took a tentative sip. He wasn't swallowing razor blades anymore. *Sweet relief.*

Cataloguing his body, the first thing he noticed was that he was naked apart from his underwear. *Another thing I don't remember doing.* The shivering was gone, his skin no longer clammy and the muscle aches had faded, but the dull throb that pounded in his skull rattled his brains. He moaned, falling back on to the sheets and gripping his forehead.

"Hey, you're awake." Mace's words were soft, but they cracked like thunder in the quiet and Reef instinctively reached up to protect his head, turning away from the noise.

"Head hurts."

Mace's grip on his wrists was firm, but gentle. Two pills fell onto his palm and Mace passed him the water in the other. Reef cracked open his eyes and saw Mace holding the bottle of Tylenol up for Reef to see. He sighed in relief. Tentatively, he lifted himself up onto his elbow to swallow the pills and drain the rest of the water, before easing himself back onto the pillow.

The tablets worked quickly, his headache fading fast, but it only served to focus Reef on how hungry he was. "What time is it? I'm starving."

"Three a.m."

"Cool, I feel heaps better." Reef stood slowly, and apart from being a little lightheaded, he felt pretty good. He reached for the tee that was sitting on the bed, but got a whiff of himself and nearly turned green. *Damn.* Changing his mind, he added, "Might have a shower, then get some room service. You want some?" Reef was surprised with the look Mace tossed his way—his brow furrowed and head tilted to the side. *Confusion?*

Reef internally shrugged his shoulders, and continued,

"At least I'll have plenty of time before I have to get ready for the heat."

"You don't remember do you?" Mace's tone was incredulous. Eyes wide and mouth open, his trainer shook his head. "Unbelievable."

"Remember what?" It was Reef's turn to be confused. *What's there to remember? Shitty time at the competition, getting on the bus, sleeping, waking up thirteen hours later.*

"You've slept for a day and a half, Reef."

What? A day and a half? What the fuck? Reef opened his mouth to speak, but Mace clearly wasn't finished. He held up his hand, stalling the words Reef's brain was still trying to come up with. "You've been in and out since you got on the bus. You haven't eaten, barely had any water. You were delirious."

"Seriously?" Reef sunk back down onto the bed. He wasn't that sick, was he? Ford had commented a few times that he looked tired and Reef's throat had been hurting for a week or so, but apart from being cold—something he rarely experienced in full ski gear—he didn't think he was that bad. At least he thought he was okay.

"Your fever broke about four or five hours ago. I've had the tour doctor in here three times since you passed out to check you over and decide whether you needed to be admitted to hospital. Between her and Ford, you've had pretty much round the clock medical support. You'll need to take it easy for a week or so, but you should be right for the last comp."

Reef shook his head. *I'll lose the points.* "But—"

"There was a lay-day yesterday. The snowstorm got worse and the road up the mountain was closed. You weren't penalized for missing the second round, but you're going to forfeit points for the rest of the competition."

"Like fuck." Reef's tone was indignant. "I'm fine, I'm competing."

Mace stood and towered over Reef's still-seated form. He clenched his jaw tight before shoving his hands in his pockets. He was pissed, his tone cutting. "No, you aren't fine, Reef." Visibly taking a deep breath, he blew it out. His voice was quieter with his next words, almost pleading. "You've just spent over thirty-six hours in semi-consciousness. Ford and I both thought you should have been in hospital. He's been watching you through that fuckin' monitor for hours, sick with worry and Momma Bear has racked up hundreds in international call costs while I've been updating them both. I don't care whether you think you're fine, you're not. As your trainer and your friend, I'm telling you, you're *not okay*."

Reef sighed and rested his elbows on his spread knees, letting his head drop down. He knew what Mace was saying was true, but the knowledge that he'd lost the world championship because of a fucking head cold was hard to take. "I've worked so hard, Mace and it was all for nothing. I can't win anymore." Everything coalesced, the knowledge he'd lose piling on his shoulders and adding more weight to his already unbearable load. Reef didn't know if he could get out from under it—the news was the proverbial straw. One thing had become crystal clear to him, but he still wasn't sure if he was ready to say the words.

"Bud." Mace drew his attention, sitting across from him on the same arm chair he'd been asleep on. "I'm not just saying this to placate you, but winning this world championship isn't everything. Second place will still give you a pretty damn good payday and loads of sponsors are after you. The money you could earn in endorsements is good, probably higher than what you earn on the circuit—it'll set you up nicely. And there's always next year."

Reef huffed out a breath and stood before pacing the width of the room. "I need to think about my options."

————

IT'D BEEN two hours since Mace last checked in with him. Ford paced the room restlessly, but he was exhausted. Shaking the tremor out of his hands—the one he got when he'd barely eaten and his blood sugar was far too low and he was operating on no sleep—Ford sat on the end of his bed. Resting his elbows on spread knees, he worked out the time difference between him and Reef. It was eight hours—well after midnight in Sapporo. *Is it too late to call Mace?* He pondered the question a moment more, toying with the idea of sending a text to see if he was awake. *Fuck it.* He couldn't wait any longer.

He dialed Mace. When the video feed popped up after the call was answered he didn't expect to see Reef's smiling face, but there he was.

"Oh God, you're awake," he breathed, relief swamping him after what had been endless hours of frantic terror. Tears sprung to his eyes and his heart flipped seeing his man awake and flashing him a crooked grin. Every tense muscle unknotted. Reef was going to be okay. Every frustrating minute of the arguments he'd had with the team doctor dissipated into a puff of smoke. Their butting heads to try and get him admitted into hospital faded away. An eternity had passed waiting for Reef to wake up, watching him through the very monitor he was staring at him through now.

"I'm sorry you were worried, hon."

Ford sniffed and wiped away the tears, trying to get a hold of the emotions overwhelming him. Happiness filled the void left when the fear and angst evaporated. "S'okay, sweet. How are you feeling?"

"Surprisingly good. A little lightheaded, but I think it's because I haven't eaten anything in a while. I've just downed a bottle of water so I'm not as thirsty anymore, but Mace has given me another one and some electrolytes too. I've got a bit of a headache, but the muscle aches and sore throat are pretty much gone."

"Good." Ford nodded taking a deep breath. He was shaking, the tremor in his hands back again. "I've been so worried, Reef." His voice broke on his man's name, the tears flowing freely now. He'd been powerless to help him, able to do nothing but watch him suffer. Every protective instinct in Ford screamed at him to go to Reef and be with him, but he had obligations at the resort that he couldn't palm off this time. Add zero sleep into the mix and Ford was a mess.

"Shhh, hon, it's okay. I'm okay," Reef murmured soothingly through the connection. Ford again dashed the tears with the back of his hand and smiled tentatively at his man.

"Sorry, I'm a wreck, but don't mind me. Did Mace tell you he'd pushed back your flights so you can take it easy for a few extra days?"

"Yeah, he also told me about the lay day and that I was gonna have to forfeit the rest of this heat." Reef paused and Ford could just see the wheels turning. "Do I have to forfeit? Can I compete?"

"What?" Ford asked incredulously. "Are you serious now? You've been in and out of it for a day and a half. Mace and I were begging the damn doctor to admit you into hospital and you want to up and compete? Are you insane?" Ford pushed his computer off his lap, dropping it onto his bed, so he could stand and pace again. Truth be told he wanted to shake some sense into Reef.

"Hon, just listen to what I'm saying. And can you pick up your computer again so I can see you, please?"

Ford shook his head at Reef's words and took a hold of the laptop. As soon as he was in front of Reef again, his man continued talking. "I know the tour doctor can rule out my participation, but assuming she gives me the okay, what's the worst that could happen if I compete?"

"You could get sicker. And you may feel better at the moment, but you're anything but recovered. You'll be lethargic for a while yet and you're dehydrated too. You need to take it easy and let your body recover. If you push yourself too far, you could easily end up in hospital and you *will* miss the last heat. My medical opinion is watch TV for a week, get better and kick ass at The Fridge."

"And what's the best case scenario?"

"You'll wipe out your energy levels for a few days, recover and be fine for the final comp. But, Reef, you were a lot sicker than I think you realize. In my opinion, it's more likely you'll get worse. You should have been in hospital, connected to an IV and being monitored. Your fevers were far too high for me to feel comfortable with and you were out of it for so long."

"I'm okay now though."

Reef's reassurance sounded hollow to his ears. Maybe it was because he knew the human body better than that—it was nothing but a pipedream for Reef to think he'd be able to finish the season.

"The point is that you might not have been. I'm lodging a formal complaint against your tour doctor with the medical board. She was negligent in not having you admitted. Even if it was a virus like she was insisting it was, you should have been under constant observation."

"I don't know if I can give up when I'm so close, Ford. I know you think I'm crazy, but I have five competition days left for the season. And then I'm done."

If only. No matter how much Ford hated the thought of living through another season like this one, he'd never ask Reef to give it up. Ford sighed. That was it, wasn't it? He'd never ask Reef to give up competing, and Reef was right—he *was* too close to achieving the championship to throw in the towel. Ford had to support him.

"Look, I can't tell you what to do. Medically, I think you're crazy but I get it, Reef. I understand. I'm behind you, whatever you decide. But you're gonna have to do exactly what Mace and I tell you and rest in your down time." Ford continued detailing what he thought would give Reef the best chance of recuperating from the exertion of the competition.

CHAPTER FOURTEEN

FORD'S ALARM SOUNDED. Disoriented, he blinked open his eyes, reaching out in the darkness to turn it off. It was the middle of the night. *Why am I awake?* He startled. *Reef.* He sat up, the heavy covers falling low around his waist and the cool air hitting every inch of his exposed skin. Then everything came rushing back—his conversation with Reef, the relief knowing he was awake, Mace's furious call and the half hour of planning to help Reef make it through the next few days. *The competition's starting.*

Ford yawned, shivered and reached out to pull his laptop closer, yanking the covers up to his neck as he laid back down. The event was being televised live online, so at least he didn't have to get out of bed to watch it. Snaking one hand out, he opened up the feed before snuggling deeper into the warmth of the feather down covers. Stretching his long body out, he half watched, half snoozed until he heard Reef's name. Eyes springing open, he pulled the screen closer to watch his man in action. Reef was insane, absolutely crazy for even attempting to perform at an elite level when he was still sick but pride, nevertheless, welled inside Ford. He may be nuts, but that was what made him the best of the best. He was one hell of a competitor, the epitome of a sportsperson.

Reef lined up, going through his typical pre-jump routine until the buzzer sounded. Pivoting on his board, he began the slide down the run. Small powder arcs formed as Reef snaked down, hitting the launch point in the perfect position. Nerves assailed Ford as Reef—knees bent and his arms low—hit the jump. He shot into the air at one hell of an angle, sending him soaring high into the sky. He always made it look so simple, effortlessly flying, spinning and flipping before pulling off a perfect landing. Watching how Reef did it with ease almost made Ford believe he could do it too. *As if.*

Focused intently on the video feed before him, Ford could imagine the flex and play of Reef's muscles as he used the forward momentum to propel himself, flipping over and over, tumbling like an acrobat through the air. Ford counted three rotations before Reef straightened and braced for landing. It wasn't the most difficult jump he'd ever done— Reef would call it easy—but given the circumstances, Ford was happy he hadn't chosen anything too taxing. Ford huffed out a laugh—*not too taxing*. Ironic that almost anyone else would be pushed beyond their limits, but for Reef, it was simple. That was his man.

His jump was over in only a few seconds. Reef gently touched down, the thick powder at the base of the ski run left there by the recent storm softening his landing. He'd pulled it off spectacularly. Ford let out the pent up breath he'd been holding and grinned, punching the air in victory. Excitement pulsed through him. Two more jumps for the day, then another three the next. God, if Reef could hold out, if he could pull it off and get even close to the level of points he'd been scoring all season, he'd do it. He'd be the World Champion. Ford didn't want to get ahead of himself, but he couldn't help but dream for his man. Smiling, he closed his eyes and fell back onto the pillow, dropping his forearm across his face.

"You did it, sweet. You're so close," Ford whispered into the darkness.

———

"SWEET, I'm so proud of you," Ford murmured, his fingers brushing the screen where he could see Reef lying in bed. He was struggling, his fever spiking again and his energy levels completely sapped. The two days of competition had taken it out of him, exactly like Ford knew it would. Mace fussed over him off screen—all Ford could see of Mace was his hand swiping Reef's face down with a wet towel.

"Can you take a drink for me, Reef?" Mace asked gently, passing him a bottle of water. Reef took it and gulped it down.

"Slowly, sweet," Ford cautioned. "Mace, keep him in bed and check his temperature every fifteen minutes until he stabilizes. If it gets close to thirty-nine again—that's um..." Ford paused, calculating the conversion between Celsius and Fahrenheit, "one-oh-three for you—call an ambulance. Keep him hydrated like you've been doing too. I'll call for updates when I can, okay?" Ford was distracted, looking at Reef and trying like hell to remain professional to do a visual assessment. His shivering had slowed and he wasn't disoriented like he had been a few days earlier. He was tired though, struggling to stay awake.

"Ford?" Reef's words were quiet, almost pained.

"Yeah, sweet."

"Need to sleep. Sorry I ignored your advice." Reef yawned and even that small action visibly sapped more of his energy. "Love you."

"Love you too, Reef. And don't worry, we'll get you through this. You'll be better soon, sweet. I promise." *You have to be.* Reef's eyes were already closed, his body lax in sleep before Ford had even finished the sentence.

The rescue station's radio sounded in the background and Hiro leaned back in the chair waving to Ford through the open doorway. "We're up, Ford. Gotta go."

"Yeah, okay. I'm coming." He directed to Hiro, before speaking into the camera again. "I've gotta go, but call me if there are any developments, Mace." Ford stood, reaching for his red ski jacket.

"It's all good, man, don't stress. I've got this." Mace had turned the camera so they could speak and gave him a reassuring smile. Ford nodded and waved, ending the connection quickly.

"What have we got?" Ford slipped on the jacket and zipped it up, donning the rest of his gear as he went into the supply room with Hiro.

"Multiple injuries from a collision. Possible broken bones—an arm and a leg—and a kid we'll need to have follow us down. It's happened right near the middle chairlift." Hiro already had the heavy pack on his back, leaving Ford to join two rescue sleds together—forming a train—and strap them to his waist. He worked quickly, doing up the buckles and dragging the heavy gear over the linoleum floor to the door.

The air outside was crisp, the sun high in the sky. Apart from a few fluffy clouds passing overhead, the weather was flawless. A light breeze danced over his exposed skin, but Ford was too preoccupied to enjoy the surroundings as they skied to the chairlift. He had to get his mind off Reef and onto the job before them.

"Your guy okay?" Hiro asked, rousing him from his thoughts.

"I'm worried about him. He should have been in bed, but instead he was out competing. I get why he did it—he's too close to give up—but the pressure isn't exactly gonna help."

"Stubborn, determined and independent—sounds like you two are the perfect match." He grinned at Ford as they skipped past the line of skiers and waited for the chairlift to come to a stop. Working quickly, they loaded up and seated together they started the trip up the ski field.

———

FORD KNOCKED ON THE DOOR, adjusting his bag on his shoulder. Reception at the swanky little indie hotel had given him a key when he'd arrived, but it was the middle of the night. The six hour drive from Santa Caterina di Valfurva to Obertauern, the Austrian ski resort, had taken far longer than he'd expected. Blizzards had closed roads until they could be plowed again and an accident on the freeway had delayed him for hours. Sweaty and exhausted, Ford just wanted a hot shower and a comfortable bed.

He stepped back waiting for the door to be answered. It opened quietly and Mace smiled then stepped to the side to let him in. He grinned and walked forward, bumping fists on the way past. "Good to see you, dude," Mace whispered as he let the door close behind them.

"You too." Ford smiled. "I wasn't sure if you'd still be up. Were you waiting for me?"

"Yeah, but it's okay." Mace pointed to a bag sitting beside the door. "I'll head out now so you two can have some privacy."

"Don't be ridiculous, Mace. Go to bed." Ford grasped his shoulder and squeezed. "I appreciate you wanting to give us some privacy, but this is your room too. I don't expect you to up and leave every time I stay. Believe me, we're doing nothing but sleeping."

"Maybe just tonight then. It's pretty late to wake Caden."

"You two are close, aren't you?" It may have been phrased as a question, but Ford already knew the answer. Over the season, Mace and Caden's friendship had blossomed. Reef often mentioned that they'd gone out for drinks or—much to Caden's trainer's exasperation—were skiing together. Then, while they were in Italy for Christmas and Ricky had joined them, they'd become inseparable. The bromance they had going on was kind of cute.

"Yeah, but I doubt for much longer." Mace leaned against the wall and looked up at the ceiling, blowing out a long breath. Ford forgot about being tired and gently dropped his bag out of the way.

"Wanna talk about it?" he asked, moving over to lean on the back of the velvet sofa, focusing his attention on his friend who was radiating pain.

"I can't tell you the specifics. I know, morally, I did the right thing. But what I did is gonna hurt him. Badly. And it's just a matter of time before it happens. I don't know whether to tell him or wait until it blows up. Either way, he'll think I betrayed him."

"Shit, that's heavy." Ford scratched his head, trying to think. "I get that you can't tell me specifics, but can you talk to him? If you can, I think you need to try to explain things.

At least if he's warned beforehand, when it blows up he'll be prepared."

Mace nodded. "I can now. I couldn't before. But telling him now will just fuck up whatever friendship we had sooner. I don't want that to happen, you know?" When Mace turned to look at Ford, his heart hurt for the man. The normally unflappable Mace wore his emotions on his sleeve and he was heartbroken. His eyes shined with unshed tears and his lips were turned down in a frown. Mace bore the heavy burden in the slope of his hunched shoulders.

"Yeah, man, I get that you don't wanna lose him, but maybe the only way you'll keep him is to let him know what happened. It might not make things better, but if he understands why you did it, maybe he'll be able to get past it."

"I doubt it, Ford. This is big. I've pretty much destroyed him, but I had no other choice." Mace dropped his gaze and swiped at his face with the back of his hand.

Ford stepped forward, pulling Mace into a hug. The other man came willingly, resting his forehead on Ford's shoulder. "Be there to put him back together, Mace. Don't give up on him. If he's that important to you, don't let him go."

"I don't know if I can do it alone."

"So take Caden to Ricky. Then the two of you can fix him together." At Ford's words, Mace's head snapped up and he stepped back, his expression shocked. "I might be out of line, but I'm guessing that he'd want to help." Ford shrugged and raised his eyebrows, silently asking Mace for confirmation. But the other man's poker face had already slipped into place. He gave nothing away. Ford smiled gently at him and patted Mace's arm. "'Night, Mace."

"'Night, Ford. I'm a heavy sleeper, so...."

Ford laughed. "You might still need earplugs in the morning."

"Hey Ford? Thanks for listening." Mace gave him a small smile and stepped over to the only open door in the suite, closing it gently behind him.

"Anytime, Mace," he murmured in response. Ford looked around for the first time since stepping inside. He was standing in a cozy TV room, a large flat screen mounted on the wall, a sofa and two armchairs faced it. Each one was different, but they tied in together brilliantly. The carpet and walls were almost the same tone of taupe, but the velvet furnishings were in bold colors—purples, blues, green, black, and gold. Dark timber tables and the bronze lamps gave the room a sophisticated look. But what he really wanted to see was the bed. A yawn tore out of him right on cue and Ford picked up his bag, turned off the lamp closest to him and headed toward what he guessed was the other bedroom.

Ford cracked the door open a few inches and saw Reef's suitcase lying open on a stand, illuminated with the soft glow of a lamp. *The bedroom.* He entered silently and gently placed his bag down before closing the door behind him. The sight before him took his breath away. Reef was lying on his side, curled into his pillow, only half covered by the sheets. It took everything in Ford not to go to him and kiss every inch of exposed skin. Instead, he headed to the attached bathroom and closed the door behind him. A mish-mash of different sized and colored glass tiles, spanning the hues of the rainbow, lined the shower stall. The kaleido-scopic mix matched the furniture in the bedroom and contrasted with the dark grey tiles on the remaining walls to give the washroom an intimate vibe. He looked at himself in the mirror. Bloodshot eyes and lank hair, growth too heavy to even be called a trimmed beard and creased clothes made Ford look like a damn hobo. He'd trim the beard tomorrow. For the moment, shower and bed.

BARELY TEN MINUTES later he was clean and dry, had fresh breath and he'd hung the towel on the hook. Ford slipped under the thick covers, doing his best not to disturb Reef as he lay down. His man's deep even breaths sounded from next to him and Ford couldn't resist any longer. Rolling to his side, he shifted closer and pressed a gentle kiss to Reef's shoulder. Reef's spicy scent—all man and outdoors—filled his senses. *Home at last.* All that smooth pale skin was too tempting and Ford gave in and kissed Reef again. This time he swiped his tongue out, the need to taste his man overwhelming. Ford slipped his hand onto Reef's waist and shuffled close enough that he could feel the heat from his body radiating against his own. There was nothing he wanted more than to love on every inch of him, then fall asleep together, but Reef was still recovering and interrupting his sleep two days before the biggest competition of his life wasn't gonna happen. Ford pulled back and laid his head on Reef's pillow. The press of his hand on Reef's skin would have to be enough to get him through the night.

"C'mere," Reef mumbled, grasping Ford's hand and pulling him closer. He hesitated only a second before eliminating the distance between them, plastering his body against Reef's. Nose buried in Reef's hair, their feet tangled together, Ford hugged his man tight and let out a contented sigh. Closing his eyes, he relaxed until Reef reached over their heads and tangled his fingers through Ford's still damp curls. Pressing his ass back, Reef rubbed himself like a cat against him. Ford's already half-hard cock took notice, becoming painfully erect far too quickly.

Reef's quiet moan had Ford abandoning any pretense of wanting to sleep. He'd never leave Reef needy and, well, if he got an orgasm out of it too, who was he to argue? Ford gently bit Reef's shoulder, licking away the sting, and kissed a line to the sensitive spot under Reef's ear. Running his fingertips over Reef's lithe muscles, he let them dip a little lower each time he caressed him. When he hit the line of hair that framed Reef's cock, he couldn't resist any longer and wrapped his hand around the thick shaft. Pumping languidly, he set up a slow rhythm that had Reef gasping and thrusting his hips, pressing his cock into Ford's hand before pushing back, grinding against Ford's front. Pre-cum leaked from him, lubing the way for his rigid dick to slip and slide against Reef.

"Ford," Reef moaned, the sound like kindling in a tinder dry forest. Ford's growl was accompanied by his hips shifting forward, seeking out the tight heat of Reef's channel. They ground down on each other, a slow dance that had the fire raging higher and hotter with each movement. Ford needed to be inside his man, needed to make love to him, but Reef's grip was tight and Ford couldn't pull back to get the lube from his bag.

Reef turned his face and with his eyes still closed, tugged on Ford's hair, guiding him until their lips were a whisper away. Ford crashed his mouth down onto Reef's and kissed him, stealing his air and possessing him until they both had to separate or pass out. Pressed hard against his man's ass, he rocked, making Reef gasp and loosen his grip on Ford's hair. Sliding his hand between them, down Ford's body to grip his cock, he stroked him in languid pulls. Moaning long and low, Ford tried to hold off the imminent orgasm, desperately wanting to be inside Reef when he came. But stopping himself was easier said than done. Still holding his cock, Reef pressed the head of it against his channel and Ford cursed, their skin slipping and sliding easily against each other.

He pulled his other arm out from under the pillow and canted his hips, separating them enough that he could slide his fingers between Reef's cheeks. His man was already slick, the unmistakable feel of lube meeting his fingers. Working first one then two fingers inside his tight heat, Ford growled. "You want this, don't you, sweet? You wanted my cock in your ass so bad, you couldn't wait for me to get here, could you? You've already worked lube into your ass, haven't you?"

Reef's whimper was shameless, unreservedly needy, just the way Ford liked him. Using both hands, he parted Reef's ass cheeks and his man guided Ford's cock to the tight ring of muscle circling his entrance. Rocking his hips forward, he gently breached Reef, sliding in until the head of his cock passed the resistance of his sphincter. He paused, letting Reef adjust to the intrusion, but apparently Reef was having none of it. He thrust back hard, impaling himself on Ford's rigid dick. Reef's gasp was elicit and downright sexy, and it pushed Ford over the edge. Losing control, he anchored Reef to him and pounded hard. Reef turned his head and Ford attacked his mouth again, their tongues dueling in an age-old dance. Masculine grunts and growls sounded, driving Ford higher. Sex had never been this good with anyone else. And now Ford knew why. He'd memorized every one of Reef's hot buttons—endless hours exploring one another would do that—and nothing made him happier than being the one to make Reef come undone.

"Goddamn, Ford, don't stop. I'm close, so fuckin' close."

Reef had barely got out the words when Ford gripped him harder and changed the angle of his penetration.

"Jack yourself off, Reef. Slide your hand up and down your cock—"

"Oh God,'" he breathed, every muscle in Reef's body locking up tight. Ford drove deeper, harder and the final hit on Reef's prostate tipped him over, a hoarse shout rending the air. The muscles in Reef's ass contracted and literally milked the cum from Ford's balls. Shooting deep in him, Ford painted his lover—the love of his life—with his mark.

Sated, he slumped down, resting his forehead against the back of Reef's head. His heart hammered in his chest, the breath squeezed out of his lungs like he'd run a marathon. Mind-numbing ecstasy coursed through his veins as he rode the high of his orgasm. Still tangled in the bed covers, a sheen of sweat coated both of them.

"Damn, what a way to be woken up." When Reef turned his head and grinned, those sexy as fuck dimples showed in his cheeks and Ford laughed softly. Those warm brown eyes which captivated Ford and had made him fall head over heels in love, glowed with humor.

"When did you wake fully?" he murmured, nuzzling into Reef and kissing the damp skin below his hairline.

Reef sighed happily. "Right about the time you slid into me."

Ford wrapped his arm around his man, his hand wiping over the remnants of Reef's orgasm. He kissed a line up Reef's throat. "I've missed you, sweet."

"Me too, Ford. So much, hon. Lemmie get us cleaned up. You must be exhausted. You've been driving all day."

"S'okay, I'll do it." Ford yawned, his eyes sliding closed. "Later," he mumbled, sleep already overtaking him.

———

FRESH POWDER SWIRLED around him as Reef aimed his board at the ramp half way down the mountain. This was it, his first jump in the season's final competition. The world championship rested on the next thirty seconds of his life. He grinned. He *so* had this.

Reef spun one-eighty degrees so his less-dominant foot was forward. That seemingly small adjustment made the technicality of the jump multiply. He crouched lower to pick up speed and zeroed in on the launch point. The sinking feeling in his gut as he lifted off was followed by the adrenaline rush from nothing but air below him. Flying high, Reef didn't waste any time. He grasped his board and kicked into a forward roll, angling his body so the axis of the spin was off center. His concentration was laser focused, but fuck he loved this shit. Flying high in more ways than one, he counted the rotations as he tumbled through the air. Crystal clear cobalt blue sky, the pristine white of fresh powder. Blue, white. Four times he looked up to see sky, which meant four spins. The ground was getting closer by the second. A split second decision would either make him or break him, but Reef didn't hesitate, pushing for one more flip before he hit the thick powder. He'd either eat it, or kick ass. *Kicking ass it is.* Blue sky came into view above him and he knew he'd done it. The grin he'd worn on his face the entire jump spread so wide his cheeks hurt. But it wasn't over until the fat lady sung. And this jump was only the opening score.

Touchdown and Reef sunk into the deep snow, powder swirling around his thighs as he hit the snow heavily. He was upright, but it wasn't graceful. Somersaulting forward made landing a fight against the downward momentum to stop from face planting the ground. It took all of Reef's strength and balance to avoid doing it, but he managed.

Just.

The crowd of people gathering at the base of the jump were cheering and whistling. It took Reef a moment to realize what he'd done. He'd just landed one of the hardest jumps he'd ever attempted. He hadn't even been able to pull it off in practice before. And yet, even though the landing wasn't perfect, he was still on his feet. He'd done it. He'd actually fucking done it.

A sense of accomplishment filled him. He'd worked so damn hard, given up so much and everything had finally fallen into place. He'd committed every part of himself to his goal. Now his future, everything he'd done in the past—all the painstaking hours of practice, the injuries, the second-guessing himself, the travel and being separated from his friends and family—all coalesced into that one moment in time. And it was fucking brilliant. Reef let out a whoop and punched his fists to the sky. He'd done his bit, given his all. Now his fate rested in the hands of the judges. Whatever the final outcome of the comp would be was anyone's guess, but Reef knew whatever went down, he was proud of what he'd achieved there on the snow.

He skied to a stop next to the barrier in front of Ford. His man didn't even hesitate, pulling him into a fierce hug. There was a lot of back slapping and "Congratulations" spoken, but Reef had no idea who they were from. His head buried in Ford's neck, Ford's murmured words were the only thing Reef was focused on. "I'm so fuckin' proud of you, sweet. I've never, *ever,* seen anything so bloody amazing. You were fuckin' flyin'. It was perfect. You were perfect." When Ford pulled back, he looked into his eyes. Reef saw the love shining in his gaze—he guessed he was giving Ford the same goofy love struck stare—and it made his heart do the same somersaults he'd just pulled off.

Ford cupped his face with a gloved hand before stepping back and letting Mace hug him. "Well done, bud. You nailed it. You absolutely killed it out there. It's in the bag."

"Bit premature."

"No, it's not. You're the best this sport has ever seen. I'm so damn proud of how far you've come, Reef. You're a champion in the truest sense of the word."

"My boy." Momma Bear pushed Mace out of the way with a playful shove of her ample hip and took Reef's face between her mitten-covered hands. She pulled him down to her level, kissing him on the forehead. "This is it, honey. You've done it. You deserve every accolade for this. Everything—every sacrifice—was leading you to this point. Well done, Reef."

"Thanks Momma. You know I couldn't have done it without you, right?"

"Nonsense." She motioned to the air. "That was all you."

Coach stepped up behind Momma Bear, the barrier still between them and put a hand on Reef's shoulder, squeezing tight with his iron-strength grip. "You're a champion, son. No matter what the score is, you're a champion."

"Thanks, Dad." Reef reached out, hugging both of them. They may not be his birth parents, but these two people were the most important family he had. Their praise, their support meant everything.

CHAPTER FIFTEEN

His body was holding up. At least as good as could be expected when he'd been laid out by the worst virus he'd ever caught. Until a few days ago, Reef wasn't sure whether he'd be well enough to compete. But at the time, he was too damn sick to stress about it. Now, it was down to the wire. His final jump of the season. His final chance to make it, to achieve the one thing he'd dreamed of since watching his idols as a kid. Standing at the precipice, Reef took a minute to look out at everything before him. A weather front was moving in, dark grey clouds amassing in the distance. They'd be in the midst of it before nightfall. The sky, for the moment, was Aegean blue. No, it was darker than that. Royal blue perhaps? Flags flapped in the breeze, Obertauern's Fridge Festival event sponsors' signs everywhere. The combination music festival-*cum*-snowboarding competition was a party and one more jump stood between him and a cold beer to either celebrate or commiserate.

Caden had already finished his jump and to say it was anything short of spectacular would be a lie, but apparently the judges were withholding the top-three scores until the end of the competition. *Are they trying to psych me out?* Seriously, having the scores as close as they were already was insane. Not knowing what he had to beat, the uncertainty and at the same time, the challenge, caused nerves to stampede through Reef's gut like a herd of buffalo. Was he good enough to do it? Could he handle it if he lost? He'd done it before. Only time would tell if he'd have to do it again.

Reef pushed all the 'what if's' out of his mind. He *had* to focus. Nothing had ever been as important to him as the need to get a hold of his focus. *That's not true. Ford. Ford is* more *important.* Reef shook his head, trying desperately to clear his thoughts. He closed his eyes and stretched his arms out by his sides. Breathing in, he slowly raised them above his head. He pressed his palms together and brought his arms down to his chest, exhaling as he went. His thoughts slowed, his mind began to clear the images flashing before him like the opening credits for *The Big Bang Theory.* Reef repeated the action, reaching for his Zen.

Mace's words from the beginning of the season drifted into his mind. *"Seize that championship, Reef. Strap in, focus and breathe. Feel the slope. Feed off the energy. Harness the rush, channel it. Fly. This is* your *season,* your *time. You're not ready to be the best, you already* are *the best. Show the rest of the world what we know. It's your world championship. Reach out with both hands and grab that bastard. Bring it home."*

The chaos dissipated, slowly being replaced with the jump Reef had planned playing out in his head. It was the most ambitious he'd ever tried, even more so than his first jump of the heat.

He was finally centered, calm enough to push off the mountain. Reef opened his eyes and traced the line he would travel with his sight. The buzzer had long since gone off so Reef rotated on his board and started down the mountain. Knees bent, he flew down the slope, picking up speed as he neared the jump. Launching himself off the ramp, the inertia as he sailed high made his gut feel as if he'd left it on the ground. Reef shifted his weight in the air and his board spun, like the blades on a helicopter. He curled into a ball and while still spinning, flipped over again and again. Flashes of white helped Reef figure out which way was up. Seeing the snow getting closer, he pulled out of the tumble and slowed his spin, getting ready for the landing.

White powder rushed up to meet him. Arms out wide to aid his balance, he touched down, zigzagging through the knee high powder until he'd slowed. Reef blew out the breath he was holding and relaxed into the gentle slide to the barrier where his family and friends were waiting. The crowd was going nuts, screaming and cheering—chanting his name. He heard the words, saw the waves and connected with the high-fives people were giving him, but it was surreal, as if he was standing outside his own body, watching from afar. The jump replayed itself in his head, the landing. He'd done it. Hadn't he? Reef patted down his body. Yep, he was in one piece; he was upright on his board on the other side of the jump. He looked over to Ford, waiting at the end of the line with Mace, Momma Bear and Coach and saw love and pride shining in his gaze. Reef's heart fluttered in his chest, love sending a warm glow through his body that lit him up from the inside. He smiled at his man, heading over to him when he'd fist bumped and high-fived a few of the fans. It hadn't sunk in—the jump was insanely difficult and he'd pulled it off. So, why was he totally numb?

His pseudo parents were the first to congratulate him

this time, with Mace following closely behind. He listened to their words without taking them in, hugged everyone in all the right places, but didn't appreciate the warmth of their embraces. Reef was adrift, floating untethered. It was like an out of body experience, which was totally surreal and a little unnerving. But Ford would fix it, fix him. He needed his touch, his strong arms wrapped around him, his lips against his own. Thing was, he didn't want to share Ford at that moment, or maybe it was that he didn't want to be pulled away from the moment with Ford. Reef grasped the thick material of his man's jacket sleeve and tugged. "Come with me."

When Ford clicked into his skis, Reef headed for the building at the base of the slope. He needed a minute to get his bearings, to figure out whether the jump was as good as he'd hoped. Could it have won him the World Championship?

Reef unbuckled his bindings and stepped off his board while Ford took off his skis. Stacking his and Ford's gear up against the racks, Reef marched in, flashing his competitor's ID to get past security. Taking the stairs two at a time, he headed straight for the offices on the other side of the function center, seeking out any privacy they could get.

"Reef," Caden called out, stepping into his path. "Can I talk to you?"

"Gimme a few, bud." Reef dodged him and kept walking, waving his friend off. "I need a minute with Ford."

"It's about the scores." His response was quiet, but the sound echoed like a gunshot in Reef's brain. He stopped walking. Ford staggered, barely avoiding crashing into him. He looked at Caden, really studied him. The tense set of his jaw, the slump of his shoulders, the utter defeat in his usually bright eyes. Something was wrong. Very, very wrong. Reef grasped Ford's wrist and squeezed, needing the strength of his touch, even if it was through their heavy clothing.

Ford moved to stand in front of him and clutched his biceps, studying the confusion Reef's eyes no doubt held. "Go, sweet. Talk to him. And I'll be waiting here when you're ready for me."

"Thank you," he whispered before pivoting on his heels to face Caden.

"Can we sit? Somewhere private?"

Reef didn't know what to say to that, so he nodded. Caden was withdrawn, pale, and the knot in Reef's gut grew.

They exited at the other side of the function center and headed down the corridor Reef had intended taking Ford into. Caden directed them into a small room, entering first and held open the door for Reef as he walked in. Sitting in one of the executive chairs surrounding the small, round table he waited as Caden closed the door and sat next to him. He watched Caden knead his hands together, the whole time looking down, not meeting Reef's gaze.

"Dude, what's goin' on? What's the deal with the scores?" Reef asked. He was surprised that his voice sounded so level, calm even.

"I fucked up, Reef." Caden blew out a breath and finally lifted his gaze. A look of utter desolation met him. Caden shook his head. "I failed my last drug test. They're withholding the scores because they just got notification of the results from WADA. I've been disqualified. You're being announced as the winner."

Reef was stunned silent. Caden failed his drug test. He'd taken drugs. He'd cheated. And Reef was winning because of it. Not because he was good enough, not because of his own talent, but because Caden had been disqualified. Reef opened his mouth, but closed it again when no words came out. How the hell was he supposed to respond to that? Sorry you got busted, you lying sack of shit? Reef clenched his jaws together and blew out a breath. He shook his head and stood. Paced the room searching for something, anything, to say to the man before him, a man who he'd once thought of as a friend. Now he wasn't so sure.

"Why?" His tone was harsh, and the question surprised him. Did Reef really want to know?

"I..." Caden's shoulders slumped. "I couldn't handle the stress. Mom dying, the competition, the fundraising, all the other stuff I have goin' on and now I find out my sister's pregnant...it was too much. I couldn't sleep, I was so fuckin' anxious all the time, even knowing this is the last season I was competing in. Nothing calmed me down, except weed. Smokin' a joint fixed it. For a while at least."

Reef was angry, there was no doubt about it. He wanted to hate Caden for cheating him out of the win he'd worked so damn hard for, but he couldn't. Reef understood what it was like to be overwhelmed and Caden had his grief to deal with too. He sighed and sat down again. "That was the positive result? Weed?"

"Yeah." Caden ran his hand through his hair. "I'm sorry, Reef. I know I was wrong. Even if I hadn't been busted—especially if—it still wouldn't have been a fair comp and you deserved better than that. Everyone did."

"We did deserve better, Caden." Reef nodded. "I'm so fuckin' angry right now. I've worked to get myself into this spot for well over a decade. I've given up so much to be here and the one year I'm actually competition to you, you cheat and get yourself disqualified. I suppose I'll never know whether I could've beaten you."

"Reef, you deserve this. You're the best snowboarder in the circuit."

"Yeah, well, I guess we'll never really know that, will we?" Reef stood and went to the door. With his hand on the knob he said, "Caden, you need to get help to learn how to cope. I don't know what you're doin' after this season's out, but you need family and friends around you. Promise me you'll do that."

"I will, Reef." He didn't hear if Caden said anything else; he was out the door and down the corridor searching out Ford. He met him in the doorway to the function room and dragged him back into the semi-private walkway.

"What's going on?"

Reef rubbed his forehead and leaned against the wall. He sounded defeated even to his own ears. "Caden's out. I've won."

"What the hell? What are you talking about?"

"Disqualified for a positive drug test. That's why the officials withheld our scores, not because they were so close. I'm the winner by default." He wished that numbness had persisted a little longer, because now he was hurting. Anger, despondency and frustration warred for top spot.

"Oh, Reef," Ford murmured before stepping in close and cupping his face with warm hands. "Don't let him take away from what you've done." When Reef raised his eyes to Ford's, questioning him, he continued. "You don't get it, do you? You won, not because he cheated and got caught, but because you deserved to win. I don't believe for a second that you're the winner by default. That jump you just pulled off was better than anything I've ever seen. You're incredible. You deserve to win. Don't let anybody tell you otherwise."

Reef shook his head, fighting back the hopelessness and

disappointment that the one thing which meant so much to him—his chance at a lifetime achievement—had been reduced to naught. "But I didn't win. Not outright anyway. I'm only getting it because Caden isn't."

"Do you know that for sure? Have you seen the scores?"

"I don't need to."

"No? Do you think that Caden would have asked for them? He's convinced he would have had you beaten because he's done it in the past. But, sweet, your jumps were out of this world—so far above and beyond anything he's ever done. Talk to the officials. See what they say before you assume you would've lost." Ford unzipped Reef's jacket and slowly ran his hands down Reef's chest then around his waist, pulling him close. Reef moved willingly, holding Ford tight.

"What did it feel like when you landed the jump?"

"Honestly? I was kinda detached, as if I was observing what was going on. Didn't even feel like me standing there getting congratulated. I couldn't tell you what anyone said."

"Sweet..." Ford breathed, a pained note to his voice as he pressed his lips to Reef's throat. Reef lifted his chin, wanting more of those intimate touches. This is what he needed—the warmth, the love that Ford imparted with every touch of his mouth to Reef's sensitive skin and the strength of his embrace. He shivered when Ford rained a line of nips down to his collarbone, moaning quietly as heat passed through his body, chasing away the remnants of the fog which had surrounded him from the moment Reef had landed his jump. Ford captured his lips, swallowing the needy sound he made.

"Love you," Reef breathed between kisses, finally pulling back to rest his forehead against Ford's.

"Before you speak with one of the officials, I need to show you something, okay?"

Reef wanted to rail against the added distraction, but he had faith in Ford. His man wouldn't have told him to wait unless he thought it'd help Reef. So he nodded and let Ford lead him into the meeting room across the corridor from them. It was much like the last one he was in—cream colored walls, a round timber table, and black leather chairs. But unlike the other one, this room had a high window. Reef sat and watched as a fluffy white cloud rolled quickly from one side of the window to the other, marring the bright blue sky. Ford played with his cell momentarily, before sitting down next to Reef and taking Reef's hands into his. He held tight, Ford's touch grounding him, giving him the quiet confidence to face his crumbling career head on.

Less than a minute later, the door burst open, Mace already talking as he powered through it. "Reef, we need to find out what the hell's going on. It's not on that the scores are being withheld." Reef cut him off, holding up his hand in a stopping motion.

"Caden's told me a bit of what's happening. We'll look for one of the judges in a minute. But first, Ford wanted to show me something."

Ford rose and motioned for Momma Bear to take his place, closing the door behind Coach as he entered at a mellower pace than Mace had done.

Reef was clueless and Mace looked just as confused until Ford spoke, a small smile tilting his lips upward. "Momma Bear, I think Reef needs to see the letter."

"Finally. You've been holding out on me, boy," she said playfully. Momma Bear smiled and reached inside her bag, producing a white envelope which she handed to Reef. He looked it over, noticing the sender's information first—

Department of the Prime Minister and Cabinet, New Zealand.

"What's this?" Reef shifted his gaze up to Ford, to find him grinning. He paused for a moment, committing the image to memory. A happy Ford was one hell of a sight to behold, but this was different. It was the same sense of pride he'd seen in Ford's eyes when Reef had caught up with him after his jump. Whatever the letter was, it was something big for Ford.

"Open it."

He slid his finger under the already opened seal and pulled out the single piece of thick card stock. As a matter of course, Momma Bear opened his mail and emailed copies of anything that needed his attention. She obviously knew what it was and from the looks on everyone else's faces, so did they. He unfolded the paper and found a smaller burgundy and gold card inside. Putting it aside, he read the letter.

DEAR MR. REED

The Department of Prime Minister and Cabinet has received a nomination on your behalf for the issue of a Bravery Award to you. It is with great pleasure that the Honours Unit has, after consultation with the United States Government, resolved to grant the award to you. We congratulate you, and thank you on behalf of Her Majesty, The Queen, the New Zealand government, and its people for your selfless act of bravery in the rescue of Mr. Stratford Wallace. Your disregard for your own safety in digging Mr. Wallace from the avalanche debris field and your strength in carrying him to safety, showed a great degree of courage.

The enclosed invitation contains details of the ceremony

in which the Bravery Award will be bestowed upon you. If you are unable to attend, the award may be presented to a nominee on your behalf, or accepted in absentia.

Yours faithfully,
Prime Minister of New Zealand
The Hon Bill English MP

REEF READ IT, then read it again. He looked up at Ford, sure his shock was obvious. "You... How... What the fuck?"

"You saved me, Reef and you were so fuckin' brave. Every handful of snow you moved, every step you took with me on your back, you put yourself at risk. And you never hesitated, never once complained even when you were falling down from exhaustion. You're a hero. My hero. No matter what happens today, you'll always be the best in my mind."

"Ford," Reef started, but had no idea what to say. Didn't he understand that right from the beginning, he knew? It was Ford, the other half of his soul. Reef may have pulled him from the snow, but it'd been Ford who'd saved him, given him the love that he'd only ever dreamed of having.

————

FORD WATCHED Reef place the letter carefully on the table and turn to him. Reef's warm fingertips running down his cheek to his chin had Ford's eyelids fluttering closed. Damn, his man's touch was like nothing else. Soothing and igniting a fire within him all at the same time, Reef brought their mouths together for the sweetest of kisses. A slow melding of their lips and gentle touches of their tongues followed as Reef gripped the curls at the base of Ford's neck, pulling him close. Ford held his man tight, communicating through his body the love currently doing cartwheels in his belly.

He'd needed the importance of Reef's actions that day to be recognized for what they were—heroic. It wasn't just something small between lovers, or in their case future lovers. No, his actions were dangerous, selfless. More courageous than anything Ford had ever seen. Nature's fury unleashed in an avalanche and Reef hadn't batted an eyelid, giving her a giant fuck you when, without a second hesitation, he'd stepped onto the unstable debris field and shifted the freezing snow with his hands to get Ford out. And then to carry him for hours on end to safety was superhuman. Ford was ecstatic when the Prime Minister's office had contacted him to confirm Reef's citizenship, letting him know their preliminary assessment that Reef's actions were worthy of recognition. Then Momma Bear worked her magic on the US Embassy, getting them to sign off on the award to one of their citizens and all the pieces fell into place quicker than Ford had ever imagined. Even if he didn't have the World Championship, Reef would have the Bravery Award. Hopefully he thought of it as a decent consolation prize.

"I can't believe you did this for me," Reef whispered, awe in his voice. Ford held him close as Reef buried his face in the crook of his neck, small tremors passing through his man's body. Ford knew instantly what was happening—the adrenaline high from Reef's jump was wearing off, the shock of the afternoon's events setting in. Ford's protective streak flared to life and he pulled Reef closer still, tightening his grip.

"Ford," Mace murmured quietly. "I'm gonna get the officials. We need to give him some answers."

"Yeah, go. I'll stay here with him," Ford whispered, then to Reef, "Hush, sweet, I've got you." Ford ran his hand up and down Reef's back, but it wasn't enough. The shudders wracking his body were getting worse. Ford looked around him and spied the chair.

"Ford, sit with him. I'll hold it steady while you get settled," Coach instructed him quietly. He shot the man, who'd become his father for all intents and purposes, a grateful smile and tugged Reef onto his lap. He curled into Ford's embrace and Ford breathed him in. His favorite scent —outdoors and man surrounded him and Ford closed his eyes, ever grateful to the snow gods for delivering his man unharmed after such a complex jump.

"Thank you," Reef whispered, nuzzling his throat.

"Always, Reef. I'll always do everything in my power to make you happy." Reef looked up at him and then around the room. Ford flicked his gaze to Momma Bear and Coach who were sitting together watching them, Coach's arm around his beloved wife, Momma Bear with tears in her eyes.

"My boys," she cried, droplets falling down her cheeks.

"I love all of you." Reef smiled at them. "You have no idea how much it means to me to have you with me." Reef reached out, taking Momma Bear's hand in his. "Today was supposed to be my chance. Whether it happens or not." Reef shrugged one shoulder, feigning a casual air. But Ford knew him better than that. His mood dropped—he hung his head a little and let his shoulders slump. Ford hated that he'd gone from being quietly confident to facing the possibility of another year with the world championship remaining a pipedream. But Reef didn't let his disappoint-ment linger and Ford loved him even more for it. "The award is just...wow. I'm so privileged to have you in my life, so damn blessed that all three of you saved me and accepted me, see me for the man I wanna be."

"For the man you are, Reef. Your momma and I couldn't be prouder of you."

"Thanks, Dad." Reef smiled, those gorgeous dimples making an appearance and Ford couldn't resist kissing it chastely. "Hey, where's Mace?"

"Gone to get an official," Coach supplied.

A knock sounded on the door a moment later and Reef stood tentatively, opening it for Mace and one of the judges. He smiled at Reef, before holding out his hand to shake. "Reef, well done. Amazing jumps this heat." He introduced everyone and motioned for Xin Li, the judge, to take a seat.

"I'm glad Mason came to find me. I wanted to fill you in."

"Yeah, thanks," Reef started. "I've spoken to Caden and he's updated me a little on what's going on, but I was hoping that you could give us the official version."

Ford held his breath. There was only one thing he was interested in hearing from the judge—whether Reef would have won regardless of what happened to Caden.

"Sure. I'm assuming Caden explained that he's been disqualified?"

"Yeah, he said that. He also told me I was being announced as the winner."

"That's correct. He was to be awarded second place in the competition. That spot will now be forfeited." The judge paused for a moment, looking thoughtful. "I'm not sure how he found out you'd won. We didn't release that information to him, but it doesn't matter for your purposes. Congratulations, Reef. You're our new World Champion."

Ford's heart stopped beating as the elation of what Xin Li had said sunk in. His gaze flicked to Reef who sat staring at the judge with wide eyes. "Sorry, what? Can you say that again?"

He smiled broadly and Ford could have cried with joy. He wasn't imagining what he'd just heard. "It's a well-deserved win, Reef. Your jumps over the last few heats in particular have been nothing short of incredible."

"Are you telling me that I won the championship outright? That I beat Caden's score regardless of his disqualification?"

"You beat him by quite a bit actually." He nodded, still smiling. "The heats are finished, so we'll be crowning you in about half an hour. There's a bit of a media storm out there. The Anti-Doping Agency's press release was made public about ten minutes ago and the reporters have already caught onto it. They'll probably want you to comment on Caden's disqualification." He fished out a page with a few bullet points printed on some sort of letterhead and handed it to Reef. "Here's the International Ski Federation's stance on it. We'd appreciate it if you could keep your comments in line with this."

"Yeah, sure. Whatever you want," Reef replied absently, dismissing him. Ford couldn't tear his gaze away from his man. Seeing the understanding of what he'd achieved dawn on Reef was fucking fantastic. His mouth, which was turned down when the judge began explaining, had slowly morphed into a wide smile. His eyes sparkled with wonder and his laugh made all the gooey sweet feels in Ford's heart dance. His man had done it. He'd persisted through one challenge after another in an incredibly long and trying season and he'd come out victorious.

"See you in a few, Reef. Congratulations again." The judge shook Reef's hand and left the room. Ford grinned at Momma Bear and Coach who were looking between each other and Reef with shocked, but ecstatic, expressions. Mace was smug, like he knew it all along. And the dude probably did. He was a master at getting the best out of Reef and he'd seen enough competitions in his time to know a winner.

When the door closed, the room was silent for all of half a second until Momma Bear's "Yeehaw," sounded. Ford laughed, his heart light with the joy of everything that had gone down that day. Their celebrations could easily have been commiserations, especially with Reef having been so sick only a couple of weeks earlier, but that night they were going to party like it was nineteen ninety-nine.

Reef laughed and jumped out of his chair, into Momma Bear's embrace. He picked her up, and despite her squeals of protest, spun her around in circles. He'd barely put her down before Momma Bear succumbed to her excitement and started jumping up and down. With her arms still around Reef, he did the same and soon they were laughing uncontrollably. Coach joined them, dancing what looked like the moves of a mascot in an NFL game, making Reef laugh even harder.

Between the three of them, their differences and the lack of familial relationship was obvious, but it didn't matter. Coach and Momma Bear loved Reef like their own and Reef adored both of them. Ford envied their relationship. He'd never known that kind of love and support from his own parents, he'd never believed that they'd have his back no matter what. And now he knew the truth about them, knew that they'd sooner walk away than accept him for who he was. While it hurt to realize that, the three people before him had filled the void they'd left and more. They'd reached out when he'd needed them most, drawing

him in and giving him a family who knew true uncondi-
tional love.

Seeing him standing to the side, an observer in Reef's
moment, Coach wrapped a beefy arm around him, bringing
him into the fold. Together, they enveloped Reef in a hug,
his man melting into Ford's embrace. Mace hadn't joined
them in their celebrations, but Ford wasn't about to stand
for that either. Pulling him by the arm of his jacket, Mace
stepped closer and high-fived Reef. "Well done, bud. You
did it— total whitewash. How's it feel to be World
Champion?"

"I fuckin' love the sound of that, Mace. It'll never
get old."

"You did good." He nodded, smiling.

"You helped more than you'll ever know. I couldn't have
done it without you. You're the best trainer out
there, Mace."

"I'll take that." Mace laughed and joined their hug-fest
properly, squeezing Momma Bear tight.

FORD STOOD in the front row, cellphone in hand ready
to record Reef getting his prize. He gave his man, who was
on the sidelines waiting to be announced, the thumbs up
and began filming when the International Ski Federation's
chairman started speaking. Camera flashes erupted around
Ford as the third place winner, Adriano Bertucci, was
announced. The Italian man stepped onto the lowest
podium to receive his check and trophy and raised it high.
As the cheers died down and Reef was announced, Ford
held his breath, waiting for his man to appear on-stage. He
wasn't disappointed when the roar from the crowd was
deafening. Reef had just pulled off an incredible achieve-

ment and he deserved all the accolades he could get. Reef waved to Momma Bear and winked at Ford—his smile causing Ford's breath to catch—as he strode across the stage to stand on the highest step of the podium. Pride welled in him when the chairman lifted the massive trophy—a crystal globe the size of a basketball mounted on a foot-long matching crystal pillar.

"Let's give it up for World Champion, Reef Reid." The Chairman passed the heavy World Cup to his man and Reef held it up high above his head, causing the crowd to go wild again. The smile on his face was one Ford would remember for the rest of his life. As corny as it sounded, Ford was completely smitten, convinced that those popping cartoon love hearts would be floating above his head, giving away their not-so-secret secret. Ford was beyond caring, he wanted to shout it from the rooftops, let the whole world know that the man standing on that first place podium being crowned as World Champion, was his. Being a part of the biggest moment of his life was the best thing Ford could ever ask for. "Well done, sweet, well done," he breathed before whistling loudly and cheering, trying to keep his cell steady as he continued to record the ceremony.

Reef motioned for Momma Bear and Coach to step onto the stage with him and after helping them up, he began his speech. "I dreamed of this moment from the first time I saw a freestyle snowboarder as a kid. I worked hard and got myself into a competition when I was thirteen and that's when these two amazing people came into my life. Give a round of applause to Momma Bear and Coach, my parents." The crowd went nuts, cheers, whistles and clapping continuing long after politeness dictated. Only when it died down a little did Reef continue, "They gave me everything, but most of all they gave me their unending love and support.

They took me in and turned me into the man I am today. I'll always love you both. This championship is for you Momma, Dad." Reef hugged them as Ford blinked back tears. He wasn't the only one fighting his emotions. Reef had a way with words that had just moved an entire crowd of strangers.

"To my support crew, I'm more grateful than I could ever hope to convey." He listed his sponsors and thanked them individually, and then he spoke about Mace. "My trainer, Mason Canning, without you I would have been lost. You're not only the one who gladly picks apart every trick I do to make me a better snowboarder, but you're there for me through thick and thin. Seriously, holding a cold compress to my forehead and feeding me through a straw when I was dying from whatever hellish virus I had a couple of weeks ago was going above and beyond. You're my BFF dude." At that, the crowd roared with laughter and Reef gave Mace a wicked grin, his dimples showing as he snorted out a laugh at Mason's embarrassed eye-roll and shake of his head. "There's only one other person I want to thank. Hon, you mean the world to me. I love you more than life itself. I can't wait for forever with you."

"Love you too, sweet," Ford whispered.

"Let's get this party started," Reef shouted, lifting the trophy high in the air again.

EPILOGUE

FORD HELD the door open for him as Reef stepped into the restaurant, the heated air warming him. The wind buffeted the door in Ford's grip until he forced it closed, its howl suddenly silenced. It was only April, probably too early for snow, but there was every sign a front was about to hit. Reef looked around the large open space. Out of the floor to ceiling windows he could see New Zealand's Parliament House and its manicured gardens. Their friends and family were already sitting at the table he'd booked for the post-Bravery Award ceremony celebrations. Apparently the casual drinks he'd organized had turned into a party with a 'Congratulations Reef' banner hanging from the wall behind them and bunches of colorful balloons tied together along the length of the table.

Momma Bear and Coach sat in the middle, beaming at Reef when he waved to them. Mace was huddled with Caden and Ricky talking, each of them with a beer in hand. Angelo was there and Trent too. He and Ford were slowly repairing their relationship—baby steps and all that. It warmed Reef's heart knowing that Ford had his friend back.

It'd been awkward as hell the first time they'd caught up, but something had changed in Trent while they were gone.

Momma Bear hugged him again when they stepped up to the table. "My boy." Adjusting his tie and smoothing the lapels on his suit jacket, she added, "I'm so proud of you, honey. The award ceremony was beautiful. And you and Ford looked so handsome during all the photos."

"Yeah, it was cool. And the medal's pretty special, too." Reef blushed. "I kinda don't wanna take it off."

"You *should* be proud of it, sweet." Ford slipped his hand below Reef's jacket, resting it on his lower back, holding him close. Reef leaned into him, but they couldn't stay cuddled up. Jeremy, the reporter Reef was meeting, was already seated at a table waiting for him to get their interview started.

"Are you sure you're okay starting without me? The meeting won't take too long." Reef hated ditching them for it, but between his and Jeremy's schedules, it was the only time they could swing it.

"Go ahead, son. We don't mind waiting until you get back to order." Coach patted him on the back.

"I can order for you, sweet," Ford offered.

"Yeah, that'd be great, thanks." Reef smiled at him. "Get whatever you think I'd like." He squeezed Ford's bicep before stepping away. "Won't be long, hon."

Reef undid the buttons on his jacket and loosened his tie as he moved across the restaurant to Jeremy's table. The bronze medal caught his attention. It was pinned to his lapel, and Reef wore it proudly. He'd been on a high for weeks since he'd won the world championship. And now the Bravery Award and getting to spend some quality time with Ford after having been separated for so long—it was all freaking awesome. And to top it off, they were heading on vacation in two days. Weeks of warm weather, swimming in the ocean with a vibin' city as the backdrop lay before them. Reef couldn't wait to get to the Gold Coast, but first he had an interview for Snowboarder Magazine to do.

"Jeremy, hey." Reef shook the retired snowboarder, now reporter's hand. "Good to see ya, dude."

"You too, my man. Congrats on the Bravery Award. Pretty awesome stuff." Jeremy motioned to a chair. "Grab a seat."

"Thanks." Reef sat and picked up the drinks menu scanning it quickly before ordering a beer. Jeremy was cool. He knew exactly what snowboarding at competition level was like, he'd lived it for years. They chatted easily for a few minutes, breaking the ice and Jeremy started recording on his cell after Reef gave him the okay.

"Awesome job on the World Championship, my man. What was different in your preparation this year to the other years you've competed?"

"I think the season I took off last year made all the difference. I was burnt out, had a lot of shit happenin' that I needed to work through and get sorted out. Until I did that, I couldn't focus completely on what I wanted. I came back bigger and better, had a rockin' pre-season. Then all the hard work paid off and everything just fell into place."

"Yeah, I've seen some footage of your pre-season jumps. Pretty sick."

They spoke for a while about training, equipment, his workout regime, eating plan and how Mason's influence helped him gain the winning edge.

"By the looks of the banner over there," he pointed to the table where everyone was gathered, "you look like you've got a few friends waiting for you to start the party. Is there someone special in your life who you'll be celebrating with?" Reef would normally steer clear of giving details of his private life, but he jumped at the chance to answer this question.

"Yeah, I do have someone incredibly special to go home with." Reef smiled as his cheeks colored. "Working through all that stuff with Addilyn, my ex, gave me the mental space to be able to move on."

"Another congrats is due then." Jeremy smiled and raised his beer in a toast. "Your breakup with Addilyn was pretty widely publicized. Is your new lady in the public eye too?"

"Ah, no. He's alpine rescue, but we met snowboarding. He was my heli-skiing guide. I ended up digging him out of an avalanche. Got this to prove it." Reef pointed down at the medal on his chest and smirked.

To Jeremy's credit, his shock only lasted a second. Reef wasn't sure whether it was because of his sexuality or the way he and Ford had met, but ultimately whether Jeremy was surprised or horrified didn't matter. He was ready to come out, haters be damned. "Wow, what a start to a relationship. The obvious, though crass question is, were you hiding your sexuality in the past by dating women?"

"No, not at all. I'm bisexual, so I've dated women in the past and now a man. You wanna meet him?"

"Sure." Jeremy nodded, smiling genuinely. "As long as I can ask him to give me the low down on you." Reef grinned and nodded, unworried about any answers Ford would give him.

"Sorry, I'm hijacking the interview aren't I?"

"S'all good, dude. You don't talk about your personal life much, so the readers will love seeing this side of you." Reef called out to Ford and waved him over when he looked across at them. It only took him a moment to join them at the table.

"This is Ford Wallace. Hon, Jeremy Vaucluse." Ford reached out to shake hands with Jeremy but froze midway, his eyes darting to Reef when he'd obviously realized how Reef had referred to him. Reef smiled and nodded. "It's okay, I outed us."

They sat down again and Reef curled his fingers around Ford's, squeezing them. Jeremy started, "So, Reef you have hijacked the interview. Your coming out wasn't what I was expecting today."

"I'm surprised we managed to keep it quiet. Our relationship has gotta be one of the worst kept secrets in history. All our friends and family know. We tried—and I think failed more often than we succeeded—to keep it quiet from everyone else during the season."

"Is there a reason why you didn't make your relationship public earlier?"

"We decided that the focus should be on my performance, rather than on us." Reef shrugged. His answer was as simple as that. If it weren't for the likely shit storm his coming out would have created during the tour, he would have had a sky-writer paint it across the heavens. When Jeremy remained silent, he added. "I dunno if there have been any other snowboarders who've come out, but I'd say I'm one of the first. Every competitor on the tour had worked too damn hard for the focus to be on who I was sleeping with, rather than our jumps, no matter how good he is in bed." Ford's eyes bugged out and he blushed a furious shade of red. Reef couldn't help but laugh at him.

"How have people reacted to you two being a couple so far?"

"The people who matter to us have been incredibly

supportive." Ford was unequivocal, leaving no room for discussion on their decided lack of support from others that should—and as much as Ford hated to admit, even to Reef—did matter. He did a good job hiding the hurt he was still dealing with from Jeremy—it broke Reef's heart knowing that Ford would never count his parents as their supporters.

"We've had a bit of shit to deal with, but what can you do? Haters are gonna be haters. I wouldn't give up Reef for anyone." Ford smiled at him and brought their joined hands to his lips, kissing them softly. Reef was lost, staring in those brilliant blue eyes. He was sure he wore one of those love sick grins, but that was okay, Ford was looking at him in exactly the same way.

"What he said," Reef murmured, when he realized no one had spoken for a while.

When Jeremy laughed, they turned to him. "I can see why it was the worst kept secret around. You guys aren't subtle."

Reef snorted out a laugh and Ford chuckled, adding, "He's in love. He gets all starry-eyed."

"Like you can talk, Ford. You literally ran across the hotel lobby to hug me the day before a heat began. There had to have been a hundred people in there with us."

"If memory serves, it was you who ran across the lobby. I kissed Mace to deflect everyone from your *Baywatch* moment." The look of smug satisfaction on Ford's face had Reef laughing again.

Reef rolled his eyes. Ford was right, but there was no way in hell he'd admit it. "I'm pleading the Fifth."

Turning to Jeremy, Ford added, "The reporter who published the stories about Reef's break up with his ex was there taking pics. Mace planted one on me so our lack of subtlety didn't turn into a headline. He figured no one would care if a trainer wasn't strictly straight, but the guy vying for world champion might have been bigger news."

"A lot of people like to think snowboarding's a pretty accepting sport, that we're all laid back—very live and let live. Do you disagree?"

"Mace, Caden and his trainer are the only three people associated with snowboarding who officially know about our relationship. I think everyone else has been happy to pretend not to have seen anything. Dunno if that's 'cause they don't care, or if they don't want to see us together. Either way, it makes no difference to us. Like Ford said, the people who matter have been great, haven't they?" Reef leaned into his man, enjoying the touch of his strong muscles playing under the silky cotton of his button down shirt.

"You mention Caden as being one of the people who matter to you. What's your take on the drugs scandal?"

"Look, as a competitor, I can't condone what he did. It was against the rules, plain and simple, but he's still a good guy. It hasn't affected our friendship, nothing could. He was there when I needed a bud and I'll stick by him no matter what. He's said that he believed the penalty imposed by the Federation was fair and I agree with that. He was obviously disappointed his career didn't end on a high, but, you know, sometimes fate intervenes for a reason. He was always gonna retire at the end of this season. Losing the crown, being disqualified didn't change that. Now he's figuring out what he wants to do with the rest of his life, which is a good thing, ya know?"

"Yeah." Jeremy nodded and Ford squeezed his hand, shooting a smile at him. The relief coursing through Reef was palpable. He knew the question had been coming—every reporter who'd interviewed him so far had asked him the same one. He'd been nervous about hearing it from Jeremy though, because unlike the other times he'd been questioned, he didn't intend to follow the Ski Federation's spiel. Caden wasn't a monster and the sooner the sporting press remembered that, the better. Snowboarding's golden child had fallen from grace, and now his friend needed a hand to get back up.

Jeremy seemed happy with the response, smiling, and nodding his approval. And why wouldn't he be happy? Reef had just given him a scoop. Well, another one.

"Speaking of ending the season on a high, you've been shortlisted for snowboarder of the year, Reef. What do you think your chances of winning are like?"

"I'm stoked about getting nominated. It's one thing to be recognized through points in competition, but it's another thing altogether for the best of the best to put me forward as a contender. The idea that they think I influenced snow-boarding's progression is pretty freaking cool. It's the icing on an otherwise mad year. Winning would be great, but if it doesn't happen, that's okay. This year has been pretty perfect either way—got the guy, got the championship, got the medal." Reef grinned. "Yeah, everything I ever wanted and more."

Jeremy's final question was another one Reef knew was coming. But like the question on Caden's positive drug test, Reef wasn't giving the stock standard answer he'd given in all the other interviews. Apart from wanting Ford to know he'd come out, the answer to this question was the main reason he'd called his man over to join them. "So, what's in store for you next, Reef? When do you head out for pre-season training?"

"No pre-season training for me anymore." He let that

bombshell sit for a moment while Ford absorbed it. "This year was it. I'm out."

He'd been toying with the idea for a while, but hadn't made his decision until Christmas, when he'd been making Ford's bauble. He was cutting up photos, sitting cross-legged on his bed, shirtless wearing ratty old sweats in some random hotel in whatever country Reef was in at the time. All he wanted—the only thing—was for him to be in *their* bedroom and for Ford to walk in and surprise him with something as simple as a kiss. That desire to share his home —to *have* a home—with Ford, was palpable. At the time, the idea he could have a Christmas tree, something he hadn't had in nearly a decade, struck a chord with Reef. God, he wanted it. But not just the tree. That'd be a simple fix. No, he wanted it all—the white picket fence, the family, his happily ever after. And when he imagined all that, it was Ford he pictured it with.

Reef had anguished over the decision and finally asked for advice. He surprised himself when Momma Bear picked up the phone and he'd asked for Coach. But his father's insight was exactly what Reef needed. Instead of being surprised, like Reef thought he'd be, Coach expected it, reminding Reef of their conversation in Fernie. *"I knew when you found the right person, you'd stop being a nomad in a heartbeat if it meant having the home you'd always dreamed of."*

Coach's words, his quiet strength, were exactly what helped Reef make the decision. It'd come easily after that. He hadn't wanted to carry the secret around, but the time to tell Ford never seemed right. But not telling him had made Reef question whether it was the best decision to make over and over. In the end, he knew it was right—keeping the secret was the hardest part. So, he'd spoken with Mace, wanting to give him the heads up to find another competitor to train. Turned out that Mace had the same idea as him—retire at the end of the season and settle down. Sitting in that interview and announcing his plans to the world made a weight lift off Reef's shoulders.

"What?" Ford asked, turning to him, surprise and confusion in his voice. "What are you talking about?"

"Hon, I'm retiring." He smiled at Ford and turned to the reporter. "Jeremy, you've got your scoop. I'm done. I'm not contesting the championship next year. I've found something, someone, more important to me than competing."

Ford spun in his seat and grasped both of Reef's hands. Concern pulled his brows low, marring his features. "Sweet, you can't give up your dream."

Reef squeezed Ford's fingers before pulling a hand free and running his fingertips along Ford's jaw. "I've achieved it, hon, I'm not giving up anything. I'm gaining so much more." He smiled, wanting nothing more in that moment than to kiss his man. "Now, I'll get to chase the snow with you and teach kids. I'm the new ski instructor at The Remarkables."

"Serious?" Ford breathed, hope shining in his eyes.

"I'm not doing another season without you." Reef shook his head and laced his fingers through the newly trimmed curls at the back of Ford's head, no longer able to resist kissing him. Their lips brushed together gently, sending a spark of electricity straight through Reef before Ford pulled back.

"I love you, Reef. I can't wait. Forever's gonna be fan-fuckin-tastic with us together."

––––––

THEY STEPPED out into the cold night air. The wind had died down leaving Wellington's city center quiet. An ethereal glow lit up the normally lush green lawns of Parliament House, the fine coating of white from the first snowfall of the season giving the manicured gardens a storybook feel. The magic of the snow never ceased to amaze Reef.

Ford clasped his hand and tugged Reef into his arms. Smiling, Reef closed his eyes and tilted his head back, letting the big snowflakes fall onto his face. Their family and friends had carried on ahead to waiting cabs and Uber rides but Reef still held back, wanting a moment of quiet with his man. The voices faded into the night and the unmistakable near-silence of falling snow descended on them, enveloping them in a bubble—a perfect moment in time captured like a still frame. Reef leaned into his man, nuzzling his neck while they held each other close on the cold city street. Fingers tangled in his curls, Reef pressed a languid kiss on Ford's throat, breathing him in.

"I had a dream last night," Ford murmured, the vibration against his lips making Reef shiver. Pulling back to look at Ford, he couldn't resist touching him. Running his thumb down Ford's cheek, he brushed away a snowflake caught on his closely groomed beard. Ford's smile made Reef's heart stutter, then thud harder in his chest, his blue eyes captivated him. Desire and love coursed through his body, leaving Reef breathless.

"What was your dream, hon?"

Ford leaned in and brushed his lips against Reef's, the barely-there touch making Reef moan. "Me and you lying in bed together. Our little girl woke us up jumping all over us." Ford's smile turned wistful. "She had your eyes, your smile. She was feisty, so sweet. The dog, this big furry thing, slobbered all over us and our shy little boy waited at the door. We had a family, sweet. It was the most amazing thing." Ford mirrored Reef's action and brushed a snowflake off Reef's cheek, the move tender.

"That sounds pretty damn good to me, hon. Like everything I could ever wish for."

"I love you, Reef."

"And I love you." Looking at his man, Reef was struck again by how insanely gorgeous Ford was. With his fingers tangled in Ford's hair, their bodies pressed together and puffs of their warm breath fogging the small space between their faces, Reef knew this was exactly where he was supposed to be.

He sealed their lips together slowly. The intensity of their kiss stole Reef's breath. Wrapped in his lover's arms, the other half of his soul, Reef knew he'd done it—arrived in paradise. A year ago when he hopped on his flight, he thought he was headed to the tropics. But he hadn't needed a holiday on an island. He'd needed the detour to Queenstown, to meet this man before him. All the tests of their strength they'd made it through were so they could find themselves, find each other and their place together in the world. Falling in love with a man was unexpected. But it was also perfect. Fate had intervened to give Reef everything he'd ever dreamed of. And damn, their future together looked bright. He couldn't wait to live it with Ford by his side.

THE END

MEETING CONNOR

MEETING CONNOR – TEN DAYS LATER

Their hotel was directly on the beach. They could literally step out of the elevator and walk onto the sand. The ocean, the heat—it was heavenly, exactly what he and Reef had needed after a long winter. And what a place to do it; Surfers Paradise was hoppin'. Buskers played on street corners and they'd already discovered so many great little hole-in-the-wall food joints, not to mention the mad nightlife.

He and Reef had been there for a week and he was loving every minute of their holiday. A morning run along the beach, breakfast in one of the little cafes dotted around town, followed by lunch on their private balcony and late afternoon swims had kept them busy during the day. By night it was candlelit dinners and dancing.

Ford smirked as he watched Reef stretch out on the sun lounge a few feet away from the pool he was floating in. God, he was a beautiful sight dressed only in his Oakley sunglasses and tiny black swim trunks. Reef had tried them on in the department store. Seeing the way they hugged his barely covered ass, had Ford's dick like steel. He'd been hard pressed not to sink into Reef right there and then in the dressing room. Instead, Ford barely stopped to pay for the tiny trunks before he dragged Reef back to their hotel. He'd tried every one of the dirty fantasies which had paraded through his mind on the light rail trip back to their room. They'd christened so many surfaces in the suite and on the balcony that Ford lost count of how many times they'd come together. Twenty-four hours later and they'd only just managed to resurface. He smiled at the memory as his cock perked up.

"Coming in for a swim, sweet?" Ford called out, splashing him.

Reef downed the rest of his rum and Coke before he looked at his watch. "We gotta go, hon. We told your cousin we'd meet him in ten."

"Only takes five to walk to his buddy's." As much as Ford wanted to catch up with Connor, he was enjoying their alone time, well, their naked time really. Wearing clothes in the autumn heat wasn't the problem—pretty much everywhere was air-conditioned. Nope, it was having Reef's perfect bubble butt covered up by anything more than those sexy-as-sin trunks that rankled him. Knowing he had to wait to see him bent over another surface or legs splayed out wide, his hole beckoning Ford to fill him up had Ford almost begging out of the beach party his cousin had invited them to.

"I have to get dressed." The tone in his voice had Ford reacting quickly. Reef was nervous; he really wanted to make a good impression on Connor. Ford took advantage of Reef staring at him to tease his man. He lifted himself from the pool with ease and stalked over to him, rivulets running down his not-so-pale skin. Still dripping wet, he straddled Reef's thighs, the cold water settling between them and warming with the intensity of their combined body heat. Ford cupped his man's face with both hands and leaned in close, brushing his lips tenderly over Reef's.

"Sweet, this is gonna go well. Con's cool, he's not like my parents. At all. He's gonna love you."

"I'm just a little nervous, ya know?"

"Yeah, I get it. Come on, you don't need to get dressed up. Its just drinks on the beach—really casual. Throw your shorts on, grab your flip flops and we'll swing by the liquor store on the way there to get some beer."

Reef smiled at him. "As long as I can ogle your ass when you get up."

Ford wiggled his eyebrows before swooping in and biting Reef's bottom lip, sucking it into his mouth. Reef moaned and Ford's dick thickened as Reef palmed his ass and brought him closer, aligning their bodies. Reef's hard length met his own as Ford rocked against him. The tease complete, Ford chuckled and released Reef's lip, letting it slide through his teeth as he let go. His voice was rough with desire when he spoke, "Let's head off, or we're gonna be late."

The hard, wet sand under his toes was cool, refreshing. So unlike a ski field, the deep blue of the ocean with its crashing waves was stunningly beautiful. It beckoned him. Shooting Reef a wicked grin, he slapped his ass and took off, running toward the water. Reef dropped the beer and sprinted after him. Ford laughed, the playfulness between them so freeing.

Water lapped at his calves as Ford lifted his strides, losing ground on Reef. He knew the crash tackle was coming, but he was still caught off guard, letting out a surprised shout when Reef collided with him and they hit the water. The sand coating their feet was washed away, the salt water cold against his heated skin. Spluttering, they resurfaced, Reef's arms still wound tight around his body. He shifted, lying on top of Reef, embracing him fully as he leaned down to kiss his man. Lying in the shallow water, the waves rolling over them had Ford battling the desire to kiss his man stupid or laugh. "I can't decide whether we've managed to do a perfect Baywatch re-creation or the opening scenes of Grease."

Reef snorted out a laugh as he pushed Ford off him and stood up. Holding his arms out wide, he belted out, "Those su-umer ni-ights." Ford left him behind in the crashing waves, jogging over to the warming beer and picking it up.

"You're a dork," he shot over his shoulder as Reef followed him.

They held hands as they strolled, a comfortable silence falling between them as they looked for the white three-story house Connor had directed them to. Ford turned his attention to Reef and marveled at his luck. How had he been so fortunate to land this man? He stopped walking and yanked on Reef's arm, pulling him flush against his body. Untangling their fingers, Ford wrapped his arm around Reef's waist and crushed their lips together, his tongue dancing with his man's. A needy moan tore from Reef's lips when Ford slid his hand down the back of Reef's shorts and palmed the globe of his ass.

"Ford, my man," a dude called out, "that you?"

Ford growled and punched his hips forward, letting Reef know in no uncertain terms how much he wanted him. Pulling away to address the man who spoke, Ford's smile was instant. "Connor, great to see you."

"Likewise." Truth be told, Ford was a little nervous seeing his cousin for the first time in over a decade. He wouldn't hide his relationship with Reef—couldn't even if he wanted to. The magazine article had gone live the day after Reef's interview with Jeremy and the news had quickly been picked up by the mainstream media, making international headlines. But with Connor before him, grinning like the cheeky kid he'd been the last time Ford had seen him, the remaining nerves disappeared on the salty breeze. Ford stepped away from Reef momentarily to hug the other man.

"It's been far too long," Connor added, his Australian accent so different to Ford's British one.

Stepping back to Reef, Ford took his hand. "Sweet, this is my cousin, Connor O'Reilly. Con, my boyfriend, Reef Reid."

Reef held out his hand and shook it, staring between the two of them. Ford smirked. He and Connor looked alike—the same dark curly hair, the same nose, jawline and lips, the same build, albeit Con was a few inches taller than him now. The only major difference was their eyes. Where Ford's were blue, Connor's were a deep brown, almost haunting in their depths.

"Holy shit." A lady behind them breathed. "And you think my cousin and I look alike. You guys could be twins."

"Right?" Reef said to her smiling, as she hooked her arm through Connor's. She was tiny, barely over five-foot, with flowing long brown hair, bright blue eyes and pouty lips that were totally kissable.

"Good to meet you, Con," Reef added.

"I'm Katy, Con's friend." Ford saw the fireworks when she turned and smiled at his cousin. The way they looked at each other, their eyes glued to the other, the way they stood so close—they had some serious chemistry going on between them. Ford was happy that Connor had someone in his life so soon after finishing his latest enlistment and returning home.

"Come inside and meet everyone," Con murmured without taking his eyes off Katy. He motioned to the white three-story mansion with Flo Rida's, *Good Feeling* blasting from outdoor speakers. Ford followed them, his hand once again linked with Reef's as they passed through the low gate. A garden stretched before them, thick palm trees casting shade over patches of grass and the sparkling pool. A hammock rocked in the breeze and people mingled around the table on the back verandah.

"Guys, meet Ford, my cousin, and his partner Reef. They're here from Kiwi land for a few weeks." Turning to Ford and Reef he grinned. "We'll test ya on names later, but the only other person you really need to know is Levi, my best mate and Katy's partner." Connor motioned to a dude who had the looks of a James Bond model walking up to them. Ripped but not thick muscles, dark blond hair, smooth skin.

"Damn, you're all freaking beautiful," Reef muttered under his breath. That earned a hearty laugh from Levi who held out his hand in greeting. "G'day, Reef. Hey, Ford, nice to meet you. Nick, Katy's cousin, is gonna throw some burgers on the barbie in a few. Beer's in the Eskies over there. Chuck yours in there too, if you like." Levi motioned to a few open coolers filled with ice and bottles lined up in the shade. "We're about to play a game of footy. You guys in?"

Reef's wicked grin was contagious. Ford was totally down with tackling his man.

ABOUT THE AUTHOR

By day Ann Grech lives in the corporate world and can be found sitting behind a desk typing away at reports and papers or lecturing to a room full of students. She graduated with a PhD in 2016 and is now an over-qualified nerd. Glasses, briefcase, high heels and a pencil skirt, she's got the librarian look nailed too. If only they knew! She swears like a sailor, so that's got to be a hint. The other one was "the look" from her tattoo artist when she told him that she wanted her kids initials "B" and "J" tattooed on her foot. It took a second to register that it might be a bad idea.

She's never entirely fit in and loves escaping into a book —whether it's reading or writing one. But she's found her tribe now and loves her MM book world family. She dislikes cooking, but loves eating, can't figure out technology, but is addicted to it, and her guilty pleasure is Byron Bay Cookies. Oh and shoes. And lingerie. And maybe handbags too. Well, if we're being honest, we'd probably have to add her library too given the state of her credit card every month (what can she say, she's a bookworm at heart)!

She also publishes her raunchier short stories under her pen name, Olive Hiscock.

Ann loves chatting to people online, so if you'd like to keep up with what she's got going on:

Join her newsletter:

http://anngrech.us8.list-manage2.com/subscribe?
u=0af7475c0791ed8f1466e7fd9&id=1cee9cdcb6
Like her on Facebook:
https://www.facebook.com/pages/Ann-
Grech/458420227655212
Join her reader group:
https://www.facebook.com/groups/1871698189780535/
Follow her on Twitter:
@anngrechauthor
Follow her on Goodreads:
https://www.goodreads.com/author/show/7536397.Ann_
Grech
Follow her on BookBub:
https://www.bookbub.com/authors/ann-grech
Follow her on Instagram: @anngrechauthor
Visit her website for her current booklist:
www.anngrech.com

She'd love to hear from you directly, too. Please feel free to
e-mail her at ann@anngrech.com or check out her website
www.anngrech.com for updates.